ARTIFICIAL INTELLIGENCIA

RICHARD A. CLARKE

ARTIFICIAL INTELLIGENCIA

a novel

RARE BIRD
LOS ANGELES, CALIF.

This is a Genuine Rare Bird Book

Rare Bird Books
6044 North Figueroa Street
Los Angeles, CA 90042
rarebirdbooks.com

FIRST HARDCOVER EDITION

For more information, address:
Rare Bird Books Subsidiary Rights Department
6044 North Figueroa Street
Los Angeles, CA 90042

Set in Dante
Printed in the United States

10 9 8 7 6 5 4 3 2 1

Publisher's Cataloging-in-Publication Data available upon request.

For Alan Turing, Carl Sagan, and those scientists and engineers struggling to improve humanity's lot.

1

Eluosi Fengqing Jie
Dalian
Liaoning Province
People's Republic of China
Wednesday, November 12
2105 hours

He heard the gulls and smelled the ocean as the breeze picked up, the mix of the wet, salty air and diesel blowing a chill up the street from the sea six blocks away. That meant, he knew, it would rain and soon. Before midnight. Wei Bao had lived most of his life in this harbor town and he knew its smells, its streets, and some of its secrets. This neighborhood, Eluosi Fengqing Jie, Russian Street, still held a secret from Wei, but that would end tonight. He would see to it.

Wei was walking with another man whose height, bulk, and clothes contrasted with Wei's skinny jeans, short black leather jacket, running shoes, and baseball cap. The larger man, Yao Guang, looked and was older, his bulky parka hiding a blazer and much more strapped and buckled on underneath.

Guards were locking the doors on the Moscow Shopping Center as they walked past, dimming the lights on the outside signs in Cyrillic and Hanzi.

"Why, Yao, would anyone want goods from Russia?" Wei asked.

Yao Guang exhaled a cloud of gray-white smoke. Like many of the veteran police, he could not kick the habit. "A nation past its time." Seven years older than Wei, he appeared more the part of a police detective, deceptively dull looking. Although Wei was the senior officer, he was still learning from his older partner. "That's why guys like these have to hack us. We have so far surpassed them as a nation, as a people," Yao declared.

"In some things, yes," Wei agreed. "In software. In electronics." The two men learned from each other. It was an unlikely, but successful partnership. Wei had his foreign graduate degree in computer science and looked the part of the management consultants who filled the slick malls and bars of Pujiang. His partner, Yao, had years busting drug and sex shops near the Dalian wharfs and tracing the paths smuggled goods moved on, including to the ever-growing well-to-do classes elsewhere on the Liaoning peninsula.

"Shit, where did he go? He was right there." Wei started to run, but Yao's hard left claw grabbed his shoulder.

Yao was giving the tutorial now. "Don't blow cover. We will find him. Big Russians stand out, even around Russian Street. We ask the camera girls, your camera girls."

Instincts, Wei thought. He still did not have Yao's natural, automatic, appropriate response to situations on the street. Chagrined, he punched a number into his mobile.

"Zhēntàn jîng du Wei." Detective Inspector Wei, he said, and recited his credential number. "The target RU21-351. He was just on Russian Street. What shop did he enter?"

Two miles away, in the Ministry of Public Security's provincial headquarters for Liaoning, a shift of twenty young technicians, mostly women, sat row upon row, slightly separated by barriers that prevented them from seeing each other's screens. They wore headsets and chattered softly to officers in cars, on foot, even one in a helicopter, across Dalian and the nearby suburbs.

Wei's first project when he returned from Canada had been to introduce an artificial intelligence program for recognition, identification, and tracking in Dalian. Police cameras had always been ubiquitous, but after COVID-19, most Chinese people wore face masks. Wei's software overcame that obstacle. The citywide surveillance system Wei had created used hidden and overt cameras all over the city to capture faces. The AI then compared the faces with the National ID photos to guess at whose face they had just seen on the street or in a bus or in an apartment building lobby or on a metro platform. The AI looked especially at their ears and their way of walking, both of which were usually unique to each person.

To confirm the identification was correct, the AI then looked for where that person's mobile telephone was, what tower it had pinged last. Wei had supplemented the telephone towers with hundreds of police devices that also captured all mobile phones, which quietly pinged the police receivers every few seconds.

The AI compared the identity guessed from the cameras with the location of that person as indicated by their phone. If the two sources agreed, then the AI had identity confirmation. It learned from these comparisons, and its error rate of guessing at faces declined over time. His AI program integrated data from cameras that looked at license plate numbers, matched them with the car's registered users and the mobile telephone signals emitted by the driver and passengers. If a citizen moved by mass transit, as most did, the AI system followed the rider by knowing when they used their smart transit card to get on a bus, a tram, or a train. Cameras matched their image when using the transit card with images on file from their national identification card, military ID, and other instances of positive identity proofing.

Thus, Wei's program knew where every person in Dalian had been seen. Every person, all the time. If you gave Wei's system the name of someone in Dalian, it could tell you not only where they were at that moment but where in the city they had been over the past month, day by day, hour by hour, sometimes minute by minute. The software Wei had perfected showed whom a targeted person had been near in a train, a bus, a car, an office, a store, a bed.

Despite the centralized power of the Beijing government and the Party, the rulers allowed major cities to experiment, to develop their own systems. No one used the old Maoist phrase of "let a thousand flowers bloom," but the semi-autonomous cities had on some issues produced innovation and proved which approaches worked best. Wei's system had worked so well in Dalian, a second-tier city, that the AI software had been adopted by other, larger metropolitan areas. It was also put into use in Xinjiang monitoring the Uighurs. Wei, however, was given no reward. He did not own the patents, the Ministry did. Wei did not even know where outside of Dalian his system was being used.

The young woman in the police camera operations room answered Wei's call and acknowledged his request. She pulled up the identifier RU-21-351 and pronounced his name into her mouthpiece. "Ruslan Dragovich, merchant seaman?"

"Yes, yes. He was just on Russian Street, passed Halyang moving toward the water. He must have entered a shop. Less than three minutes ago." Wei looked down the street. There were cameras all along the pedestrian mall, including some, he knew, that did not appear to be cameras. There were mobile phone antennae, including those operated not by the telephone company but by the police, who had enough antennae to triangulate any mobile to within three meters in most of the city.

The technician typed into her keyboard. An image appeared on her screen. "Yes, he was walking east, alone. His phone record appears to be off. Wait. Wait." She typed again, pulling up other views, other cameras. "Is he a priority one, Inspector?" she asked. If he were, she could task all cameras in the neighborhood to scan for anyone with his size, his coat, his gait. Even without seeing his face, they could identify him.

Wei ran his left hand through his thick, jelled hair and looked at the ground. "Yes, yes, of course he is." He waited, deeply sucking in the increasingly cold, salty air. He immediately regretted being short with the camera woman and made a mental note to apologize later.

"Target acquired," she chirped. "Live coverage. Leaving what looks like the back door of a shop. White Birch shop. He is now walking south in the Guanghui Alley, toward the Technical School."

Wei turned to his partner. "Now can I run?"

Yao frowned. "We bike. Faster." With that, the detective sergeant moved on two high school boys coming toward them on bicycles. His police credentials appeared to materialize from the palm of his hand, and with fewer than a half dozen words spoken, he and Wei were pedaling around the block to the Guanghui Alley.

"Keep following him, please," Wei instructed, holding his phone with one hand and the handlebar with the other. Wei hated earbuds. They kept falling out when he was running or biking. He had lost four sets.

Wei knew that later Yao would complain that he had said "please" to the camera woman. Everyone in Canada said please all of the time. Please. Forgive me. May I? Sorry? Do you mind if...It was one of the things he learned from their culture during his graduate school days that he wanted to bring back, to introduce into China. He knew it was a losing cause.

They rounded the corner to an empty alley. "Are you the two men on the bikes just entering the alley, Inspector?" the young woman on the camera desk asked before Wei could inquire what had happened to his Russian. "On your left, two, no, three doors down. He went in there. Two minutes, twenty seconds ago."

"Thank you," Wei said, hopping off the bike. He pointed Yao to the right door. Naturally, it was locked, but Yao, without hesitation, pulled a tool from inside his jacket and expertly popped the mechanism. Wei made a mental note to ask Yao later for tips on lock picking. He also noted a covert camera above the door. They would know inside that two men were entering, but Yao had already descended down a stair, toward the muffled sound of an alarm bell.

Wei followed closely behind and could see three men in the basement pulling hard drives from computers and three more ready to pounce on Yao when he stepped off the bottom stair and into the room. "Police! Stand still," Yao bellowed, and then quickly ducked as one of the Russians swung an ax at his head, barely missing him. Another of the men swung a steel pipe through the air, this time hitting Yao behind his knees, collapsing him onto the bottom of the staircase.

Time slowed almost to a stop for Wei. The basement room filled with an acoustic wave, enveloping everything, creating a sound barrier that drowned out all other noise in a long, pain-inducing roar. Wei realized it was him. He had fired four 9mm rounds from his NP34. The explosive sound, bouncing off the concrete walls of the basement, had deafened him. Yet, he could somehow still hear his own high voice yelling, cracking, "I have nine rounds left. Who wants one? Everyone on the floor, face down. Hands behind your head."

He was aware amid the rush of adrenaline, through the entire out-of-body experience, that he actually must have some instincts. They had just kicked in, spring-loaded. He had not thought about a response. It just happened. His subconscious had taken control. Some part of his conscious mind now registered regret at the loss of self-control, but that thought was quickly banished by the overpowering, demanding urgency of figuring out what to do next.

Yao rose slowly from the floor, pushing the dead body of one of his assailants off him and kicking the ax behind him, his pistol drawn. Both attackers were dead, their brains sprayed in two splatters of blood and other matter running down the white block wall. Wei realized he had double tapped them both, aiming for their heads. His arms were heavy now, and he tasted something vile in his throat. Then he noticed the smells, sulfur and blood, and he felt his own fear like an icicle jabbing in his stomach, a chill tingling his skin.

Yao was standing stably now, back from the four men lying on the floor. With his gun in his right hand, Yao was talking into a microphone on a cord he had pulled from an inside jacket pocket. Wei heard the words "…transport for four, full crime scene team, uniforms outside, two dead bags…"

2

Dalian Police Headquarters
3 People's Square,
4th floor, Computer Crimes Branch
Thursday, November 13
0630 hours

THE BLACK TEA WAS too hot and the sweet roll too sticky, but Wei Bao knew he needed them both to stay awake until he had finished filling out all of the forms and had given the twins their instructions for the first forensic passes on the Russian servers and laptops. "Thank you, Yao," he said and tried to smile at his partner in appreciation of the breakfast.

"You saved my life, boss. You get free tea and tián tián quan. At least the first time you save my life. Maybe not every time. Working with you, I think it might get expensive." Then, to Wei's surprise, Yao actually winked.

"No one told me the cyber squad would be dangerous," Wei replied. "And no one told me that if you killed people there would be so much more paperwork." He spoke as much to himself as to Yao, forcing his eyes to stay open, looking out at the signs of imminent sunrise over the sea.

The one nice thing about their office on the fourth floor of the Ministry building was that from one of the windows you could just glimpse a slice of the ocean. Orange and pink pushed up from below on the purple and gray. The rain had come after midnight, as he knew it would, but it had stopped sometime in the dark depth of the night as he was rewriting, editing, after he had left Yao and the others to run the interrogation rooms process.

More than anything, he wanted a hot shower. It was the goal, the reward, that had kept him going for the last few hours. And a shave. He normally only shaved on Saturdays. He really didn't need it more often, but this day, a Thursday, he would shave while having a long shower. That was the plan.

Then a nap, a quick one, lying next to Fenfang, who would be tired from her night shift at the hospital, and then he would come back in to see how the computer forensics was going. The twins would have results by then.

When he looked up, what he saw before him made him think quickly that none of that might happen anytime soon.

"Chief Inspector, sir!" Wei spat out as he stood quickly to attention behind his desk.

"Sit, sit, Wei Bao." Dalian's criminal police Chief Inspector Wang Niu was rarely seen in the offices before sunrise, and never in the worker offices like Wei's at all.

"Were these pastries made overnight? May I have one, Inspector? I need to be fortified for the call I have to make to the Russian Consulate. To tell them that one of my officers killed two of their citizens. And that we have four more of them in the lockup. My vodka deliveries may stop coming because of you, Inspector Wei." Despite the deep voice and grave tone, there was a shifting way to his eyes that said he might be playing with his young subordinate.

Wei was still standing. "It was most unfortunate, Chief Inspector, but we did not anticipate a violent reaction, not an attempt to kill an officer, or I would have entered with uniformed, armed support. But they were about to—"

"Kill Detective Yao." Wang cut him off. "I read the draft incident report on the way in. You had no choice. Besides, if it were up to me, these Russian scum would all be taught a lesson. They think they can come in here, drill into the network of the Technical School, tap into its fibers, and run their crimes online from our territory like they still occupy it. This isn't Vladivostok or one of their Siberian shit mounds. This is Dalian. They do not own it anymore. We say who works from here and who can be attacked from here, not some oligarch in St. Petersburg. They are such an uncultured nation. They make only oil. And the vodka, of course. Sit, sit."

Wei noticed how perfectly the chief inspector's uniform fit, how neatly it was pressed, how the many medals were in such straight lines. When he wore his own uniform, Wei always struggled not to look like he had borrowed it from his dad or older brother. He had neither—no siblings, no parents left alive. Through his semi-stupor, Wei realized Wang was waiting for a reply to a question he had just asked.

"Do I know Huang Qiang?" Wei said, repeating what Wang had just asked him. "No, no, I don't think... Is he under arrest?"

The chief inspector bellowed a laugh, the first one that Wei had ever heard emit from his boss. "Huang Qiang is the most powerful civilian after our beloved president," the chief inspector cut him off. "People here don't know his name, but in Beijing, everyone bends to his will, even ministers."

"I am sorry, sir, I should know..." Wei tried.

"Huang Qiang is the president's chief of staff. What the president thinks comes out of Huang's mouth as orders not to be questioned, only to be carried out successfully, fully— sometimes quietly, always with precision."

Wei struggled to follow the conversation. "Our nation is so fortunate to have such leaders," he recited, not knowing what else to say, not wanting to say the wrong thing.

"He destroys lives, lives of those in the way, those out of step with the latest direction. But, if you can, you will tell me what he wants," the chief inspector replied. "If you cannot, then do not. I may not have need to know."

Grabbing for his own tea, Wei took a sip, trying to delay answering. He suddenly realized that he had no idea what they were talking about. "Of course, Chief Inspector, but..."

"Yes, Bao, what is it?"

"Of course, I will try, but I do not know how I would even go about learning what such an august man would want and how..."

"He will tell you. Huang himself. I am told he is very direct, almost like an American. No polite talk or ritual. Personally, I cannot even imagine why he would want to see a relatively newly minted inspector from the Dalian police. I offered to go myself, but his office said it must be you. They asked for you by name. How do they even know you exist? Do you know?"

Wei sat silently. He looked into the black tea in the paper cup in his hand. There seemed to be only one meaning that the chief inspector's words could have. "No, no, sir. I do not know anything about this. I am to meet the president's chief of staff? He's coming here?"

"No, you idiot, you're going there," Chief Inspector Wang said, standing up and brushing pastry powder from his pants. "You are to report to his office to meet with his people at five o'clock this afternoon. That gives you almost ten hours to get to Beijing and then into the Zhongnanhai. My adjutant will have all of the papers for you, the tickets, the passes, ready by nine."

Wei leapt to attention again. He saluted, not knowing what else to do or to say. The Zhongnanhai was the part of the Forbidden City not open to citizens. There, the rulers lived and worked. The Zhongnanhai—he was going there, today?

Wei Bao realized his boss was still talking. "And, Wei, get a shower before you fly away. You smell." On his way out, the chief inspector took the last pastry.

3

4 Dasheng St, Apartment 606
Shahekou District
Dalian
Thursday, November 13
0745 hours

DR. YANG FENFANG WAS in the shower when Wei Bao entered their tiny high-rise apartment near Zhongshan Park. The steam from the hot water filled the small bathroom. Fenfang was the most junior attending oncology physician in the Sino-German Cancer Center at the university's Second Hospital and had been at work for the past two days and nights. When she realized there was someone else in the bathroom, she began to scream, but then a naked Bao quickly pulled back the shower curtain and stepped into the tub with her.

They left the shower only when the hot water turned chill, then they ran down the cold corridor to the bedroom and dove quickly under the covers, there recreating the warmth of the shower. Wei Bao wanted to remain there all day, but this day was taking him to Beijing, indeed to the Zhongnanhai.

"Stay in bed with me. You need sleep; I can tell," Fenfang urged as Wei rose and began to look for his best suit, the one he wore a few years ago at graduation in Toronto. He still had the same build, slight but tightly muscled. "I don't have to go back into the clinic until midnight Saturday. Take a nap with me, and then we can go to the fish market. We could make something special tonight. Take a nap. As your doctor, I order it."

Wei looked at her, with the thin sheet pulled up to her chin, looking just as she had after their first time, a month after they had met in Toronto, at the Chinese Student Association mixer. She had turned down residencies in Toronto, Shanghai, and Beijing to be with him in Dalian. Now, it was he who was going to the capital, at least for a day.

"You are an oncologist, not my doctor. I don't have cancer, and I have to fly this morning, but I should be back tonight. I will let you know as soon as I get the flight back booked," he said as he struggled with his tie.

She rose from the bed, came to him, and fixed the knot.

"Fly? Where?" she asked, her naked body pressing up against his tight black suit. As a detective, he usually wore casual clothes, seldom a uniform. She hated it on those rare ceremonial occasions when he had to "dress up like a policeman." Fenfang loved her policeman, but not the police.

"Beijing, but that is not something anyone else needs to know, chatterbox." He remembered her fellow oncology residents from the crowded dinners in tiny apartments she had dragged him to, gossiping and giggling like teenagers. She had always introduced him to the other residents as an IT specialist with the provincial government, and he had always played along.

"Beijing! As an oncologist, I can order you to stay away. The air there is carcinogenic this time of year. And it's so poisonous in other ways too," she said before kissing him. "I won't marry you if you get lung cancer, so no Beijing."

Wei Bao was not much taller than Fenfang, but he had on shoes and she was still in her bare feet. He looked down into her eyes and gave her a disapproving look that said "be serious."

"Okay, go if you must, Mister Policeman. I will buy the fish by myself. It will be ready when you get back, even if it is a midnight meal."

"Then I will buy a white French wine in the airport there, a Sancerre like the one we had in Quebec. And I will do it while holding my breath or wearing my mask," he said, moving to the door. "And keep your opinions medical, Miss Doctor. It's better for your own health. That's my professional opinion."

Fenfang frowned at him and stuck out her tongue as Bao blew her a kiss and pulled the apartment door closed behind him. Yao was waiting downstairs in their beat-up undercover car. He had volunteered to drive Wei Bao to the airport for the flight to Beijing, for the visit to the Zhongnanhai, the political heart of the nation. As the elevator descended, Wei's body gave an involuntary shiver at the thought of his destination.

4

The Zhongnanhai
Beijing, PRC
Thursday, November 13
1520 hours

He felt odd, uncomfortable sitting in the back seat. He had tried talking with the driver, but might as well have conversed with a stone dragon. So Wei closed his eyes as the car moved deftly through Beijing's afternoon traffic, blue and red lights blinking behind its grille.

Sensing the car speeding up, he looked out and saw they were quickly moving past Tiananmen, where he had been only once, as a high school student twenty years ago. Adrenaline pumped to his brain. Tiananmen. They really were taking him to the heart of the nation. This was real, but what was this? Why was he being brought before the throne? Not because he had killed two Russians, the chief inspector had assured him. So, why?

There were, he noticed, cameras on almost every street pole near the square, overtly displayed. Wei realized he was silently identifying them by manufacturer and model. He was surprised by how many were older versions, far less capable than the ones he had ordered for Dalian. These older cams would not be able to do high-quality facial recognition beyond ten meters, but maybe that didn't matter, there were so many of them. Maybe just their presence was a deterrent. He wondered how many of them were actually online, recording, sending data back for analysis and storage. The storage requirements would be too immense.

The driver turned onto West Chang'an Avenue and then, remarkably, he spoke, startling Wei. "You do not get to come in through the Xinhua Men gate." Wei thought he heard a suppressed chuckle. The New China

Gate, Wei remembered from a long-ago class, was the formal entrance to Zhongnanhai, the vast administrative park filled with lakes west of the Forbidden City. The leadership of the entire country met there, had their offices there. Some said the leaders lived there. Chairman Mao had.

The gate at which the car did eventually stop was decidedly not ceremonial, not the Xinhua Men. This gate was small, modern, and staffed by the People's Liberation Army Unit 68199, the Praetorian Guard. Some carried automatic weapons. Wei recognized the weapons as the QBZ-95. He had trained on it but had never been issued one. Politely, the guards asked him to step from the car and enter one of the gatehouses. Inside the door was a stylish young woman with an iPad. She could have been the greeter at a five-star hotel.

"Inspector Wei Bao." Her tenor suggested it was not a question, but an announcement. She knew in advance what he looked like. Her name, she said, was Biyu. No family name provided. "I am so sorry, but even the esteemed inspector must pass through security. It is very rigorous here, of course. Are you carrying firearms?" she asked in such a cheery tone that she might have been asking how his flight had been. It had been bumpy and crowded. No, he was not armed today. He knew that would have been a complication.

After the very intrusive pat-down by one of the PLA and now on the other side of the airport-style magnetometer, his charming young escort led him out of the back door of the guard house and to a larger, blue car, which he later identified on the web as a BMW 7-Series. His original car, the one with the blinking grille lights, and its driver stayed outside the gate. "How was your flight from Dalian?"

She did ask it after all, as they settled into the car's orange-tan leather bucket seats. He knew she would ask about the flight. Some people were good at small talk. He wasn't. Either she would ask about the flight or the weather in Dalian this time of year. "Punctual. Indeed, we landed a few minutes early." He did not add the fact that they then had waited thirty minutes for a gate to open and finally were assigned to a pad from which they were bussed to the terminal. And it's beginning to be cold there, he thought, practicing his small talk, but we have not yet had snow. Yes, we do normally get a lot of snow up there, usually, but less in recent years. Maybe it was better he didn't say that.

There was no traffic inside the park, though the driver moved slowly past the gardens. Biyu was providing commentary. Qing Dynasty this, the Revolution that. Her voice sounded like the recorded passenger instructions he had ignored on the China Eastern Airlines flight from Dalian. His focus was inside his own mind, idling high but failing to generate scenarios, reasons why he might be here, as they moved closer by the second to the seat of all power.

"...actually not in the Hall of Diligent Government, the Qinzhengdian, but behind it in a small building near the Huairen Hall. I will not accompany you. Just walk in and tell the officer at the desk in the lobby your name. They know it, of course, but you must tell them. Then you will sit in the lobby until he is ready for you. Have a good meeting."

Wei realized the car had stopped and his door was being opened by the driver. "Yes, yes, of course. Thank you, Biyu," he stammered. Huairen Hall, the Hall of Cherished Compassion he recalled from school, was the home of the Politburo. He was going to the building behind it, he told himself. Biyu's smile seemed sincere, and as he stepped out into the chill air, he recognized for the first time how beautiful she was. Then a guard shut the car's door.

The building to the rear of the resplendent Huairen Hall was indeed small and plain by comparison to the monumental gates and halls in the vast garden and the Forbidden City to its east. Three stories of gray painted blocks topped by the traditional artichoke-leaf upturned roof. It was one of several identical structures in a row and marked only as BUILDING 8. Of course it was. Eight was the luckiest number.

He had turned in his phone, which the guard had placed in one of a series of small lockers, and since he never wore a watch, he had no precise sense of how much time passed as he sat in the dimly lit lobby, slowly turning the pages of a large-format, glossy picture book about the water features and gardens of the Central and South lakes. The lakes, he read, were officially called seas. Where he was sitting was near the Central Sea, and it...

"Inspector Wei, please follow me." The young man in the gray suit was on the other side of the lobby, holding open a door. During a quick elevator ascent to the third and top floor, his escort avoided small talk and eye contact, tapping into his mobile. The escort apparently didn't need to have his device put in phone jail. Stepping off the elevator, the escort—no name at all provided—placed a badge attached to his waist up against a card reader, then placed his eye up to an iris reader, opening an opaque glass door. No Name looked up from his mobile long enough to say, "Please go in," in a tone that implied Wei should have known and already walked through. How many more escorts would there be, how many more hand-offs before what he now regarded as "The Meeting," the session where he would learn the reason for his presence?

This room was larger and better lit than the downstairs lobby, and it held a small conference table with six chairs, a desk in the corner by the window, and by the door Wei had just entered, two red leather couches with matching armchairs. The leather, he noted, was cracked in a few places. The old furniture must have been handed down from a more important office. This did not appear to be a waiting room for distinguished visitors. Wei automatically looked for the cameras. They must have been very well hidden.

An older, bald man in a black suit sat quietly on one of the couches, intently paging through papers in a red file folder. He did not look up at Wei, who settled himself in the chair nearest the door, satisfied that even old bureaucrats were kept waiting here and made to sit anxiously studying their papers. Seeing the English-language *South China Morning Post* on the coffee table, Wei eagerly picked up the newspaper, only to find the speed of his reading in the Western language had clearly slowed somewhat in the last few years since Canada. The headline was about the APAC meeting in Manila, which followed the president's successful two days of meetings and tours in the Philippines. Wei flipped inside the paper, looking for the sports pages, hoping to see how the Toronto Maple Leafs were doing in this year's hockey season. Poorly, was the answer he found in the NHL standings chart.

After scanning the sports pages, Wei threw the Daily back onto the coffee table. The motion seemed to startle the bald man on the couch, who suddenly looked up from his file and at Wei. "You are an honest man, clean. A good citizen. And have cracked many cyber cases that others could not.

Even North Korean cases. Now these Russian criminals." Wei realized the man had been speaking in English and talking to him, about him. "You love the motherland, the zuguo?"

"Of course, I love my country."

"Good. This file is for you. All you will need." He thrust a thick green folder at Wei and was moving across the room toward the desk in the corner. He was short and moved quickly for an older man. "Come, sit over here with me," he said, pointing at a chair opposite the desk.

"Cigarette?" the bald man asked, thrusting a package of Gitanes at him. "French. They kill you quicker." Wei declined and found himself staring at the man's stained teeth and wondering why, when everybody in Beijing smoked Zhongnanhai brand cigarettes, in the actual Zhongnanhai, they smoked something from France.

"My boss, the boss of us all, is determined to weed out corruption. It sucks the lifeblood out of the economy, mal-distributes resources and rewards. It prevents us from being a well-functioning machine responsive to the needs of the people, to the directives of the Party." He had spoken that in Chinese, and he looked at Wei for agreement.

"Bìxu táotài fubài." Corruption must be weeded out, Wei parroted. He had seen that phrase in the airport and on billboards along the highway into the city. It was the latest mantra of the Party. "Bìxu táotài fubài," he repeated.

"Yes, correct, especially in the companies owned by the State. There, corruption is theft from the people, from the Party," the bald man continued in Chinese. "Corporate managers hire their cousins, their brothers-in-law, their neighbors, and give them No Shows. That is what the president believes. That is what he hears. That is what you will prove. And stop. You will stop the No Shows. And we will arrest them and all the bosses who gave them their jobs." He had said "No Shows" in English.

"Yes, sir. No Shows." He had almost said No No Shows. What were No Shows, exactly?

"Good, son, good. You must also prove that the managers are skimmers, getting kickbacks from their No Show cousins."

"They are skimmers. No Show skimmers. Yes, sir." Slowly, Wei was beginning to think that this man might actually be Huang Qiang. Wei should have looked for a photograph of him online before leaving Dalian, but now he saw a picture on the bookcase behind the desk, in a silver frame. It was the bald man standing with the president, the two laughing at some unknown joke. What Huang, the president's chief of staff, thought, those words came out of the president's mouth, Chief Inspector Wang had said. Or was it the other way around?

Huang Qiang spoke quickly, in bursts, with a high-pitched, nasal sound. "Questions, then. Any questions? Answers are in the file I gave you and other things you need are in here," he said, passing Wei a leather briefcase. "But while you are here, what questions?"

So many, beginning with *are you really Huang Qiang* and *what are No Shows and skimmers*. "Why me? I mean, sir, there are so many good police and intelligence officers."

"No, there aren't," Huang shot back, then smiled, a twisted, thin smile. "Everyone is suspected of corruption, even some in Intelligence, the State Security. We cannot use them for this special mission.

"You are not from Beijing or Shanghai. That is a plus. You have no connections. You are not yet a Party member, but you have a clean record. We have checked, carefully checked. You are an expert in artificial intelligence and its application to databases for identities, for facial recognition. This will be most helpful in tracking these No Shows and proving they do not appear, do not work. Instead, they probably spend their days in parks or in bars. That's where your cameras will find them."

"Yes, sir. Cameras."

"Besides, nobody knows you. They won't see you coming." A grin spread across his face and quickly ended. "A company, Blackberry, offered you a job if you would stay in Canada, but you returned to the motherland and to the police who paid for your graduate work. You could probably be working now for a Chinese company, Baidu or Tencent or Alibaba, but no, you work for the police, for the country."

"It's not about money for me, sir. It's about service," Wei Bao heard himself saying. He didn't mention that the real reason he returned was that his sick mother had needed him.

"Yes, but we must be careful with police and with people from Dalian," Huang mused. "You know about Bo Xilai? He was mayor of Dalian. He had Wang Lijun create a high-tech surveillance system in Chongqing, but they also used it to surveil our leadership for political purposes. They went to jail."

"Sir, they were when I was in high school."

"I know, I know. That is why you are approved. We checked your connections, but I suggest this as a cautionary tale. Bo also had a coconspirator, Zhou Yongkang. He was the minister in charge of all police nationwide."

"I never heard of him, sir."

"He went to jail too. For life. All of them. For life."

"I will learn their stories and their crimes, sir."

"They are colorful stories." Huang laughed, again showing his stained teeth. "Bo Xilai's wife killed an Englishman. Left his body in a hotel. Incredible. They were all corrupt. Stole millions of yuan."

Wei again said, "I love my country."

"And the president loves AI and machine learning. You are one of the AI people his program sent overseas to learn, one of those who can get us to the two goals," the man who apparently actually was Huang Qiang continued.

"The two goals, sir?" Wei asked, quickly regretting it.

Huang frowned. "AI will make the Chinese people's economy number one in the world and the People's Liberation Army's strength number one on the planet. These are the Party's AI goals. You do not know them?" He shook his head at Wei. "However, you are still a good young man, Chief Inspector Wei Bao. Do this job right and you will be in the Party."

"Chief Inspector?"

"Yes, while you are on this assignment, temporarily, you are a Special Chief Inspector, assigned to my office. You report only to me. You will have a new badge and credentials that say you are to be given all assistance you request. Do not abuse these powers, Wei."

"No, sir." He was aware that sweat was running down his back.

"Questions, other questions?"

"May I have help, a team?"

"Yes, of course, anyone. There are forms in the folder for you. Requisition forms for people, money, things you need. Computers, of course. Work from Dalian. Make that your base. It won't attract attention. Other questions?"

"What city, what company do I investigate?"

"Everywhere. All of them. State-owned or controlled companies. Any industry. Any city. Other corporations, too, where the State owns a majority or substantial minority share. Bring me the proof. Then we arrest them all. All at once. At the right time." Huang Qiang smiled and bared his yellow teeth, but it was the smile of a mongoose who had just spotted a snake. Wei Bao felt cold at the same time he was sweating.

"Go, then. Get started. Come back to me in ninety days." The bald man then reached for another large folder and looked down at it as he spread the content across the desk. Their meeting was evidently over.

Chief Inspector Wei Bao left the office and the building quietly. He had no escorts on the way out, no beautiful Biyu Last Name Unknown, no man in a gray suit with No Names. The guard in the lobby told him where to wait outside for a shuttle bus that would take him to the Lingjing Hutong metro station. He handed Wei a metro pass. The large blue car and its driver were not outside waiting.

5

Dalian
Saturday, November 15
Xuni Shije (Seekers World Arcade)
2330 hours

THE PURPLE SEEMED TO ooze from the walls and ceiling, barely illuminating the large space, except in glowing pools of brighter violet light above scattered podiums where the controllers monitored the players. On the far wall was an image of a building, dimly illuminated by more purple light. He recognized the building; it was one he had seen in the Zhongnanhai in Beijing, one of the temple-like edifices they had driven past. Biyu had called it the Ziguang Ge. Of course, Hall of Purple Lights. And that was also this room, arcade of purple lights.

Grunts were the only sounds Wei could hear. Then one man about twenty feet away jumped and screamed. A pool of red light developed around the screamer, who slowly removed his helmet, which then shot out of his hands and up toward the ceiling. The player had died, virtually, a victim of a dinosaur. A controller appeared and whispered to the screamer. The two then walked off toward a podium to select another reality for the player.

Wei counted over thirty helmeted bodies standing, scattered about the vast player space of the warehouse. He knew that in an hour or so, after midnight, their number would likely be three times that or more. Which ones were the twins? Everyone seemed to be wearing dark jeans and black T-shirts. Wei realized he should have paid more attention to the twins' running shoes. There were a variety of brands and colors among the players' footwear. Bright oranges, greens, yellows, and reds that glowed in the purple light. He could not remember what either of the twins wore at the computer lab and, in any event, those were probably their "work" shoes.

He thought about showing his badge to the controller and asking for the twins, but he realized it might cause a commotion if the players thought the police were raiding the arcade. Most of them were high on something. Instead, he walked among the players, each lost in the virtual reality that could only be seen inside their helmet, all moving their arms and legs interacting with things that looked very real to them. He stood close to one player after another, each of whom was oblivious to his presence. There was one young woman in a short leather jacket he was sure was Guo Chunhua, the woman he had arrested along with her twin brother two years ago when they were just eighteen. They'd been arrested, but never processed, never prosecuted.

He hadn't filed paperwork on her. Instead, he had fixed her abysmal Social Credit Score and then hired Chunhua and her twin brother, Bohai, whose score he also had to adjust, as "administrative assistants." They had been hacking for him ever since. They were the ones who had discovered the Russian hacker crime gang that had physically tapped into the Technical School's network and used it to launch cyberattacks in America. The twins had given him the lead that sent him to the basement where he had killed two men.

"What the fuck, dude!" Chunhua screamed in English as Wei pulled the virtual reality helmet up and off her head. "Oh, it's you, boss," she said in Chinese. "It's our night off, man, really."

"I know. And you can enjoy it for a few more hours, but don't play all night. I need you and Bohai to get some sleep and see me in the morning, at the office, at nine." He moved closer. "We have a lot of hacking to do," Wei said quietly into her ear.

"Not more Russian creeps," Chunhua moaned.

"No." He smiled. "Chinese corporations, big ones."

"That's illegal, boss. We don't want to get arrested, again."

"Not if I do it, it's not illegal." As he moved away, he turned back to Chunhua. "Besides, you have never been arrested. Your papers got lost, remember?" He wanted the twins fresh Sunday morning, which was a good time to hack, when few people were at work. "Don't come to the Lab. I will text you two the address on Signal. New digs. Remember, get sleep tonight. Bohai too. See you at nine. Nine in the morning."

Wei, however, had no plans to sleep. He had a lot of coding to do, a new AI program that he would insert into the corporate networks after Chunhua and Bohai hacked into the companies. And he knew they would get in. They were the best Chinese hackers he had ever seen, better than the PLA guys in Unit 52181, the elite army unit in Pudong, outside Shanghai. The Americans could see the PLA guys sometimes, they had even put some of their pictures online and issued arrest warrants for them. Guo Chunhua and Guo Bohai were ghosts.

Yao Guang was outside the augmented reality gaming arcade, waiting in a royal-blue BMW X5. He dropped the driver's side window. "You need a ride, mister?" he asked in English. Wei got in the vehicle and smelled how new it was.

"I assume you were here looking for the twins?" Yao asked as they pulled out. "You find them?"

"Found Chunhua. Told her they should both be at the new place at nine tomorrow morning. We're going to need them."

"I know you think you can trust those kids because you can bust them anytime, but are they really that good? You know neither of them finished college?"

"College bored them. In this business, the best are self-taught. And those two? They are among the best. And, yes, I trust them. They just needed to be put on the right path. They're really fucking good."

"Hacking, okay, but you said we were going to be doing stuff with AI?" Yao asked. Wei was constantly surprised at Yao's breadth of knowledge.

"Says the man who is more self-taught than anyone I know. By the way, since when do you speak English, Guang? 'Want a ride, mister?'"

He answered in Chinese. "I don't, but I remember some words from university classes, even though that was over twenty years ago. But look at this ride, Bao—I mean, Chief Inspector Wei. X5. I like our new job already."

"You didn't get this in the police motor pool."

"No, but we do have a big budget, and I got a good lease on this. And I have most of the equipment in the new office installed. Doesn't look like a police office, for sure. You want to see it tonight? They should be almost done."

"Tomorrow morning is soon enough. I have some coding to do tonight, best done at home."

Yao started up the BMW. "Your doctor friend may be a little distracting."

"She is back at the hospital at midnight," Wei said, reminded how much information he shared with Yao. "By the way, how did you know I was at the Seekers Arcade just now?"

"Simple. We have a real smart detective on the force who wrote some sort of AI program, so all I have to do is call in to dispatch and give them a name and they tell me where that person is. Almost always works. Who was that guy? Bao somebody?"

"Well, that's the first piece of code I write tonight. I am going to create a new category of person: untraceable." Wei, Yao, and the twins were all about to become invisible.

6

Dalian
Changjiang Road
Sunday, November 16
0945 hours

WEI ALIGHTED FROM THE light-rail car at the intersection of Changjiang and Shanghai roads and walked across the slick pavement and down a side street toward the football field, where later that day there would be a game between two local clubs. As the city recovered from Saturday night out, there were few people on this wet Sunday morning, few on the tram, even fewer on the streets in this old neighborhood just over the freeway from the docks.

The four-story building Yao had chosen for their operation dated from the 1920s. Yao had taken the entire top floor. A Danish shipping firm had moved out to a fancy high-rise in Eton Place only a month before, leaving a vast loft space with a kitchen, dining area, and large open-plan work area. In the back there was a server room with a reinforced floor and separate air conditioning, as well as fiber connections to two local Internet switches. The Danes had spent when they fixed up this space years before, but the lure of the new and prestigious glass towers had been too strong.

Yao Guang had ordered the four executive offices on the floor converted into bedrooms. He knew they would be sleeping, eating, and working there for the foreseeable future. Most importantly, the fourth floor had its own small side entrance and elevator, a legacy from a time, almost a century before, when the Japanese import-export firm that had designed the building wanted to keep its executives well apart from their Chinese staff who worked on the first three floors.

The sign Yao ordered had already gone up on the separate entrance: ReGlobal Audit Department. That should be boring enough to keep people away. Wei looked like he could have been an auditor finishing up his books on Sunday morning, carrying his laptop in his backpack, wearing reflective sunglasses. He had also donned a baseball cap with a weird design logo instead of his usual Toronto Blue Jays hat. The hat's tunnel image and the reflective glasses were designed to throw off the facial recognition system he had helped design and was now intent on stumping. He didn't even want his own Dalian Police to know where he had set up shop.

The old elevator moved slowly, and the door opened with a loud chime. "Be there by nine o'clock, you tell my sister, and then you show up a half hour late. Late night, Inspector?" Guo Bohai teased Wei, as he, clad in his usual red sweats, greeted his boss and savior with a hug. Bohai was a hugger. It drove Yao crazy that Wei allowed that behavior, but Wei tolerated a lot from the twins because they were his secret weapon.

"Very. Been writing the AI code all night. You like your new playpen? Tell Yao if there is anything else you need here. To do the job, I mean—not for fun." The vast open space on the top floor had been fitted out over the past forty-eight hours with glass tables, ergonomic chairs, laptops, servers, printers, large display screens, and whiteboards on wheels.

"You like it down here by the docks? Stinky old buildings? We couldn't be out by the university or in the tech park?" Bohai kept needling Wei, who glared silently back at him.

The elevator chimed again. "Sunday breakfast for the chief inspector and his team," Yao bellowed as he appeared from the elevator, carrying two grocery bags.

"Chief?" Chunhua repeated from her perch on a high stool in front of three computer monitors.

"Special Chief. It's just temporary," Wei explained, suppressing a smile, "while we do this job. It's so we can get whatever we need to succeed. This is an important task, important for the nation."

"So it involves AI, you said, but what exactly is this job?" Yao asked as he spread out the breakfast foods on the counter of the open kitchen area. "Or is it another special need-to-know case?"

Wei had already given Yao some idea of the task, but Yao was setting his boss up to tell the story to the twins. Wei hopped up on a seat by the kitchen bar and indicated to the twins to do the same. Yao stayed on the other side of the counter, leaning forward, his two large hands on the counter, propping up his wide frame.

"Here is the problem," Wei began. "There are managers in state-owned companies who are hiring their deadbeat relatives for jobs that really do not exist. The relatives never come to work, but they get paid, then they give some of the money back as a bribe to the managers who hired them."

"How do we know this happens?" Yao asked. "I mean, it might, but does it happen enough for us to set up this special taskforce?"

"Our leaders, in fact our very top leader, thinks this happens a lot. Knows it does. So it is up to us to prove him right. 'Corruption must be weeded out.'"

"I saw that on a sign once," Chunhua said, turning to look out the window at the sea. "Or was it a thousand signs."

"Our leaders in Beijing, the guys who want the weeding out, they call these people who get paid by state corporations but never come to work 'No Shows,'" Wei explained, using the English term as Huang Qiang had.

"Nosho," Bohai mumbled and tapped into his smartphone. "Japanese word. Means 'place,' according to the translation app."

"No Show, it's English." Wei corrected.

"English," Bohai tapped again. "No Shoes. App says it means barefoot."

"Que xi gongren," Wei screamed using the Chinese phrase. "No Shows, those who do not show up for work."

"Oh. Why didn't you say that?" Bohai laughed.

Wei ignored him. "And their bosses, who get a cut of their salaries as a kickback, are called 'Skimmers,' pie zha qi. They skim off some of the No Shows' paychecks. No Shows and Skimmers. We have to identify them. Then, all at once, in a big show, arrest a lot of them all over the country."

"Why you always speak English to us, boss?" Chunhua chuckled in English.

"Dalian not your Canada." Bohai giggled.

Wei glared back at the twins. "I've been working on an AI algorithm. It will hunt and find the employee roster and the payroll list on a company's network. Then it will find the company ID card photo of each employee. Next it will find the surveillance cameras in the company, especially the ones at the employee entrances. We identify everybody who shows up at work each day."

Yao snapped his fingers. "You subtract the people who show up and we see on camera from those on the list of who gets paid and the names that are left are the No Shows!"

Wei Bao snapped his fingers back at Yao. "Precisely."

Chunhua shook her head. "You two are funny together. You make it sound so easy. First, you have to go to all these companies and ask them to let you run your little AI tool. That will tip off the No Shows. Second, some people work remotely, like we did during the virus, not just at the big plants and office blocks. They may not show up on the cameras, but they may be working somewhere."

"I thought of that. We aren't going to let the companies know what we are doing. Not going to ask. You two are going to hack your way in. Here's an initial list of the firms. You up to that?"

Chunhua looked up from the list of target companies. "Hacking into these guys is a crime. You sure we're okay doing this?"

"I told you last night, we have orders to do so. Orders from the top. That makes it legal. Still, cover your tracks. Make it looks like Russians or Americans are doing it. Use their attack tools, their techniques, staging servers in Vietnam, Philippines. Use Cyrillic keyboards. Think you can do this?" Wei asked, knowing the answer.

"You kidding me, boss?" Bohai laughed. "These are state-run companies. Our baby brother could get in, and he's only twelve."

"Bohai! Mother said Zixin is not allowed to hack yet," Chunhua scolded. Then the twins erupted into shrill laughter, sharing another joke only they understood.

It happened a lot. They had no baby brother or living parent. Although the two now tried to dress differently than each other and had recently acquired very different frames for their glasses, the tall, skinny twenty-year-olds were almost an entangled pair in some quantum sense. The boy, Bohai, affected what he thought was a rapper-gangster style of speaking, a mélange of Mandarin and intentionally broken English that he hoped made him sound much dumber than he was. Wei had seen right through it. Both twins would score near the top of any pool of test-takers on any verbal or quantitative aptitude test. In fact, when in school, they had.

Yao and Wei exchanged a familiar glance and Wei continued, "As to people working remotely, the company records should show their location of employment, whether they work from home or what office they are supposed to be in. But also, we use the surveillance cameras in every city to look for the workers who are not showing up at the factories. If they are at another job or in a park, at the cinema or bars all the time when they should be working..."

"City surveillance cams use National ID card photos to identify people on the street. Company ID photos may be different. Differences may screw up the AI," Bohai said, looking up from the notes he had begun taking on an iPad Pro.

"And to prove that they are kicking back money to their managers, we would need their bank records, their WeChat and Alipay account data," Yao added. "Please don't tell me you are going to hack them, boss."

"I can get all that, no hacking needed," Wei said, his hands gesturing, as though he were using sign language to translate his words. "You and I, Yao, we get the permission to access those databases, get clerks to copy records into our data lake, while these two hack into the other companies and pull the workers' names, images, pay records, and surveillance footage. Then we run the facial recognition program."

"That's a lot to compute." Bohai shook his head. "But wait. What? Did you say data lake? Our data lake? You got us a data lake, boss?"

"Yes. It's in the Alibaba cloud, but right now it's empty. It's your job to start filling it." Wei reached out for the tea that Yao offered him. "Nobody likes a dry lakebed."

7

Dalian
ReGlobal Audit Department
Changjiang Road
Monday, November 17
0800 hours

"It's called Autonomous Tiger, Zizhi Hu," Bohai explained, over another brown bag breakfast in the loft, "because it runs on its own and rips like a tiger."

"Otherwise known as Offense AI," Chunhua deadpanned. "OAI. We developed it yesterday."

"We finished it yesterday, late," Bohai clarified. "Early this morning. We sleep here now. Nice. Bigger beds than on our boat. But we've been working on this OAI for months."

"Okay, since June," Chunhua admitted. "We knew you would need it someday. That's why we did it. Not for us to use. We don't hack anymore, except for you. Just you. Really."

"Right. That better be true. Okay, so show us how the tiger hunts. Walk us through the steps on the Dalian cyber range," Wei said. The special chief inspector had used his "provide all assistance" card to get priority access to his undergrad alma mater Dalian Technical University's high-in-demand network simulator, a cyber range that was used to test both offensive and defensive apps and to teach students how to use them.

Bohai pointed to one of the large screens on the wall. He used a pull-down menu to select Model Large Corporate Network. "Sure, boss. First, our tiger runs external scans. It identifies all of the block of IP addresses the company has. External scans can tell a lot, like what operating system they have, Kylin, Red Star, Windows, regular Linux, whatever. Then we ping them to see what defenses they have up, Huawei firewall or Checkpoint, maybe Cisco clone, possibly Palo Alto clone."

Yao Guang stared at the screen as Bohai's tiger simulation played. Yao seemed genuinely interested in the technical detail. "Won't pinging alert them?"

Chunhua shook her head. "Not really. They get millions of pings a day from bots that just go round the internet pinging IP addresses to see what they are and if they are wide open."

Bohai clicked the simulation to continue. "Then the tiger AI runs the probabilities. What known vulnerability in their OS or firewall can we get in with? Probably newly discovered ones that not even good-hygiene sites have patched yet. Maybe old ones they never got around to fixing. It tries one after another until it gets in."

"But we may not really be in. Could be a trap." Chunhua picked up the story. "So, it checks if this is a honeypot, a sandbox, a fake network where we have been shunned off to where the defenders will watch us to learn our tricks? It checks how much activity is really going on in this network. Are the servers real or simulated? If it's real, it goes ahead. If it's a honeypot, it drops a wiper and destroys the sandbox. Then it tries another way in."

On the large screen, a box on the simulated network map turned red and a beeping sound chirped out. "Ha, their intrusion detection system discovered you. Now what?" Wei asked.

"No problem, boss. That thing goes off a lot. It just sends a work order to the guys in the Security Operation Center, where it just gets in the line of other alerts and work orders. Lots of others. We could even add other orders in front. By the way, Zizhi Hu already makes sure there are a lot of alerts by making loud, clunky attacks on the site for hours before, during, and after the real one. It does website defacements, denial of service attacks, all sorts of tricks to keep them busy in the SOC." Bohai was on a roll.

Wei smiled and sat back, enjoying the show, knowing he had done the right thing when he had hired these two rather than turning them in.

"It sees they have internal firewalls to prevent lateral movement. Good for them, but no problem for Zizhi Hu. It pops firewalls using known vulnerabilities and moves on, mapping the entire network, sub-nets, endpoints, shadow IT." Bohai passed the clicker to his sister to continue.

Chunhua spoke slower and softer, making Wei and Yao lean forward in their chairs. "Now the Zizhi Hu gets credentials. In this case, the company is fancy and has an Israeli application called a Privileged Access Manager, PAM. The Hu knows a vulnerability for this PAM that the Americans, NSA, use, and the Hu uses it to get control, establishing a new Super User. This Super User gets very special qualities. It is not listed in the directory and its activities are never logged, or if they are by mistake, they get erased right away. We call this Super User the Yinxing Shen, Stealth God.

"Stealth God now creates a workspace for itself on a server, naming it something boring like Archived Net Logs. It then uses your new AI program, boss, beginning by going to payroll and copying over the database. Then it goes to personnel and copies over that database. Finally, it goes to security and gets the pictures of all employees from their access cards.

"Now back to our stuff, the Zizhi Hu. In a workspace it created for itself on the network, the AI breaks these files up into smaller ones, then compresses them, then encrypts them with its own algorithm it imported; now it exfiltrates those files off the company network to a staging server in Vietnam like the NSA would, then to one in the Azure cloud in California, then bounces them to an Amazon cloud in Virginia, then to a Rackspace cloud in Texas, then back to a new one in Vietnam, and then to our data lake."

Bohai resumed. "Then all of those virtual servers we just used in the clouds, all of which we bought with fresh stolen credit cards and turned on an hour before, they all disappear. Poof. No way to trace the bounces."

Yao and Wei exchanged a glance. "Okay, then. Enough for the cyber range, let's go out onto the Internet. Live. Let's try it first on only one company. How about Manchurian Steel and Metals, probably not well defended?" Wei guessed aloud and looked at a file. "IP address block in 27.113.19.255."

Bohai repeated the IP address back as he tapped it in. "Okay to hit send?" Wei nodded. Yao stood up and began to walk away from the wall-mounted screen.

"Where you going, Yao? Don't you want to watch the Zizhi Hu show?" Bohai called after him.

"I am going to empty my bladder, which doesn't take me that long. I will be back in time for your show."

"Already happening. See?" Bohai pointed to the screen, which was quickly changing, with symbols for network devices appearing, blinking, turning various colors. "You pee now, you miss it."

Chunhua was clapping and hooting. Yao turned around and came back. The screen was getting covered with a network map. A box at the side gave a rolling tally of numbers for endpoints, firewalls, servers, file sizes. Now another map appeared as files left the company network and bounced across the internet. Something on the other side of the room beeped. Then the screen switched to a depiction of Wei's own new data lake. It was filling up.

"Nobody likes an empty data lake," Bohai said, proudly standing in front of the big screen.

"Nobody, especially not Zizhi Hu," Chunhua added.

"You're done? Already?" Yao asked. "That took like ninety seconds."

"Wrong. It took three and a half minutes. It only seemed like less, but it was still some kind of world record," Wei said, walking over to the twins to bow to them.

"Chunhua could do almost as good," Bohai said of his sister. "She does tap faster than anyone."

"Would have taken me eight minutes, maybe more," she joked.

"Maybe way less." Wei laughed. "Amazing. Can I get into the data now?"

"Can I pee now?" Yao called over his shoulder as he moved quickly to the WC in the corner of the loft. "Everybody likes an empty bladder."

Wei took a keyboard from Chunhua and opened the data lake. File names appeared on the big screen. "Personnel database, payroll database, access badges, R&D? Why did you take their R&D database?"

"Zizhi Hu left breadcrumbs from the R&D file to the Equation Group, one of their staging servers everybody knows about. So when they wake up in Manchurian Steel a month from now and realize they were pwned, and they call in the Ministry, those guys will think it was the Americans," Chunhua explained in an exasperated tone, like a teacher to a dumb student. "We used

American attack tools to get in. Let's say maybe Americans want to see if China is using stolen Yankee R&D again so they can sanction the company."

"Equation Group?" Wei asked.

"NSA, boss. That's their handle," Bohai added. "It will look like NSA hacked Manchurian Minerals or whatever it was we just popped. Not us. NSA. The Americans. We don't go to jail, even if you get run over by a tram. We didn't do it. They did. NSA. Bad American imperialists."

Wei shook his head in amazement and started going through the payroll database. "Looks like everybody who works at Manchurian does direct electronic deposit to their banks. Nobody is paid in cash anymore?"

Yao was back. "No, part of the crackdown on corruption by our president. No cash. Electronic fund transfers only for all payrolls everywhere in China. Everyone uses WeChat or AliPay anyway. Everything is traceable."

Wei handed back the keyboard to Chunhua. "Okay, next steps. Run the facial recognition program on the video files from the employee entrances and figure out who the records say works at the plant and is showing up for work. And who isn't. Do that for the Manchurian Steel and Metals and then the next nine companies on our initial list. Once we know the people being paid but not showing up, the No Shows, then we see what happens to their money in the banks. Does some of it go to their bosses? Are their bosses related to them?"

"So we really don't get to hack the banks?" Chunhua complained.

"No, you don't. I told you, Yao and I are going to go serve notices on the banks to give us access to their systems. After all, as you said, I might get hit by a tram. We wouldn't want some new cop to arrest you for breaking into banks, not again."

"We were never prosecuted," Bohai called out from his keyboard. "And it wasn't a bank, anyway."

8

Dalian Police Headquarters
3 People's Square, Xigang District
Chief Inspector's Office
Friday, November 21
1530 hours

Chief Inspector Wang did not rise from his chair facing the bay window, looking out across the city from the top floor of police headquarters. An aide indicated that Wei should sit in the leather chair next to Wang, then withdrew to the far end of the large wood-paneled office to get the tea. Sitting close by the chief inspector, Wei noticed that the older man looked fatigued. For the first time, Wei did the math and realized that his boss was almost exactly thirty years older than him. And now they held the same rank, almost.

"You can see it all from here—the downtown, the wharfs, the harbor. You can see the car crashes, the fires, our patrol cars blinking on their way to a bar fight. You can see thousands of people," Wang said as he put down the binoculars he had been using, "but you can't tell what they are thinking. Cigarette? Or are you only smoking Gitanes now? Thank you for coming. I know you must be busy."

"I don't smoke, sir," Wei replied, remembering where he had first seen a box of Gitanes a few days ago.

"Yes, you should stay healthy. After all, you have your own doctor. Fenfang would not like it if you smoked. She is a woman of strong opinions?"

"The air is bad enough without adding more particulates to our lungs, sir." Wei's eyes narrowed, looking at the sharp pleat of the chief's uniform, the sparkling black shoes.

"You must not call me sir, not now. You are now also a chief inspector, I am told. A special chief inspector, but that is a chief nonetheless, no?

You are a colleague, and I am to grant you any assistance you may require from our force here. So, what do you require from us?"

"That is very kind of you, but at the moment I am not in need of help, Chief Inspector."

"We all need help, Wei. We all have to help each other. No man can get along by himself. That is what the Party is all about, everyone working for the people. That is what this police force is all about, too. Maybe I can help you with your enemies. Who are your enemies, Wei?" Wang asked as he sipped a small cup of the hot tea his aide had left on the table between the two seats.

"I don't believe I have any enemies, except a few men in prison."

Wang stifled a laugh. "And the friends of the Russians you killed. Dead enemies are the best kind, but Wei, we all have enemies. You just don't know yet who yours are. Tell me when you do know, and I will deal with them, as friends do, as police colleagues do. We help each other, especially," he lowered his voice, "when a fellow officer is in trouble."

There was a brief silence. For the first time in the conversation the two men stared into each other's eyes.

"Well, Wei, don't let me keep you from your important work." Chief Inspector Wang again picked up his binoculars.

Wei stood. "Have a good day, Chief Inspector." As he said it, he realized it was something Canadians said, not Chinese. He also realized that Wang had not asked what Wei's mission was, did not inquire about the Beijing meeting at all, but he had known that Wei could requisition assistance, known about Fenfang, about the French cigarettes.

At the far side of the office, the aide opened the door for Wei, and as he did, Wei heard Wang's voice from across the room. "Corruption must be weeded out."

9

Dalian
ReGlobal Audit Department
Changjiang Road
Friday, November 21
1830 hours

YAO GUANG STARED AT the whiteboard with his hands on his hips. "It makes no sense."

Bohai sat on a stool next to him. "We did everything right. We proved there are No Shows; we just can't find where they are at the times when they should be at work." Chunhua sat next to him, tapping quickly onto a laptop balanced on her knees.

Wei looked at them. "So, what you are telling me is that these people, thousands of them, at ten big companies, have company IDs and national IDs, but the cameras at the companies never see them walk in the doors, never see them in the cafeterias, never see them in the offices or on the factory floors. And they are not in work-from-home jobs.

"Yet, every month they get paid, salaries flow into their bank accounts, and the records we got from the banks and WeChat and AliPay show them paying for mobile phone bills, buying transport cards. They have phones and transit cards, but we never see them use their damn phones and none of our cameras pick them up using the transport cards in the metros or on buses. In fact, we never see them anywhere—parks, bars, cinemas."

"It is weird, boss," Bohai agreed. "They all have National IDs with photos. Their employee files have copies of their birth records, school records at a bunch of high schools and some at colleges. We hacked the schools to double-check they went there. They did. They have grade transcripts. Their National ID pictures are identical to their company photos. We run the images through photo recognition systems where their jobs are in Beijing, Guangzhou, Shanghai, even Dalian. Nothing. They are never detected out and about. They never appear on the street, in the metro, in stores, at games."

Chunhua looked up from her keyboard. "We know where they live, and we even hacked the cameras in their apartment buildings, but we never see faces in the buildings that the facial recognition software can match to the workers' ID photos. Even though they live there. Do they sleep all the time? Do they never leave their apartments, like during the virus?"

"We've done something wrong." Wei said each word slowly, looking up at the ceiling tiles.

Yao turned to face his boss. "What we've done wrong is stay in this damn office all week, day and night, while these two plus our half-dozen clerks played with databases. We need to get some air, walk the streets, pound on doors just like we were police."

Wei came out of his semi-trance, jumped off his stool, and snapped his fingers at Yao. "Right. Exactly. Bohai, print out the home addresses of the ten No Show employees who live closest to our location here in Dalian. Yao Guang and I are going for a walk."

Bohai took a sheet from a printer and handed it to Wei, as the two detectives were donning their jackets. "What do you want us to do?" Chunhua asked after them, as Wei and Yao moved to the elevator.

"Find more databases where they show up. Medical, automotive, border controls, credit cards. And find some databases where they don't appear but should," Wei instructed as the elevator doors closed. "See if we can find other photos of them to use in the facial recognition algorithm. Grab them from their social media."

"We really going to walk the streets?" Yao asked in the shaky old elevator car as it descended. "After you pulled off a fancy German car for being a chief inspector?"

Wei shook his head, knowing that it made Yao's day to drive the BMW X5. "Fuck no, it's raining out there tonight."

They drove west on Renmin Road toward Zhongshan Square, which in winter was laced with thousands of small white lights on bare trees and strung between streetlights. "Nicholas Square," Wei said, "our own Red Square courtesy of the Russian occupation. They did like to do things big."

"Nicholas Square is a better name than what it was during the Japanese times," Yao replied, proving he too knew his city's history.

"Which was what?"

"Largest Square." Yao laughed.

"Very poetic people, the Japanese," Wei said, sharing the laugh. He was finding it easier to banter with his partner, who seemed to revel in Wei's temporary promotion. Of course, it would also help Yao's performance evaluation that he had been the deputy to a chief inspector during a major national investigation. Unsaid between them was their shared knowledge that what they were onto would also likely be a nationwide scandal, with many heads rolling, some of them important ones with influential friends.

Yao turned south toward the Qingni residential district and the high-rise apartments overlooking Laodong Park. The first address they were going to was a high-priced one belonging to a senior research scientist at the state-owned pharmaceutical firm Sinopharma Technology Holdings. The building was less than five years old, a thirty-story glass wall now twinkling with living room lights, kitchens where dinners were being readied, bedrooms where students were doing homework. Yao drove the X5 in front of a No Parking sign near the lobby doors. He threw a police placard and a blue rotator light into the BMW's front window. There was no need to be undercover tonight.

They strolled through the sleek lobby with its lightly stained wood paneling and a small jungle of ferns and palms. A man in a deep red jacket with the name of the building stitched on it stood by the elevator bank. He asked whom they were visiting.

"What, you don't think we live here?" Yao barked back.

"It is my job to recognize my residents and to assist their guests," the lobbyman responded, respectfully, sensing the two men in leather coats had an official air to them. "And I believe you must be guests. How may I help you?"

"Dr. Liu isn't expecting us," Wei said softly, flashing his badge. "It would be best for you if he were not made aware we were coming up."

"I don't know a Dr. Liu, so I won't be calling him. But by all means, officers, please visit our building and let me know how I can make your visit successful."

They were on the twenty-seventh floor in less than two minutes, looking for apartment 2704, home of Dr. Liu Honghui, the well-paid researcher at Sinopharma.

There was a 2703, a 2705, a 2706, but no 2704. The residents of the neighboring apartments were all at home, all cooperative with the two police detectives, all willing to look at the National ID file photo of Dr. Liu Honghui that Wei popped up on his mobile.

"No Dr. Liu, and no one who looks like that picture by any name. We know all the people who live on twenty-seven. We rotate who holds the Saturday drinks party, just a jump start before our weekend evenings out and a way to stay in touch, so we can complain together about the noise from those elephants on twenty-eight stomping around and partying late. It would be good for the police to visit twenty-eight and ask questions up there late Saturday night, I can tell you that." Mrs. Ho of 2703 would have talked longer had the detectives had the time.

They did visit twenty-eight, but found no elephants, and no Dr. Liu, nor anyone who had ever known him. There was also no 2804.

"There are no units with the number on any floor," the lobbyman explained when they returned to the ground level. "Who wants bad luck? Who wants an apartment that sounds like death? No one will buy a four."

The two policemen walked through the lobby to the car. Wei stopped outside, hands on his hips, and exhaled deeply, creating a breath cloud in the night air. Yao turned back toward his partner. "Want me to have uniforms visit these other Dalian addresses?"

"Sure, why not? I'm not going to. It will all be the same. No such address. None of them use their real addresses. But we need to have tried for our report, so yeah, start tomorrow night at the home addresses they used, which won't exist or won't belong to our No Shows. Maybe our No Shows don't exist. What if they're all fake personas? We need to think this through. Let's go get a Snow Beer."

"Baijiu for me," Yao countered. "It always helps me solve problems."

On their drive to the Xigang district, Chunhua called. "I had an idea, boss. Remember when Taiwan was using bots, having fake people posting things online against the Party?"

"That was a rumor, Chunhua. The Party never confirmed that such a thing happened," Wei replied because they were talking on an unencrypted phone. "Let me call you back on another phone. This one is running out of juice."

As Yao maneuvered the slick pavement, Wei took an encrypted handset out of the car's locked glove box and called Chunhua at the loft. "Why is what Taiwan did with the trolls relevant?" he asked her.

"I started to think it's odd that the company ID photos of the No Shows are identical with their National ID photos. So just maybe I have a relative who works for a certain ministry in Beijing, and maybe she worked on finding the fake Taiwan accounts back when they were posting what, of course, must have been lies about the Party."

"Okay, I'm listening," Wei said as he flipped the phone to speaker so Yao could hear her.

"Maybe she and her team identified the trolls posting on Weibo by realizing the faces on the accounts were AI generated, not real people, and maybe her team came up with an algorithm that could spot AI-generated faces."

"AI-generated faces, yeah, I've heard of that. Russia does it too, against the Americans on Facebook. They look very real. We should get that algorithm and run it against the No Shows. Maybe their ID pictures aren't real either. That would explain why we never see them walking around. It's not their real pictures. Could be," Wei said, turning to Yao as they drove through Friday night traffic. Yao nodded. "I could use my special writ authority to get the State Security Ministry to give us that software that detects AI-generated faces. Just let me know who to call. Good thinking, Chunhua." She didn't answer. "Chunhua?"

Bohai came on the line. "She gone. She mad at you now. Sister already got the algorithm, without you and your special writs. We already ran it on the Nosho ID photos. They all AI-generated. All them."

"That's great work, guys," Wei said softly into the encrypted mobile. "But, Bohai, why is Chunhua mad at me?"

"She's my twin, yeah, but I don't understand her sometimes now. She said something in English about 'mansplaining' and stomped off to her bedroom down the hall. You understand women, Inspector, don't you? You have one, right? A doctor lady? Anyway, No Shows faces are all AI-generated. Case solved. Now we can go back to get ready for the AR tournament at the arcade?"

"Not quite yet. We need to figure out whose AI it was that created the faces and got them into the National ID system and then into the companies' databases. Tell Chunhua I need you two to figure that out."

"Yeah, when she comes out. I'm not going in there. Meanwhile, I can start myself to try to figure out whose AI did the faces. Some people we know in Berlin, we can ask them to find guys who do best quality AI-generated faces, Chinese people faces and can make lots of them, all different. Need to know who can do that. I may need to spread around some Euros. Germans all about the money sometimes."

"You can spread, Bohai. Just don't spread it too deep. My new friends in Beijing all about the money sometimes too."

10

Dalian
Brooklyn Bar and Pizza
184 Bulao Jie, Xigang District,
Friday, November 21
2145 hours

"You have reservations? It's Friday. We're full," the doorman on Bulao Jie said, standing on the sidewalk in front of the closed door to the New York–styled bar.

"I can see an empty booth from here," Yao replied, looking at the closed door as he pressed his police credential against the doorman's nose.

"So can I, boss. So can I now. Enjoy," he said, stepping aside and opening the door.

In addition to the Snow Beer, Wei ordered a bacon pizza. "It's the only place in the city that gets pizza right. And it has the best toppings. Canadian bacon."

Yao ordered pork dumplings, steamed, with his Baijiu. The waiter frowned. The din from the crowd and a dozen screens showing sports from around the world provided enough cover noise that the two men could talk without being overheard in the next booth.

Wei had wanted to find a relaxed time alone with Yao. He was still thinking about the difference in their instincts and how human brains worked. "Instinct is a funny thing. You can't measure it, but it's real. You have it, Yao. You have street instincts. You know immediately what to do when you are dealing with bad guys, how to move your body, how to check them, take them down, disarm them. It just happens, it kicks in."

"You seemed to have it too back there, boss."

"No, but I have something like instinct. I have my subconscious. I feel like it's a separate brain, always running in the background, observing, analyzing, reviewing. Sometimes it speaks to me and shares its analysis. Usually it's slow to figure shit out, but when it does, it tells me something that my conscious mind had not worked out. Then, sometimes it screams at me, like when I am about to do something stupid, like pick up something hot or go out without my gun or badge. Sometimes it's a blink response and I know the right answer without thinking. I know it right away."

Yao laughed. "I only have one brain. You have two and yet you want artificial brains to help you. How many brains do you need?"

"Right now, I need a brain that will figure out what is going on with the No Shows. I am not getting a blink response, no matter how many times I blink."

"Here's what I don't get, boss," Yao said as he stacked beer coasters into a small tower. "If all of these No Shows are really fake people, and let's say you are a small-time Party member running a state-owned company's factory somewhere, and you are corrupt, but I repeat myself, and you want to make the wife happy by giving her no-good brother a job he doesn't have to show up for, just do that and get your handful of cash from him every month when he comes by to play with his nephews. Why hack into databases outside the company like transit cards, universities, mobile phones, birth records, and why create false identities, phony personas with AI-generated faces? Besides, that's too hard for those kinds of guys."

Wei was texting Fenfang. He looked up. "I don't think it's corrupt guys at the plants. You're right. This requires AI that is too sophisticated for them. And it's a nationwide pattern. You add up all that these thousands of No Shows are earning, Yao—it's a lot of money. Somebody is skimming billions of yuan."

Wei Bao pocketed his mobile. "If you are a corrupt Party boss high up, you can have State Security send money overseas for a 'special project' to a secret bank account, or you have the Foreign Ministry procure some piece of overseas property that doesn't exist from a front company you set up in Singapore and the Ministry sends the purchase price to a bank account there, or better yet to a bank account in Tuvalu. Nobody in Tuvalu ever looks out for money laundering. Have your ministry overpay for a foreign procurement, say, from Italy, where everyone will take a kickback and create a phony receipt. Or fly Central Bank gold bars to a bank deposit box in the Seychelles where all the Arabs stash their gold. That's the usual stuff. Been going on for decades. But creating phantom citizens, giving them a digital backstory, and even harder, giving them ever-changing records that create a pattern of life? Why bother?"

Yao stopped building his beer coaster tower. "So it's not corrupt Party bosses. That narrows the field to around a billion other citizens of the People's Republic. Or at least the ones who can hack databases, which is still probably only a few tens of millions of people these days."

The pizza and dumplings arrived, and they ordered a second round of drinks. "That's actually a good way to go at it, Yao. Who could do this? Who has the skill sets? You know, when you think about it, it would either take an army of people to do all that hacking to generate the accounts and faces in all these companies, keep the identities up to date, or..."

"Or two twins working for us?" Yao joked.

"Not even close. The twins are great hackers, but this requires the very best AI masters to keep up all of these databases so it looks like thousands of phantom citizens are real. That takes advanced AI programs and machine learning algorithms, and the programs must be talking all the time to the databases, the bank accounts, paying bills, moving money, creating a pattern of life.

"What if an employee is ordered to show up in person for a physical or training? The AI would have to know about that and alter the records to show that they had the physical, took the classes. That is a lot of work, one hell of an AI program, and a lot of computing power. You'd need a ton of servers."

Yao placed his oversized hand above his coaster tower, crushed it, then looked across at Wei Bao and smiled. "Simple detective work, then. Where are there a lot of servers, and who has access to them? The PLA, State Security, Alibaba, Baidu, half a dozen universities. We look there. Or forget about where the computers are and ask who could write all of that AI and keep it going? We could drive out to Dagong and ask the AI professors there who the best guys doing this in China are."

Wei considered the idea. Dagong, Dalian Technical University, did have an advanced AI/machine learning research program. He had been a minion for the program when he was an undergrad. "Why just in China, Yao? Sure, the best guys in China could be at Alibaba and Baidu, but just as likely to be Chinese people at Google or even Microsoft in the US. Or at a dozen other universities in China, the US, the UK, Israel, and Canada. Maybe they aren't even Chinese people."

"There you go again with your foreign education, suggesting Chinese people are not always the best people in every field." Yao smirked.

"Professor Pandry taught us there are journeymen, there are extraordinary coders, and then there are a very few people in the world who are AI and machine learning masters. This project would have taken an AI master. Pandry used to go to an informal club every summer in some Redwood forest in California. They actually called themselves the AIML Masters. He said there were only twenty-four of them, the best from all around the world in AI, machine learning, neural networks."

"This Professor Pandry, he's an Indian?" Yao asked as he reached across to take a pizza slice from Wei's plate.

"Born there but grew up in Canada. He was my professor at Toronto."

"He's an AIML Master, one of those top twenty in the Redwoods?"

"Oh, yeah. Definitely," Wei said, retaliating by grabbing a dumpling.

"Any of the AIMLs Chinese people?"

"One of them. Professor Zhu in Beijing. We can get the twins to hack and monitor him, but he doesn't have the time for this kind of scam. He's always trying to save the world."

"Then ask your Canadian professor who the others are, which of them might be doing this," Yao suggested. "And where somebody would get access to that many servers without being caught misusing them for this scam."

Wei had been staring into his drink but shot up and cocked his head toward Yao. "Repeat what you just said. The last part."

"Ask your professor where someone could get control of a bunch of servers and not get caught misusing them."

As a broad smile crossed Wei Bao's face, he pumped his right hand as if cheering on his team. "You know what Pandry would say to that? You know what he would say?"

Laughing at his young boss, Yao replied, "No, Chief Inspector, I don't. That's why I asked you."

"You really need only one or a handful of computers, not hundreds, if you use a Pandry Q-Compute. See, Pandry, he's the guy who designed the only stable quantum computer that exists so far. It works at room temperature and can run indefinitely without reset. All the other quantum computers are stable for only seconds, and they need to be frozen at minus 40°C. His fame comes from writing AI software that runs on quantum computers. His own programming language. His own computer design."

"Great, so email him and ask him where he has sold those computers in China."

"He hasn't. Canada would never allow him to sell to us. Besides, they're new, really only perfected since I left Canada, and they're almost handmade. There are just a handful. I think he has loaned them to a few AIML Masters, colleagues in Canada and the US, to play with before he settles on a final design and figures out who could mass produce them. That's what my friend Diana told me. We were his students together. She still works for him."

Yao picked up a paper napkin and pretended to be writing on it. "Note to file: the chief inspector admitted that he was still in touch with a girl in Canada." Wei knocked the napkin out of his hand. Laughing, both men took a swig of their drinks.

"You know, Yao, I bet it's some of Pandry's machines that somebody is using to run the No Shows. Maybe CIA or NSA and the professor doesn't know it's them that he loaned a machine to. You now, like, Pandry loans it to a fellow AIML Master, and they give it to the CIA. The CIA uses it to run a program to bleed our economy, to steal billions of yuan they can use to fund their secret projects without using money from their Congress. Too crazy?"

"Seriously, Bao, if you think only one of these AI Masters could be doing this and if you think it might be on one of your professor's machines, just send him a fucking email and ask him for help."

"It would be complicated to explain the scope of this thing in an email, and besides, I don't trust email. I'd have to sit down with him for a few hours, but he would definitely know who could do this and he could find out if one of his machines was doing it."

"Then go sit down with him for a few hours. You can write your own travel orders now, Chief Inspector. Go see your AI Master, grasshopper. Just write down what you want me to have the twins and the clerks doing while you are gone, and write it in a way I can understand it."

"That's an idea." Wei paid the check. "I would have to persuade Fenfang. She may not like me going back there without her. Let's swing by the loft and see what else the twins have found while we have been out."

On the sidewalk, Yao asked, "By the way, what did Chief Inspector Wang want you to visit him for, to pay homage?"

"He said he wanted to be helpful."

"That would be a first," Yao said as he got behind the wheel of the X5. "Have I told you how much I love this car. When this case is over, can we keep it?"

11

38,000 feet above Alaska
Aboard Air Canada flight 62, 777-800
Seat 1K
Sunday, November 23

HE FELT HE WAS nowhere specific. He was in between places, and a kind of freedom seemed to come from not being within the confines of one place. Wei looked down on the clouds. Was it that the gravity was lighter up here, or that the free single malt had calmed him enough that he could finally think clearly?

The business-class seat with its little pod had seemed an extravagance, but Yao had insisted that it was authorized for chief inspectors. He was glad now that he had relented. The single bulkhead seat gave him a privacy he had not had in weeks, maybe longer. He was thinking without distraction, sipping the nectar, watching the cirrus. His mind wandered. He saw scenes from the past week, whirlwind days that had brought him to the nation's very control center and were now ejecting him at nine hundred kilometers an hour across the northern Pacific. And he saw Fenfang.

Surprising him, she had not seemed to mind his leaving, perhaps because he said it would be just five days or seven. They barely saw each other these days, with her long night shifts and his erratic movements, brief moments together before he got out of bed and as she got in. She had asked him to bring back real maple syrup and bacon. If he did, she promised to make pancakes with Canadian bacon. Wei put bacon on everything.

He had told her he would pour the maple syrup first on her breasts and then lick it off before the liquid hardened. She made a joke about licking and hardening and then asked that he also bring back that special Reif Estate

Icewine they'd had in Niagara as they looked down at the falls and across into America, a country they'd never been allowed to visit.

It was a fun conversation before he left, until his suggestion that perhaps she might skip a few meetings of the book club. At least, she had agreed not to host a meeting in their apartment. "We just appreciate literature from around the world, in English, in French. And we discuss it to ensure we have not missed the layers of meaning." They were not political books, she assured him. But of course, they were. They were books that the club members brought back from trips abroad, books unavailable in the People's Republic.

He couldn't stop thinking that there was something in what Chief Inspector Wang had said, some meaning he had missed. Maybe Wang was warning him of jealous fellow police?

He knew that he was swimming in new and deep waters, waters he was unaccustomed to. He felt some unidentified threat, like a shark in the shadows. He had asked Yao to use his own boys to sweep their new offices for bugs. Wei and his team began to keep their mobile phones outside the suite in Faraday cages. The microphones and cameras on all of the laptops had been physically and logically disabled. He also asked Yao to have his and Fenfang's apartment swept when she was at work to make sure no one was attempting to listen to them there.

If Wei had enemies, as Wang said everyone did, maybe jealous police, they could try to follow him. Try, but when you design the facial recognition system for the police, you can design a way to disable it for special people, just in case anyone senior ever asks you to do that. Oddly, no one had ever wanted that. After Yao revealed that he had tracked Wei to the AR arcade using the police system that Wei himself had devised, the special chief inspector had personally made sure it was no longer possible for the Dalian police system to track Wei and his team, their phones, or even Yao's prized car.

Wei had made sure that his own face and Yao's and the twins were never correlated by the AI with a name or stored in the police database. Wei and his team also often blinded the system with the special baseball-style caps, which made the wearers into ghosts to the electro-optical scanners.

Wei's facial recognition software running the cameras would zoom in on a blurred image on the cap that looked like a tunnel to the software. The software would then move on because people's heads did not have tunnels on them. If there were a tunnel, it was not a person.

Wei and his team sometimes also wore special reflective sunglasses which registered them to the cameras as windows, not people. People complained about facial recognition software in the West, said it had many false positives. Maybe Western programs did. Wei's had few mistakes because of the fusion of many data sources and the machine learning program that kept self-correcting. Only he knew how often it had false negatives, as it did when tracking him and the team.

Just before he left, Wei had added Fenfang to the null set list in the facial recognition AI. Her face, if identified by a camera, now triggered a command not to record the fact that she had been seen. Therefore, the software never went to the next step to correlate where her phone was last detected.

While he was at it, Wei had also modified the metal detector scanners to first detect a special dongle he always carried on him whenever he entered the metal detectors. The device signaled to the scanner not to scan, but to project a clean image. It was less time-consuming than going through the protocol procedure every time he carried his handgun into a building with scanners, but it did not work everywhere. He had not carried a sidearm to Beijing, and he wasn't carrying a gun to Canada now. He didn't think he would need one there.

He had been sure to inform his new boss of his trip to Canada and the reason for it. Chief of Staff Huang had only replied "noted" when he had texted him on the specially encrypted phone that had been part of the kit given Wei. "Noted" meant not approved, but not disapproved. You may go outside the country. You may go back to Canada, briefly, because you made a credible case that your "contact" there would know the names of the very few men in the world who were AI Masters capable of designing a system such as the one you have uncovered. The very few men, likely all men, but perhaps a woman or two, in one Cambridge or the other.

The "contact" in Canada, Professor Ramesh Pandry, his academic mentor, might be able to confirm Wei's theory that only a quantum computer running advanced machine-learning algorithms could create and maintain as complex a scam as he had uncovered. A friend still at U Toronto had told him that the very best such systems had been designed and were actually owned by Pandry through his private startup companies. Maybe someone working in one of those companies, someone with access to a quantum machine learning generator, was behind the theft.

At least that was what Wei had written Huang. Wei was, in fact, actually less sure than he had let on to Huang that Ramesh Pandry would devote enough time to Wei's puzzle to answer those questions. Wei would have to intrigue him with the challenge.

It had been easier than he thought it would be to get the professor to take his call. Diana, his friend from grad school days, had helped. That was probably the reason it had worked. Diana McPherson had been part of the small cabal of Pandry graduate student acolytes of which Wei had been a member for three years. She had stayed on, becoming Pandry's surrogate for the things that bored him about being at the university, things like normal graduate students and their pedestrian research projects. She freed the professor to do his own explorations and projects, of which there always seemed to be a plethora, each vaguely described and likely beyond the ken of all but a few human minds that had the genetic oddity of special synapses, not unlike the artificial neural networks Pandry designed.

Wei had not said much on the call, just that he needed some help on a complex problem. The professor had been warm and gracious. "I love a complex problem. Come visit. Stay at my home. It will be so good to see you again, Bao."

How should he describe the problem to Pandry when they met in person? Catching criminals would not intrigue him, too banal. If he could describe the task as deducing the architecture of this particular complex AI system of systems from its actions, if he could make one of the questions how many AI experts and with what level of skill would it take to design and operate such a network of programs and apps, perhaps that would lead to a discussion of which specific AI Masters could do such a project, who would do such a devious defrauding scheme, perhaps under duress.

Yes, that was an angle that would attract the professor—is there an AI Master under duress somewhere, forced to help some criminal group steal money in such a bizarre way.

What he really wanted was for Pandry to confirm that a quantum computer was being used to manage the vast, ongoing theft of the No Shows. If it were commercial, conventional servers or even mainframes being used, it would require a vast installation of equipment to do all of the tasks necessary to manage this elaborate scheme in near real time. On the other hand, if it were a few quantum computers running the operation, there was only one source Wei knew of that made stable quantum computers that were reliable for continuous operations. That source used the special design that Pandry himself had created. If it was one of the handful of advanced quantum computers Pandry and his companies owned, a quick audit of their logs should be able to find out which of Pandry's partners or employees was involved, and maybe for whom they were working. If it turned out to be the CIA, Pandry would pull the plug. He was no fan of those parts of the US government. He had heard Pandry rail against the NSA and the backdoors it had put into encryption programs.

Wei also needed a plan B, in case the professor was not interested in helping or turned out not to be the oracle that he was assuming him to be. Wei could not return home empty-handed, or just with maple syrup, bacon, and ice wine. But plan B would have to come later. The thin air, the whiskey, the hard charge to get things set up and then get on the plane from Dalian to Inchon, the almost-missed connection in Inchon to the Air Canada flight, they had all worn him out. The last ten days had been all adrenalin and caffeinated tea.

The clouds seen through the window rolled gently by, and the flight attendant who came to refill his whiskey found Wei Bao asleep behind his mask.

12

International Arrivals Hall,
Lester Pearson International Airport
Toronto, Ontario
Canada
Sunday, November 23
1740 hours

He looked into the camera lens that he knew was behind the one-way mirror in the kiosk. He placed his fingers on the horizontal glass window below the mirror, as the diagram on the kiosk indicated he should. A message appeared on the mirror and a text which displayed a question in English and French, then Mandarin: "Are you Wei Bao, citizen of China?" A green "Yes" button and a red "No" appeared below the question. This was a new system to Wei. It had not been in use when he was in Canada three years ago. How did they know his face? They had not even asked him to scan his passport.

The kiosk printed a form with a red stripe across it. The screen message changed to "Please present this form to a Border Control officer at booth three, four, or five."

Other arriving passengers were streaming into the country, Canadians and Americans, mainly. They were simply standing before a camera kiosk, which then printed them a green-striped card to open the turnstile. These travelers were already registered in the system.

But since he was not registered in this system, how had they known him? Of course. They had his Ontario driver's license and his student visa from three years ago that had his facial image. The Canadians had entered all of that information into their national facial recognition database and kept it in an active file. Now, when he appeared back in the country, the Canada Border Security Agency's AI knew who he was.

He was glad that he was traveling on a passport in his true name. If he had not been, since they knew his face and real name, there would have been a problem if he had a pseudonym, and he might have been barred from entry. "What is the purpose of your trip, Mister Bao?" the CBSA woman at booth five asked him.

He did not correct the officer. Instead, he said, "I am here for five to seven days on a tourist visa to visit with my old professor at the University of Toronto and thank him for all that he taught me when I studied here three years ago." The answer was comprehensive. It addressed most of the follow-up questions that a CBSA officer would normally have asked. Most but not all. You had to give them something to ask.

"Where will you be staying?"

"At the professor's house. He invited me to stay with him, just off campus."

"What did you study when you were a student there?"

"IT, information technology." It seemed less of a trigger phrase than saying "artificial intelligence, machine learning, surveillance, and facial recognition."

"Have a pleasant stay, Mr. Bao." Mr. Wei, he thought, but didn't say out loud.

For such a normally polite and pleasant people, the Canadians had always seemed to him to be unnecessarily inquisitive at their borders. What difference did it make where he was staying or what he had studied? The person asking did not know the correct answer or have an immediate way of accessing a database that might. They would neither record his replies nor seek to verify them later. Perhaps their chatter was meant to detect nervousness, like the Israelis do so obviously at their airport. The Israelis, however, induce nervousness in innocents, which makes their system somewhat self-defeating. He wondered if the Israelis were still asking if you had packed your own bag. No one had ever answered that with anything other than a "yes." No one, in all the decades they had been asking.

He had entered "IT services" as his occupation on his visa application. He had listed "ReGlobal Audit Department" as his employer, with a phone number that Yao's clerks would answer with that name. No one ever called. Canada encouraged Chinese tourists, both before and after the virus. They spent money. They were orderly. And they all returned home, unlike thirty years ago when they stayed or walked across the border into Vermont. That's what he had been told back then by Chinese Canadians whom he had met in Toronto, usually in the after-hours Chinese restaurants. The Chinese who owned the restaurants had all overstayed visas or their parents had. Eventually, Canada had given them legal status, then citizenship. Canada needed people. For a nation roughly the size of China, it had well less than five percent of China's population. And yet five times China's per capita GDP.

Both figures explained the skyline, he thought, as the Uber driver ran parallel to the lake nearing the downtown. The high-rise residential towers were beautiful, reminiscent of parts of Hong Kong, but here they were spaced well apart from each other. Ordinary people could afford large apartments, and there was enough land that there could be little green parks around each high-rise.

He asked the driver to go through Chinatown and then up by the Comp Sci building on the St. George campus, then out northwest to the more residential Castle Loma district where Professor Ramesh Pandry lived in an elegant and overly large house next to Winston Churchill Park. Clearly his investments in IT startups and his advisory boards and consulting had paid better than his university salary.

The drive through the city brought back memories, scene after scene, of parties, of dinners, of courting Fenfang. Of long hours in the computer labs, friends he had lost contact with, moments when he knew he had made a breakthrough and gained a skill difficult to achieve, times when the professor had congratulated him, and times when he had hit a brick wall in the world of artificial neural networks. They had been formative years academically, professionally, and personally.

He had arrived on campus at age twenty-nine, after six years on the force in Dalian, still a youth in many ways. He had left three years later to go home to a dying mother, passing up a great job offer from Cylance/

Blackberry and a guaranteed residency visa. He had gone back to another world, to the world of his birthplace and of his people. Now he was here not as a young student, but an officer with a charge from the highest level in the People's Republic, a charge he hoped the professor could help him carry out.

The car turned onto Spadina Road and stopped abruptly. Two black and white Toronto police cars blocked the road, their blue lights spinning and giving the quiet street a rave-like feel. The constable, however, did not sound like he was at a party. "You can't go down there. There's been an explosion. More Fire Service trucks are still coming. Go around."

Wei could see red lights and trucks in the street two blocks down Spadina Road, near the park, near the professor's house. He heard the sirens of the units still en route. "What number, what number was the house? I'm staying on that block."

"The call came in as 322 Spadina Road."

He knew it before the officer said it. Pandry's house.

"Gas leak, looks like. You can smell it up there. Enbridge is shutting off the feed to the entire neighborhood. Goin' to be a cold night up here."

Wei stepped out of the car. "That's the house I am staying at, my friend's house. Please, sir, may I get closer? I need to know he's all right."

A police supervisor overheard Wei's plea to one of the officers on the police line. He walked toward Wei. "We've been trying to contact the owner. Do you have his mobile? Can you confirm the name?"

"Ramesh Pandry, Professor Pandry." Wei opened the contacts on his mobile. The policeman looked at the contact, the address of 322 Spadina Road. Together they called the number and got the voicemail, Diana's voice.

"Please, let me go closer, to the next police line." They asked to see his ID, took a picture of his passport, and told him he could go to the next police line. Wei removed his bag from the Uber and almost ran down the middle of the street to the next line of police cars and fire trucks two blocks away. As he drew closer, he smelled the gas and the smoke, felt waves of heat moving through the late autumn chill, and saw the giant orange flames leaping up from inside the great house. It was clear the building would soon be fully consumed.

From the back of one of the police cars, she came running at him. "Bao, Bao, it's so awful; it's all burning up, and I can't find him." It was Diana McPherson, Pandry's right hand and the person who had persuaded the professor to welcome Wei's visit. She embraced Wei, tears streaming down her face, onto his cheek, in the cold night.

They waited for over an hour in a police car for the fire to subdue, calling the mobile number again and again, fearing and not talking about the worst possibility. As far as Diana knew, the professor was supposed to be in Toronto tonight, at home, but he didn't always remember to tell her when he was traveling, and he traveled often.

Finally, a constable came to the police car to tell Diana and Wei that the mobile number they had given them for Professor Pandry had pinged a cell tower in nearby Churchill Park most of the afternoon. That was the closest tower to the house. The phone had stopped pinging the tower around the time of the explosion. "So, we have to conclude he was inside the house when it went up."

They took the police officer's suggestion to leave the fire scene, accept police rides, and come by the station the next afternoon to file a report on what they knew. Before getting into the car that would take her home, Diana agreed to meet Wei at the professor's campus office at ten in the morning. Another constable offered to drop Wei off. The only hotel Wei could remember was the Four Seasons in the nearby Yorkville neighborhood, where Pandry had taken him for dinner once. Wei accepted and was surprised on the ride when he realized that the constable was never going to shut up, talking about hockey. Wei's police team would have offered up a ride to a foreigner too, but they would have used the ride to collect information. Canadians were so naïve.

Wei roused a night clerk and got a room. It was overpriced, but the hour was late and Wei was exhausted. In the elevator to his floor, he stared at the camera hidden in the ceiling. Later, as he lay in the large bed, his mind raced, and then, after a blended Scotch from the minibar, at last, he was asleep.

13

University of Toronto
St. George Campus
Monday, November 24
0915 hours

He had dressed too warmly, expecting the late November weather in Canada to be colder. Now, as he walked from the hotel across Queen's Park toward the computer science part of the campus, a wave of pleasant memories washed over him, brought on by the look of the streets, by the smell of the hot Tim Hortons brew in his hand, and by his thoughts about the late Professor Pandry. Seeing students rushing to a lecture or a lab, he had a momentary flash that he too was late for a class. To calm down, he told himself that he was no longer a student, but an officer of the police, a detective on a case, an agent entrusted by the highest levels of the People's Republic. A lot about him had changed since he had last been here, even if Toronto looked exactly the same as it had then.

The MaRS Discovery District off to his left had been a Pandry playground, a place where the professor had brought some of his many ideas and graduate students, putting them together to create startups, some using quantum computers of his design. Almost all of the startups had grown into profitable companies delving into new applications of machine learning to do things with big data that no one thought possible just a few years ago.

He cut across the broad grass commons of Front Campus, surprised that it had no snow cover on it yet. As a distinguished senior professor, Pandry had an office in the modern-looking Bahen building, headquarters of the Comp Sci department, but he used it largely for meetings with people not involved in his work. His success with startups, copyrights, and patents had plowed enough money back into the university that Pandry had been able to get his own small building a few meters away, nestled in between Kings College Road and St. George Street. Unlike most buildings on campus, his had a green uniformed private security guard at a front desk controlling who was allowed access. Diana had put Wei on the visitor list. After showing his long-expired student ID, he was directed to the corner office.

Diana rose from behind her glass desk and embraced him again. Her eyes were red and her blonde hair uncombed, tangled. "Wei, I am so glad you're here. I need someone I trust, someone he trusted. I need to lean on your shoulder. I realized this morning that he had asked me once to be the executor for his estate when he was redoing his will. I have to figure out this whole empire he built, but I still can't believe he's dead. Last night seems like a dream or a horror movie we watched."

"I had the same sensation when I woke up this morning in the hotel, wondering where I was. Then I smelled the fire, the smoke still on my clothes piled on the floor," Wei consoled her. "It was real. What a horror. He probably went quickly when the explosion happened, probably never knew what happened. Do houses often blew up like that around here from gas leaks? I don't remember it happening when I was here."

Diana lifted papers from the printer and handed them to him. "So, I had the same question. You know me, Bao. Show me the numbers. What those blog entries there show is that in the US from 1998 to 2021 an average of fifteen people died every year from gas explosions, no data for Canada. And get this: there were on average 286 incidents a year in the US, usually one house at a time, but then there was Andover."

"Didn't we drive through Andover on the way to Detroit that time?"

"Different Andover. This one is in the US, in Massachusetts. A few years ago, dozens of houses all blew up at around the same time in Andover and a couple of nearby towns. Overwhelmed the fire brigades. Human error, they said later. A contractor had over-pressured the seriously old pipes. You see the pictures there. It looks like the place was firebombed by the RAF, like, where was it Vonnegut wrote about?"

"Dresden." Wei put down the pages Diana had printed off and sipped on the last of his coffee. It had gone cold. "Diana, you can lean on me, but I may not be good for much about his will. And I can't stay long. I came here to ask him who the great minds are in machine learning who might have created the program I have discovered. He can't tell me now. So, technically, I should fly back home tomorrow."

"Diana McPherson? Wei Bao?" Two uniformed policemen had appeared in the open door. "We would like you to come down to our offices to speak with investigators and the fire marshal's people. Just routine. Won't take long." So much for their voluntarily going down to the station in the afternoon, Wei thought.

Two hours later, sitting in an interrogation room of the 53rd Precinct on Eglinton Avenue, Wei had about had it with the slow but polite pace at which the police and fire marshals had been moving. They had asked to talk to Diana separately and before they got to him. They had just started up with him, asking what contact he had with Professor Pandry since he graduated, why he was back visiting now. Wei stuck to his cover story that he was working on an AI project for ReGlobal.

They asked whether Pandry ever taught his students how to do pen tests, ever worked on AI for SCADA systems controlling utilities. They were clearly looking for a lead that his students may have hacked the gas pipeline. That seemed most unlikely to Wei Bao. Pandry didn't teach cybersecurity, that was beneath him. "He was way beyond that, at the edges of the most advanced applications combining machine learning with quantum computing," Wei wearily explained.

The door opened, and he saw a tall redheaded man walk into the room, followed closely by Diana. The man had changed a little in the last few years, aged, but he was still quickly identifiable as Rob Porter, another of Wei's old cabal of Pandry grad students. "Gentlemen, we need to show more hospitality to our fellow officer. Wei Bao is a chief inspector of the Dalian Police, Dalian, China."

Porter quickly dominated the room. He was in a civilian suit, but he seemed to have rank over the local police who had been talking to Wei. "Bao, it's good to see you again," he said, thrusting out his right hand and placing his left on Wei's shoulder. In a minute, he had talked the locals into leaving him alone in the room with Wei and Diana.

"Should have let me know you were coming to town, I'd have picked you up at Pearson. Terrible what happened last night. The guys here are just trying to clear up any possibilities it was more than an accident. It's their job. You understand."

Porter, an old if not close friend, suddenly appearing in this police station was confusing to Wei, somehow both comforting and jarring. Wei remembered him as a moderately good programmer and system architect in their classes and a fun companion at bars off campus. Wei assumed he was probably working for some tech firm in Waterloo, but he had what looked like a police badge on his belt. And he knew Wei's real job and new rank, and now so did everybody else in the room. "Rob, great to see you too. You're a cop now?"

"Yeah, I went back to the RCMP after getting my masters. I'm grandly titled the director of technology innovation and based here in Toronto, thank god, and not at Mountie headquarters in Ottawa."

"Back to the RCMP?" Wei repeated. "I didn't know you were with them when you were a student here."

"Yeah, well, I never said I was back then and neither did you. I also never said I knew you were with the Dalian Police then either. Bet that wasn't on your student visa application. Never mind that now. What brings you back here?" Porter had a joking manner that made his question seem more like that a fellow alum might ask upon running in to an old friend than an official inquiry or a police interrogation. Wei knew his answer would be recorded, that there were microphones and cameras somewhere in the room, not visible, but there.

"How do you know I am with the Dalian Police and, come to think of it, how did you know I am a chief inspector? I just got promoted." Wei tried to also be jocular as he answered the question with a question. "I didn't put that on my immigration form because I am just here in my personal capacity."

"Oh, don't worry about not revealing it. I got you covered," Rob Porter continued in his enthusiastic way. "I dunno really. I just got a message from headquarters in Ottawa that you were in the country, you were a special chief inspector, and that you were going to be talking with the Toronto PD. Some AI program correlated me and you. I may have listed you once on one of those security clearance forms where they ask you what foreign nationals you have repeated contact with, you know the drill. Anyway, they wanted me to go see if I could help you with whatever it was that brought you here in your, ah, personal capacity."

It was just possible, Wei thought, that actually it was the Toronto police who had entered his name last night into a database, routinely, to learn more about the witness they would be talking with again in the morning. Equally possible that there was an AI program that found his name in Rob Porter's security clearance forms. All governments asked what foreign contacts you had before they granted or updated security clearances. Rob and Wei had been drinking buddies when they were at U of T, and they had exchanged emails a few times since graduation at Christmas and Chinese New Year. Wei remembered Rob announcing in a group email that he had gotten married.

But none of that answered how the RCMP knew that he was in the police, let alone how they knew about his promotion to special chief inspector. Not many people in China knew about that. Did the Mounties have an AI information fusion program running that correlated enough databases to have figured that out? "I don't suppose you had anything to do with creating that AI for the Mounties, now did you, Robbie? The AI that told you I was here, that I was a cop, and that I had a new rank?"

Porter dragged a chair over and sat next to Wei. "Guilty. That's what the director of innovative technology does. It's rare now when I get out on the street, especially to a place like Toronto PD's 53rd Precinct house." Porter rolled his eyes. The precinct house was clearly downmarket for him.

Wei had been thinking that the local police station had been rather comfortable, but it was clearly not as nice as Rob Porter's usual haunts. "So you created a program, constantly running, that correlates airport immigration forms, police incident reports, accesses intelligence databases? I bet you even do your Five Eyes thing and get some access to the databases in DC and London."

"I can neither confirm nor deny that I created any such thing, nor that any other country told us about your rank, but good guesses. Sounds like you have been doing something similar since we left campus?"

So, it was possible then, as Wei had quickly guessed, that the Americans or the Brits had known about him, his job, even his new rank, and put it into a shared Five Eyes database. Had one of them penetrated the Ministry of Public Safety personnel files in Dalian or Beijing? If so, it would seem fair enough—after all, the PLA had copied the US government's entire security clearance database of personnel files, along with health insurance claims data, hotel frequent traveler files, and credit scores on all those same federal employees with security clearances. And, of course, the facial images of almost every American with a security clearance. Anonymity was getting hard to maintain, anywhere, harder to the point of impossibility.

"No, what I have been doing mostly is working to improve our facial recognition algorithms and correlating what our cameras see, all the cameras, with the data we get from mobile phone towers so that we can find any citizen anytime. It is much harder now that everyone wears face masks. Getting ninety percent accuracy has proven harder than I thought going into the project."

Porter leaned back, titling his chair onto the back two legs. "And that's why you're here? You were going to try to get Professor Pandry to help with that last tail of data. I'm not sure he would have been too eager to help you out with a surveillance system, given all we have heard about what's been happening to the Uighurs and in Hong Kong."

Wei thought of saying that he had nothing to do with surveillance of the Muslim minority two thousand miles away from Dalian in Xinjiang or down south in Hong Kong, because he in fact had no involvement, but he thought that would sound too defensive, like he was admitting something had gone wrong. Instead, he thought the best tactic was to tell the truth. There was nothing wrong, really, in him disclosing what he was working on.

"No, I actually came here to ask him about his little circle of AI Masters from around the world. I wanted to ask him about them. I wanted his opinion on each of them, wanted him to ask them to talk to me. You see, I have a case involving a very sophisticated AI program that probably involves a quantum computer like Pandry's, and I believe one of the AI Masters must know who is behind it, maybe one of their students or employees, maybe even one of them."

Diana, who had been sitting quietly next to him, listening, seemed to come alive with interest. "Really? Do tell. He was always flying off to meet with one of those guys and he loved their seances in the redwoods every year."

"Well, what I can tell you is that I think somebody with a very high level of AI skill has invented a program that has generated thousands of fake personas, complete with faces and patterns of life that are constantly updating. Personas that collect millions of yuan in salaries, but personas who do not seem to reflect actual people. We call them No Shows because they never seem to show up anywhere, including the places that are paying them to work."

Rob Porter dropped all four legs of his chair back down on to the floor. "Payroll fraud. That's weird," he said.

"Why is it weird?" asked Diana. "Only a matter of time until bots wanted to get paid, given all they do, messing up American elections, filling people's minds with all sorts of fake news and garbage hate memes all around the world."

"No, I mean what's weird is that I got hauled into a meeting on payroll fraud two weeks ago with the FBI liaison and some Homeland types from the US embassy over in Ottawa. They were looking for help on what sounds like a similar case—sort of vague the way they always are, playing hide the salami—but it did involve elaborate fake personas earning salaries at big US companies."

Wei felt a rush of adrenaline, focusing his attention. "You call it payroll fraud. We call it No Shows. May be similar. What did they want you to do to help them, the Americans?"

"They wanted us to check to see if we had a similar problem in Canada. I volunteered my colleagues in the fraud branch, but they had to get permission from some big companies first, for the firms to run a special app we created, run it on their HR databases and then agree to tell us if they see anything odd. Frankly, I have to check back and see where all of that stands."

Wei's first thought was he now had a reason for staying in Toronto for a few days, to investigate whether there were similar No Shows happening in the US or Canada. If there were, that would make this an entirely different case. Maybe the CIA had created an off-the-books funding source for itself, but would they rob their fellow citizens? Russia would.

If it was a nation-state that was behind theft in China, that would quickly make his case a major diplomatic incident. It would also disappoint Huang and the president, who were hoping for evidence of the success of his anti-corruption program. Corruption must be weeded out.

"Could you check, Robbie? And maybe put me in touch with those Americans to compare notes?"

"Be careful what you wish for. If you've never dealt with the Bureau, or even the Homeland people for that matter, you are in for a real treat."

Porter escorted Wei and Diana out of the station house. The local police just waved goodbye as they left. Porter promised to look into things for Wei, and the three agreed to do dinner that night at Diana's home. She made only one thing well, she claimed, but it was among Wei's favorites: curried chicken pot pie.

As he rode back in a taxi to the Four Seasons from the 53rd Precinct, Wei wondered if anyone else had ever before connected those two dots, those two locations via taxi. He closed his eyes, the fatigue of jet lag hitting him. He let his subconscious mind process all that had happened since he landed. It was good to be back. It felt almost like home in a way. Canadians were such nice persons. But he felt something was off. He couldn't help wondering if, under all their warmth and politeness, any of them were telling him the truth.

14

Dalian
Second University Hospital
Tuesday, November 25
0815 hours

"Your placement following your residency will be decided based on national needs. Where do Chinese people need more oncology specialists? Here in Dalian at the Sino-German Center? In Beijing? Maybe in Wuhan or Ürümqi."

Nobody wanted Wuhan after the coronavirus that had wiped through the city back in 2020. No one wanted Ürümqi because Chinese people were sometime forced to live with Uighur families, to serve as a model for them, to report on them. Beijing was too polluted. Fenfang wanted Dalian, only Dalian. She wanted to marry Wei Bao. He loved his city, and he had shown her why, introducing her to his favorite parks, restaurants, hikes. She loved them all, even the little sailboat he rented in the summer.

"Your skills and specializations will be part of the equation as to where you will be assigned, but only part." Fenfang thought the personnel officer then looked down directly at her. "You will also be judged by your social score. And as always for assignments to other cities, there will be a security review of your file."

She knew her social score was artificially high, and if she had a security file somewhere, it too would be good. There were some benefits to sleeping with a cop who was also a computer jock. In the case of Wei Bao, she thought, those benefits included the great things he did in bed, and also what he told her he did for them online. Things that others couldn't get: dinner reservations at the best restaurants, virtual private network connections to newspapers in Canada, videos from America, all that happened for Wei Bao and Yang Fenfang. And given her scores on the skills tests, she thought that she would have no trouble staying in Dalian when the assignments were handed out at the end of the year.

As the meeting broke up, one of her colleagues pulled her aside. "Another boring meeting that could better have been handled with an email or a vid we could watch while having dinner some night," Dr. Song Ju complained to her. "I wanted to make sure you are coming to book club tonight, Fenfang. We are going to show a documentary about Dr. Li Wenliang, the hero of Wuhan. It's by a documentarian based in Australia. Sun brought it back on a thumb drive when she went to the conference in Sydney on RNA treatments for multiple myeloma."

"Oh, Li Wenliang is my personal hero," Fenfang replied to her. "I can't wait to see it. He spoke out about the virus and was arrested. If they had acted when he warned them, more people would have lived, including him."

Song Ju drew close and spoke softly. "Chin also has a video about how our hospital used to sell dead bodies to a German who coated them in plastic and used them as statues in his art."

"Yuck, can that really be true?"

"Let's watch Chin's video and see."

As they left the briefing room, Fenfang's phone beeped. It was a text from Wei Bao in Canada. *May have to stay another couple of days. Will let you know when I have a return flight lined up. Be good. Love, WB.* She sighed. She had anticipated that Wei Bao would find an excuse to extend his stay in Canada. He was always telling her to "be good." Well, she might bring a bottle of Australian wine tonight to see the Australian documentary. That would be good.

As she moved to the elevators, Fenfang looked up at the camera she knew was inside the smoked glass bubble in the ceiling and smiled. She liked to think that Wei Bao was watching her through the cameras in the hospital, the cameras in the metro. Sometimes she winked at them or stuck out her tongue. She felt good thinking that Wei Bao was always watching over her.

15

Diana McPherson's home
92 Bedford Road, Yorkville
Monday, November 24
2025 hours

DIANA HAD BOUGHT THE narrow brick gingerbread home with the Juliet balcony on Bedford Road because it was only a block from the Whole Foods on the oxymoronically named Avenue Road. And it wasn't far from campus. The front door was unlocked, and as he entered the wood-paneled foyer carrying a bag with his contribution to the dinner, Wei saw Diana bending down, attending to the living room fireplace. The cedar and the pinecones she was using for kindling wafted into the foyer and caused Wei to flash back to a lodge in Whistler, where he and Fenfang had once spent a winter break not skiing.

Wei Bao admired Diana's good fortune at having a house, a three-story house, all to herself. She had filled it with palms and ferns, giving it a feeling of softness and serenity. Although small compared to the other houses on the street, it was a beautiful home. Professor Pandry must have paid her well. Someday Wei hoped to get one of the old houses in Dalian, to move out of the high-rises, but that day seemed far off. When he married Fenfang, he might be able to get a larger unit than the closet they shared now, especially if he could somehow stay a chief inspector. He had to solve this case successfully first, in a way that Huang and his boss thought was successful, in a way that made the president look good for weeding out corruption, or at least defending the nation from foreign cyber manipulation.

They sipped a Semillon Blanc from the Okanagan Valley in BC and nibbled at an Irish cheddar called ominously, Black Bomber, as they waited for Rob Porter. He had texted that he was at Whole Foods and would only be a few minutes late. Wei Bao got up to fix the fire. He wished he had a fireplace, but he suspected Fenfang would complain that it was bad for the environment. And, in any event, he had never seen an apartment in Dalian with a fireplace.

"Your mother, Bao. You went home to take care of her. I often thought about what you could have done if you had stayed here. Maybe you would have become the professor's assistant instead of me. I sensed Fenfang wanted you both to stay. How is she? How is your mother?"

"Mother died about a year after I moved back," Wei replied. "The one-child policy places a great burden on sons to provide for their parents when they get old. After my father died, it was just Mom and me. While I was here, she lived with her sister. Sometimes I think I should have stayed there for her and never gone to Canada. And sometimes I think I should have stayed here, but not to compete with you, Diana. Pandry would always have chosen you."

"And Fenfang?" Diane asked. "Are you still together?"

"We are going to be married after her residency in Dalian."

They smiled at one another, confirming that a chapter was closed. They had both at one time or another thought what it would be like if they took their relationship further, but neither had ever tried. Wei returned to his task at the fireplace. Diana looked up at the ceiling as she formulated a question.

"Bao, I want to pick up on something Rob asked you today. You are with the police back home, in China. And you are an expert on facial recognition and AI." Diana was hesitant, having difficulty in choosing her words. "Does that mean that you are helping, I don't mean to be indelicate but, the crackdown on dissidents, human rights advocates, people like that?"

"No, no. I just did the Recognition and Criminal Tracking system for Dalian, not nationwide. It needed to be updated with software that could handle the COVID masks. Every province has its own police, technology, social scoring system. There is more local autonomy than most people in the West know."

"But about the dissidents?" she pressed.

"I use my system to go after criminals, like the last group we arrested who were Russian criminal hackers using Dalian as a base so it would look like the attacks were being run by Chinese people. They even used Chinese keyboards and attack techniques."

"But, Bao bao, the software you developed. Beijing must have it. They could use it for, well, other purposes." Women liked to call him Bao bao. His mother, Fenfang, Diana.

Wei Bao had expected these questions from Professor Pandry. Now he had his friend Diana asking them. "Beijing doesn't think anything little old Dalian develops could be better than what they have in Beijing or Shanghai." He was being careful. What he said was true, but gave the impression that his software wasn't being used. He hoped it wasn't, but saying that, admitting that he did not really know, might make him look irresponsible to Diana. He cared what she thought of him and, more importantly, he needed her cooperation.

"Besides, I work for the police, the Ministry of Public Security. The people who go after subversives and terrorists are the Ministry of State Security. They sound alike in English, but they are very different organizations, rivals. They don't cooperate much."

Diana went to a bookshelf, withdrew a slim report, and handed it to Wei. "It's from Citizen Lab here at the university. They do good work trying to protect people from government spying, innocent people, human rights advocates, dissidents. The professor used to help them from time to time.This is their report on what the Ministry of State Security is doing in Hong Kong, Tibet, and Xinjiang. It says they are using a new software that fuses together facial recognition, voice patterns from iFlytek, people's walking gait, mobile phone locations, even heartbeat signatures to track everyone they suspect of being an enemy of the state; all the time, everywhere they go, no matter what masks they wear. They claim that the software was developed in Dalian."

His heart sank. Wei took the report. "I will read it, Diana, but you must know I didn't develop anything for State Security. I am just trying to catch criminals, thieves, hackers. It's my job."

"Well, I guess we all have to make compromises after we leave school."

"I am two things. I am a computer scientist. And I am a cop. I don't do politics. I do algorithms."

Diana sliced the Black Bomber cheddar with a small pruning knife. "Let's change the subject. We need to talk about what happened to the professor."

"Yes. You said the professor was constantly flying off to meet with other AI Masters and that he had an empire of startups based on his quantum computer design and machine learning algorithms. How much about that do you know? Did he keep you informed of everything he did?"

"Quite the contrary. I was always after him to tell me where he was going and why. He forgot to do that, a lot. And the companies, and his shares in them, I'm just going to have his attorney figure all that out and whether the estate can cash out so we can make some charitable contributions. His instructions were that he wanted to make major donations to a long list of environmental groups and some groups promoting space programs. He left a rank ordered list but didn't say how much to give them because he didn't know how much he was worth. Many millions, I know that much."

With one final adjustment to the logs, Wei put down the fireplace poker and, as the fire got going in earnest, walked away from the marble mantlepiece. "I know you said houses blow up all the time, or at least two hundred times a year in America from gas leaks, but I am a detective and it's my job always to be suspicious. So, I wonder, was there anybody who would have benefited from the professor's death? Any of his AI Master partners with whom he might have been working on some big breakthrough that now, with him gone, might not have to share their fame or fortune with him?"

"Good question, Detective." Rob had let himself in. "Precisely the question I was going to ask. Cui bono?"

Porter had put together enough ingredients from the salad bar for the three of them to share, to accompany Diana's famous chicken curry pot pie. Wei had brought his favorite dessert, three handmade flavors from the newly reopened Greg's Ice Cream on Spadina. He had missed going to Greg's.

"Well, I can go back through his travel receipts and itineraries and figure out who he was working most with lately," Diana offered. "I know he was going to Boston and Pasadena and Silicon Valley a lot, but honestly you guys are just professional paranoids. No one would have wanted him dead. He was so valuable to everybody alive. We have to accept that it was just a terrible accident. That's where I am."

"Nice cheese, by the way." Rob Porter took a sip of the white wine to wash down the cheddar, as he and Wei followed Diana into the kitchen and breakfast room. "But it's not just us two who are professional paranoids. You got a flavor of it from the cops today, but now the fire marshal and the gas company are coming to the conclusion that the line into Pandry's house had four times the pressure per centimeter that it was supposed to have. There is a little pump under the sidewalk that just feeds the line into his house. It's new, digitally controlled, installed in August. They were going to use it to pump to other houses when they installed new connections down the street next year, replacing pipes that are seventy-five years old. Turns out the pipe going into Pandry's was not old. In fact, it was only two months old."

"Digitally controlled and only fed his house," Wei repeated. "Convenient. I assume you are grabbing the logs from the SCADA?"

"You're right. An industrial control software runs the pumps and valves," Porter confirmed. "Yeah, I asked for the logs. Seems like they got erased somehow on Sunday evening."

"Fuck, that stinks to high heavens," Wei replied.

"I am sorry. You two are looking all ominous and I don't understand why. Can you do a little bit more of your mansplaining, Bao?"

"Ouch. Sorry, Diana. I just got accused of that recently by a woman on my team. I will have to be more careful. Okay, I think Robbie and I were just coming to the conclusion that someone might have hacked into the controls of the gas line and increased the pump rate on the line into the house. That might cause gas to leak out on the end of the pipeline in his basement, if there were too much pressure. Gas would hang low in the basement, form a cloud near the floor, and then if there were an electric arc, maybe even a light turning on..." He opened his two hands to mime an explosion.

"Right, Bao. But, look, Diana, we are not there yet. It's just beginning to look like a fact pattern that would be consistent with that," Rob Porter added. "It was an unusually big explosion, and the fire was fed by more gas being pumped into it. That's why the house went up so fast, so completely. And the gas company logs being erased is hard to explain, unless somebody was cleaning up their tracks on the way out."

Diana had been listening as she brought out the curried chicken pot pies. "It makes no sense. He was the nicest man the world, involved with NGOs, not with gangsters, not with hackers. No one would want him dead."

"Everybody has enemies," Wei said, recalling his conversation with Chief Inspector Wang. "Maybe he just didn't know who his were."

"Well, we need to find out," Porter declared. "I can have our document forensics people help you, Diana, to go through his files and figure out who his business partners were, his competitors, maybe somebody who is racing Pandry to some new achievement."

"Or, and I know this sounds self-centered," Wei added, "but maybe somebody who had created a giant network of fake personas in China and was hoping to eliminate the few people in the world who could recognize their signature, their work?"

"That theory, Chief Inspector, my buddy Bao, is a little far out there as a motive," Porter said, "but speaking of fake personas, I checked on that project we are doing for the Americans. My guys are done with it, our canvas for payroll fraud. I am going to see it in the morning, and I get to brief it to the folks from the US Embassy and Washington in the afternoon. You should join us, because it sounds like what you were interested in, what you were doing in China. You don't have to admit to them that China has the same issue, but you might get some cooperation out of them if you did. Think about it..."

"I have permission to talk to 'experts in Canada,' not Americans," Wei said, as he cut open his pot pie and a curry cloud wafted up. He smiled broadly as he inhaled its aroma, but his mind was sending up warnings. The Americans had probably been the ones who knew he had been promoted to special chief inspector and had told Porter that. The Americans might be the ones behind the No Shows. Now Porter was arranging for the Americans to meet him.

"You can tell Beijing later that you thought the FBI people were Canadians. After all, Canadians, Americans, we all look alike. Who could tell us apart?" Rob Porter joked.

"I can," Diana insisted. "We are the ones trying to save the planet. They are the ones trying to destroy it!"

Following the Greg's ice cream dessert, Rob Porter left to pick up his wife after a night class she was teaching. "Quantum gravity," Porter explained. "She tells me what that means every few weeks when I ask again, but I can't understand it for more than a minute and then it evaporates from my brain. See you tomorrow, Bao."

After Porter had left, Diana looked across the table of leftovers and used plates at Wei. "You really think somebody killed him intentionally?"

"Maybe." Wei scraped the last of the cookies and cream from the container. "What if he had been doing work for somebody who turned out to be a crook, or somebody at one of his companies was using his new quantum computers for some illegal purpose? Maybe the professor found out what they were doing and they wanted to silence him?"

"No way," Diana shot back. "He never would have worked with crooks, or with anybody without checking them out. He was a very wealthy man. There were his patents, the startups. He didn't need more money. He didn't need to work FOR anybody else."

"Maybe one of his partners in the startups, one of the AIML Masters, maybe one of the employees in one of the quantum computing companies had a reason to kill him," Wei suggested.

Diana laughed at the idea. "Most quantum computer experts can barely tie their own shoes."

Wei stacked the dirty dishes and began to clear the table. "I know you said that you didn't know all the stuff he was doing, like in California, but what did you do for him?"

Diana stayed seated and poured them both the last of the second bottle of wine. "Last real project I did for him was almost two years ago. It was kind of creepy, I admit that. He wanted an algorithm that would find every bit of digital data about someone in every database where they showed up. He said it was for the Canadian intelligence crowd, CSIS. They want to be sure to erase all digital evidence of a secret agent's real identity before they sent them abroad with a cover ID."

"I didn't know the professor helped Canadian intelligence. That must have been a fun project. Did you succeed?" Wei asked.

"Well, you never know if there is a hidden database somewhere that might have someone's Personal Identifiable Information, but I certainly found everywhere that most people's PII would be, the publicly available sources, the government's own databases, and some proprietary, corporate places."

"That would be useful if you were trying to eliminate all traces of a persona," Wei mused, "and, I suppose, if you wanted to create all traces of a new persona. I am sure a spy agency like CSIS would want to do both."

"I wouldn't know. I never talked with them, he did. But, back to the possibility, if somebody did kill him, Bao, can you and Robbie find them?"

"I think we might, together, but I doubt Robbie's document forensics people will be able to figure out whodunnit from the data in files Pandry has scattered all over his accounts in clouds and on his physical servers." Wei smiled. "But we could, or more accurately, you could. You're the coding wizard, Diana."

"Some of his servers and one of his Q-Compute devices were in the house and melted, but with a little bit of Python, we can have a bot scrape all his cloud files for contacts, projects, investments, corporations, boards. Then a quick unstructured data run, and we use a relationship program to show connections and relevance." Diana was already up from the table and moving toward a laptop. "You are pretty good at coding too, as I recall. Shall we pull an all-nighter? Just like old times. Let's get started."

16

Professor Pandry's computer lab
University of Toronto
6 King's College Road
Tuesday, November 25
1130 hours

THEY HAD FINISHED CODING a little after one in the morning and had driven to Pandry's campus lab to initiate the program on the closed loop LAN that Pandry had used for some of his personal records and special projects. With the program running, they drove to Chinatown, where the Asian Sun stayed open until three, serving "Cold Tea" after the bars closed. Wei ordered the version that was made of lemonade and vodka. Wei had hit the bed in his hotel before four in the morning, but was back at the little office Diana had created for him at the lab by ten.

Diana McPherson called just before eleven. She had slept in. She had needed the sleep. That afternoon, she had to deal with the funeral home and make arrangements for memorial services that people wanted to hold on campus and elsewhere. Wei agreed not to look at the results of their AI program that had plowed through Pandry's unstructured data, the records they could find, looking for where the Q-Compute devices were loaned out, looking for possible suspects in Pandry's ventures. They would do that together that night.

He took his laptop from his backpack, hopped on the university wi-fi, tied into a VPN that he trusted, and opened an encrypted pipe from the laptop back to Dalian. He had activated a Tencent Meeting video conferencing app modified for secure use with his team back home. He had the door to his closet-like office closed, but he popped in his AirPods anyway so that no one passing by in the corridor could hear the far end of his conversation.

He saw Yao Guang behind the twins in the ReGlobal loft space. They were working late. Guo Chunhua was eager to tell him what they had found in his absence. "Now up to twelve hundred companies where we have identified No Shows, a total of ninety-seven thousand seven hundred and three personas. So far."

"Tell him what the companies have in common," Yao urged her.

"They are all state-owned or state-invested companies, all with more than ten thousand employees. But here is the fun part," Chunhua added. "Half of them got paid last Friday, all direct deposit to bank accounts. Yao had lots of the bank accounts monitored, legally, with the banks' help. And the money didn't stay in the accounts for long. Bouncy bouncy."

"Where did it all go, Yao?" Wei asked.

"Everywhere. The twins made a program to follow the money, to hack into wherever these people transfer the funds and then to monitor their accounts there. All the accounts bounced money from bank to bank, to Alipay, to stocks, to gold, oil, to pig belly futures, whatever they are, euros to crypto currencies, to Hong Kong, Singapore, to Tuvalu, someplace in the US called Delaware, Jersey Islands, Cyprus, Cayman Islands, Doha. Most of the accounts are still moving, merging, splitting. I don't think it ever stays in one place for more than twelve hours."

"It has to settle down at some point if anybody is going to use it," Wei noted.

"It does for a few days sometimes so they can open an online account, invest, turn a quick profit and close the account. Then it's on the move again. But," Chunhua added, "we have a calculator running, showing the current net value of the money we are trailing, minus the fees, plus the appreciated value or losses. In less than four days, whatever is deciding what to buy and sell has already made eight percent growth. Four days, during which the Shanghai Composite, the FTSE, the DAX, and the Dow have all been down a little."

"We could make a day trading app that mirrors whatever they do. We could make millions of yuan," Bohai proposed, raising up both fists in excitement.

"No, you won't," Wei said sternly down the pipe. "Just keep following the money until some of it spins off to stay in one place for a while, or is used to pay for something, like an IT equipment shipment. And keep a list of all the accounts it flows through and the identities listed as the account owners. Somewhere, whoever this is, they're going to screw up and leave us their real identity or at least a path we can trace back to them. Where are the buy-and-sell, the transfer orders coming from?"

Yao stepped back into view to answer that one. "These guys are good. They have most of the accounts set up for multifactor authentication and when the bots log into them, they produce the right authentication, including passcodes that had been texted to mobile phone accounts associated with the No Shows. What we can tell so far is that the logins all come from cloud-based accounts that get taken down as soon as the transactions are completed."

"Who is paying for the cloud accounts?" Wei asked.

Chunhua had the answer. "All the cloud accounts are paid for by credit cards. Not stolen credit cards, real ones, owned by some of the other No Shows, cards associated with their bank accounts."

"Wonderful," Wei commented. "Fake persons, real bank accounts, real credit cards, cloud email accounts and platforms that they create to have other fake personas issue instructions to buy and sell real money and assets, and move them all over the world. And even after they pay all of the fees, they're still making money at a pretty damn good rate. Wonderful. Now all we need to do is figure out who 'they' are."

"Yeah, but how do you suggest we do that, boss?" Yao asked.

Wei looked down at the notes and the diagram he had been sketching while the twins and Yao briefed him. "Next Friday, a bunch more of the fake personas will get paid. As soon as an instruction hits one of those accounts to move money out, we do a near real-time trace back to the email account or browser it came from, probably in a cloud-based account. We hack that account's logs quickly and see where it's getting its instructions. Then we hack back to that location and we keep tracing back as far as we can through the bounces. Not where the money is going, you're already doing that, but where the instructions came from. No human can hack back that fast. You'll need a machine learning algorithm. You'll need to create one, or I can do that and send it to you."

Chunhua looked at her brother. "I told you he would act like only he could figure it out."

Bohai explained, "Yeah, boss, we know. We already started on that AI. We testing it on the Cyber Range now. It will be ready for Thursday night, when the pay moves to their accounts."

"Sorry, I, ah, knew you would already be on it. Of course. You're already on it," Wei muttered.

"And, boss," Bohai broke the award silence, "our friends in Berlin, the ones we asked about who could generate the artificial Chinese people faces on the ID cards of the No Shoes? They got back to us after we haggled a little about their price, but we got them down.

"These guys are the best brokers in the business, boss. You want an exploit for Android, iOS, Linux, some SCADA, they can find the guy to make it. They did get a request for Chinese faces about two years ago. They had a guy in Singapore who is the best at generating fake faces of Chinese people. He got paid, through Berlin, for three hundred thousand faces. He quit for a year after that, he got paid so much. Berlin is happy too. They take a skim."

Wei considered that tantalizing piece of intelligence for a moment, thinking it almost too much good luck that he had it, looking for the flaw, the false flag. "If the guys who are doing this are this good, why couldn't they generate fake Chinese people faces themselves?"

"The fake Chinese people faces we see all the time in WeChat, you can know real fast they're fake, with apps, detection apps like they use at WeChat," Bohai said into the screen with Wei Bao's face. "Most guys, they have trouble doing Chinese people faces. They can do ten, twenty. Somebody did three hundred thousand, right? All distinct. Not many people that good at this."

Yao Guang whistled, as he appreciated the magnitude of the fraud. "If they used all three hundred thousand faces to create No Shows, then these guys have been making a lot of money for two years. Who are they?"

"Berlin club guys don't know. The buyer hid their internet connection by coming through TOR, paid by BitCoin, picked up the files from a server Singapore guy spun up on Azure local cloud in Doha. The buyer downloaded, then terminated the virtual server. Pfft, gone."

"So who is this Singapore guy who is so good at making fake faces of Chinese people?" Yao asked.

"Berlin guys won't give up names of people they broker with, buyers or sellers, no matter how much we pay them. They got their reputation to maintain."

Chunhua was suppressing a giggle. Yao turned toward her with a questioning face. "Well?"

"There is only one guy in Singapore who is that good at AI and who has done facial recognition work. Berlin boys were telling us who it was without telling us. They said Singapore. They knew we knew." Chunhua paused for effect. "Chong Yeow."

"You know this guy? Any chance he kept copies of the faces he made?"

"Maybe," Bohai admitted. "Maybe we did a little work for him once, long ago, in a galaxy far, far away." Chunhua gave her twin a disapproving glare.

"Then ask him how much he wants for copies of the fake faces," Wei ordered.

"Doesn't work that way. He wouldn't give them up," Bohai replied. "Not for any price."

Yao looked from Bohai to Chunhua and back. He wanted a different answer. He knew he could get them to come up with some way to get into the database of the Singapore specialist who went by Chong Yeow.

"Okay, okay," Chunhua said, looking up at the yellowed ceiling tiles. "Okay, how 'bout this? I send him a deep fake video of people walking, each one of them with a data file that shows their individual gait, like Wei Bao's system that identifies people by their gait. We ask him if he wants to buy the program that generates the deep fakes of people walking? We ask so much money he won't say yes."

"I still have a way of sending to him through Tails." Bohai realized Yao wasn't following him. "Tails is a place you go to access TOR, the system that makes it impossible to trace you."

Wei, still confused, shook his head. "How does this help us?"

"Easy. We have an oh day, zero day, that we embed in videos on Tails. It beacons back to us when the video is played." Chunhua's face beamed.

"But the beacon signal doesn't come back through TOR. So we get the real IP address it came from. Bang. We got him. We got an address we can hack."

Yao placed one of his giant hands on a shoulder of each of the twins. Wei was smiling over the encrypted video connection. "Do it. Get me copies of all the fake faces of Chinese people this guy has ever made. Then we match them with faces on national ID cards, we find where these No Shows work, and we erase them from the payrolls and seize all their bank accounts."

"Then we listen for who howls," Yao said across the line to Wei.

"Exactly. Meanwhile, I will let you know what happens this afternoon when the Americans met the Canadians. And me. Goodnight, guys."

He clicked to break the VPN link and closed the conferencing app. It was afternoon for Wei, but in China they were hours ahead.

17

RCMP Division O
Toronto West
2755 High Point Dr
Milton, Ontario
Tuesday, November 25
1500 hours

"Who knew the Mounties had secret bases in suburban office parks?" Sarah Keogh asked as she walked into the conference room. "At least it's closer to the airport than going downtown."

"It's so secret, Sarah, that we put a big sign out front saying Royal Canadian Mounted Police," Rob Porter said, welcoming her, "unlike some of your FBI offices that actually are hidden sometimes, without signs at least, in suburban office buildings."

Sarah Keogh had just flown up from Washington, where she was a deputy assistant director and led an office in the FBI's National Security Division. At forty-seven, she had been a special agent for twenty-two years. She was accompanied by three people she introduced as "from the US embassy in Ottawa" and a woman from the FBI's Toronto liaison team. Porter introduced Wei only as "an expert in machine learning from the University of Toronto, who is working with us." It was also true, as far as it went.

"I just went over this data for the first time this morning," Rob began, "but from what I can tell, our team may have something here very interesting to you." He tapped his laptop and a PowerPoint briefing began on a large wall screen. "Air Canada and Shell Canada both agreed to help us on a voluntary basis with our 'research project.' The chiefs of security at both of them were Mounties once. But we still had to agree that we would only get the conclusions of their data runs, not the details, not names or images."

The "methodology" chart that Porter projected reminded Wei of the algorithm his own team had developed to look for No Shows in China. "The program we wrote and gave them to run on their corporate networks collects payroll lists, digital identities, building access control lists and logs, ID photos, some security camera videos. It then compares identities inside the company to commercially available credit reports and their images with facial identity databases scraped from social media and all sorts of sources. Yeah, there are companies that collect people's pictures and sell them, along with your name, which they get by matching your face with all the faces they scrape from social media.

"What happened at both the airline and Shell is that some employees never showed up on the building access logs, they never used their fobs to open the doors or move the elevators. Those same people were never seen on the security cameras in the parking lots or bus stops. They were also absent from the authorized Work from Home list, so they should have been working on the premises, but no sign of them there.

"So the teams at both companies pulled up the employee ID photos. The missing people also used the headshot from their company IDs on their social media pages. But there were no other pictures of them on their social media accounts, no Instagram selfies.

"So my friends over at Citizen Lab gave both companies another app they developed that helps to identify possible machine-generated facial identities, fake faces. Because, yeah, there are also companies that sell fake face photos for ads and other things.

"Citizen Lab created a program to identify fake personas spreading propaganda online, people whose faces were generated by one of these AI-for-hire companies. Just click off the features you want your headshot to have and the face morphs into that character: older Japanese woman, Arab teenager, blond with green eyes, whatever."

Porter was projecting an image of a web page from an online company called Stock Face, complete with dropdown menus to order up the person you needed: male/female, white/Asian/Brown/Black, gender, age, hair color, eye color, glasses, hair style, clothing.

"Citizen Lab discovered hundreds of fake faces used as IDs in both companies. And, of course, they were also the same people who never showed up using their building fobs or standing around in the parking lot or having Instagram selfies."

"But, let me guess," Sarah Keogh intervened in Porter's monologue, "they all got paid every two weeks to their bank accounts. They all had driver's licenses and health insurance cards and smart phones."

"You got it," Porter replied, "and home addresses that turned out to be package handling storefronts, not residences. They're all phantoms."

After hearing all of that, Wei Bao thought it was time to reveal his true identity. He had decided to try to smoke out the Americans, to see if they would say or do something that would help him figure out if the CIA was behind all of this. He would smoke them out by coming clean, letting them know most of what he knew. Most, not all. He stood up from the table. "In China, we are calling these ghosts 'No Shows,' and we have discovered tens of thousands of them, and I am sure there will be many more by the time we are done finding them. Rob Porter is right that I am an expert at machine learning, right that I went to U of T, and right that I am helping him." He paused to look at Porter, who gave him a nod to proceed. "But I am also a chief inspector in the Dalian Police, China Ministry of Public Security."

Keogh shot Porter a hard look. "Nice of you to make that clear up front, Rob."

"We agreed, Wei and me, to tell you before you revealed anything. But I think you may want to hear what Wei has found before you get upset that he is here."

Keogh nodded and Wei pointed to Rob Porter to move on to a PowerPoint slide that Wei had created from the data his team in Dalian had given him.

"As you can see from the chart, we have examined almost thirteen hundred companies so far, all with more than ten thousand employees. We have identified almost ninety-eight thousand suspect fake personas. In four companies alone, we identified over thirty-eight hundred."

The PowerPoint chart showed:

Four Largest Employers	
China National Petroleum	1,385,207 workers
China Post Group	935,191
State Grid	917,717
Sinopec	619,522
subtotal	3,857,637

"The thirty-eight hundred personas in those companies represent only one tenth of one percent of the staff on payroll. Easy to get that small a number lost in the rounding in big companies."

"How much would a group that size get paid?" Keogh asked.

"Don't know that, but we calculated that the ninety-seven thousand seven hundred and three personas we have identified thus far earned about fourteen billion yuan last year, or about two billion dollars US.

"If we extrapolate to all the major companies, just the majors, those major firms employ about one hundred million people out of the eight hundred million in our workforce. We think they may have created three hundred thousand fake personas. Whoever it is who is getting the salaries from these No Shows could be getting as much as twenty billion dollars US a year from Chinese people before the profit they make on their investments. Our first estimate is that they have been making about fifteen to twenty percent more than the base salaries for the past year when you take into account what we are learning about their investments. And we don't know how long they have been collecting salaries or investing."

"So," Sarah Keogh started. "Off the record, not for attribution, of course, we think that this sort of thing has been going on in US companies too and, ah, some government agencies, for a little over two years. Maybe thirty months back we found signs that they were operating at scale. In fact, as far as we have been able to uncover things so far, it looks like it started at scale, didn't ramp up slowly."

Wei did some quick math. "If they have been at it in China for thirty months, and I don't know that, but if they have, then they would have made at least fifty billion US dollars by now, minimum, if they only exist in the largest Chinese employers and they are only one tenth of one percent of their workers."

"David Bernstein is from FinCEN in Virginia, our Treasury's money-laundering tracking center. They have some of the best machine learning capability for tracking fund flows," Keogh said, introducing one of her colleagues.

So, Wei thought, Bernstein was not from the embassy, as Keogh or Porter had previously indicated. He looked very young to Wei. "Our assumption is that we have many fewer of these cases of payroll fraud, in absolute numbers. Our entire workforce in the US is only about twenty percent of the size of China's, but our average salary for skilled workers is about six times that of a Chinese counterpart. In the US companies and departments that do have these fraudulent accounts, it is running about the same size, about one tenth of one percent of the workforce. We assume that if this all started thirty months ago, by now it siphoned off somewhere between eighty and one hundred billion dollars in America."

"Thank you, David," Keogh continued. "We have no estimate on what they may have earned, if they are investing it. So far we haven't been able to get all the warrants we need to trace where the money goes. The few bank accounts we have looked at get cleared out of most of the direct deposit salaries pretty quickly. Frankly, we are having a hell of a time with the search warrants. I guess you don't have the same issue in China."

Wei was about to make up an explanation and then realized he would sound overly defensive as he spoke them. "For priority investigations, some privacy rules can be waived by higher authorities, as they were in the US, I believe, after 9/11?"

Rob Porter went to a whiteboard. "Seventy billion from China. Let's say a hundred billion from North America. We have to assume the same thing may be going on in the EU. Let's assume maybe another seventy billion there. They could have a quarter of a trillion dollars by now, and that's without whatever they may be doing in Latin America, the Middle East, India, Australia. How do you hide a quarter of a trillion dollars?" Porter asked.

"Oh, that's easy," Bernstein from FinCEN answered. "The global GDP crossed the one hundred trillion dollar mark last year. The three thousand or so companies on the New York Stock Exchange alone are worth over thirty-five trillion. You could invest seven hundred billion in banks and markets around the world without it ever seeming out of place. It's a rounding error."

"But enough to buy a lot of elections," Porter replied.

Sarah Keogh, the FBI agent, picked up as if she were working off the same script. "What takes that kind of money? Weapons development, specifically weapons of mass destruction research, development, and production, like the hypersonics the Russians just happen to be deploying. How have they been able to afford that? Or maybe it's all going to Putin and his mob for their personal use. We have reports that Putin has hundreds of billions of dollars hidden away for his personal use. Or enough to build an arsenal of nukes," Sarah Keogh added. "North Korea and Iran are both cranking out nuclear warheads and slapping them on new missiles that can reach North America." That silenced everybody. "That's one way huge amounts of money disappear from the financial system."

Wei looked at the Canadians and the Americans. He knew that the two countries' security services were very close, two of the Five Eyes. He assumed what he told the Canadians, they would tell the Americans. Maybe this was all a grand scheme by the Americans to make it look like they were victims too, to throw him off the scent that it could be CIA that was taking billions from Chinese corporate coffers. From what little he knew about the US, it was also possible that the FBI might not know what the CIA was doing. CIA might not tell their rivals. Wei remembered reading that the CIA had not told the FBI when al-Qaeda terrorists were actually in the US plotting the 9/11 attack. The only way he was going to find out whether the No Shows were a CIA plot was by engaging the Americans. "I think we should continue sharing notes. Continue these discussions."

Sarah Keogh looked surprised. "I will have to check with Washington." Wei thought he should probably check with Beijing before getting too close to the superpower rival, but sometimes, he had learned, it was better to succeed than to ask for permission to try. If he cracked this case, anything he did along the way to get there would be forgiven. And if he failed to crack the case, nothing that he did according to the rules would save him. The real gift that Huang had given him was the ability to be a solo operator, outside the system. The real risk that Huang had put him in was that he was a solo operator, outside of the system.

They agreed to meet Wednesday, by which time Special Agent Keogh might have permission to work on the case further with Wei Bao. Porter offered to drive Wei to Professor Pandry's office, where Diana McPherson was waiting to go over the results of their AI program that had been looking for clues to Pandry's possible murder, pieces of data scattered across the professor's files that, when correlated, might reveal a motive, a killer.

"Why didn't we talk about Professor Pandry with the Americans?" Wei asked as they drove across town.

"Oh, you mean your theory that if he was killed, it was because he might have been able to solve the payroll fraud mystery? I think you need to make that theory a little more convincing, then let them come to that conclusion. Sometimes the Americas have a 'Not Invented Here' problem."

18

Professor Pandry's computer lab
University of Toronto
6 King's College Road
Tuesday, November 25
2130 hours

THEY HAD NOT MADE much progress with the professor's files. There were references to Q-Compute machines at several locations, one in Pandry's own home and others in the US. The AI Diana and Wei had created had also gone through unstructured data and found patterns, but nothing that was useful in pointing to someone with a motive to kill. Diana told Wei he could stay and continue to make sense of it, but she needed a break. It had been a depressing day, especially dealing with the funeral parlor.

As Wei put her in an Uber, he noticed a parked car across the street, a car that started up and pulled out from the curb as the Uber drove off. Wei noticed things like that. Sometimes he was just being paranoid. Sometimes he was right to be.

Powered by his third Red Bull of the day, Wei plowed through the offensive AI algorithm bot the twins had sent him. It looked good. It would notice immediately when a direct deposit was made into a worker's bank account. Then, when "the owner" of the account logged in and started to give instructions for transferring the money, the bot would trace that connection back to where "the owner" was, then hack that account and get the traffic history. Where had communications to the account originated? The bot would keep doing that, tracing back toward the ultimate origins of the transfer orders. He wondered how many layers the criminals would use. If the number of bounces was low enough, and if the bot moved sufficiently fast before logs were erased, the bot might just work. He was pretty sure that it would lead to someone using one of the handful of Pandry quantum computers running a machine learning program modeled on Pandry's work.

He felt a presence and looked up from his keyboard. The night security guard from the front desk stood in the open doorway to his workspace. "Sir, there are two guests here to see you."

It was Sarah Keogh and one of the two unnamed women who had been with her at the RCMP briefing that afternoon. "We brought you a pizza," the FBI agent said by way of greeting. "It's from Pi Company on Bloor Street, supposed to be the best on campus."

"That would be Big Trouble," Wei said, standing up.

"No trouble, really," she replied.

"No, the best pizza on campus. It's from Big Trouble on Spadina in Chinatown, but this will do. I am starving," Wei replied. "So nice of you to stop by, although I probably should not be meeting alone with you. But how did you know I was famished, or, actually, how did you know I was here?"

The two American women sat down in the chairs in front of Wei's desk. He opened the pizza box and offered them a slice. They quietly waved him off.

Sarah broke the silence. "I grabbed your number off your mobile during the meeting at the Mounties. Then I started tracking it. We wanted to speak with you, alone, about Professor Pandry. Neither of us mentioned him today. This seemed like a good place and time to do so."

"You are tracking mobiles in Canada? Do the Mounties know that?" Wei asked pleasantly. "Special Five Eyes privileges?"

"We don't tell the neighbors things that would upset them. They get so easily upset sometimes. They are not as into surveillance as we are. Certainly not as enamored with that sort of thing as Chinese people, eh?"

Wei scarfed down his first slice of the white pizza with clams and looked at the younger of the two Americans. "I'm sorry, what did you say your name was?"

Keogh told her colleague to go ahead. "Laura Chen, CIA. I am from our Global Crime Center. We track international organized crime, narco gangs, cyber hackers, money laundering, corruption."

"Corruption must be weeded out," Wei parroted. The remark seemed to confuse Chen.

Keogh ignored it. "Chief Inspector, if I may be direct. Can we start with why your investigation of payroll fraud in China brought you to Toronto?"

Wei smiled at her. "Special Agent, I think you already know the answer to that question. In fact, I think actually the answer is probably the same reason why you came here."

"Really, Inspector, and what would that be?"

"Well, I will start by what your reason for being here is not. It is not because you rush to share your most sensitive intelligence with your northern neighbors. Nor is it because you are concerned about the few fake persona workers likely to be in Canada, or the amount of funds being taken up here. California alone has a GDP twice that of all of Canada."

"Don't talk like that around Rob Porter. He will be hurt."

"Really, Sarah. There are more people in metropolitan Changqing than in this entire country. I came here to see my old professor, to ask him if he could guess who might be behind this sort of massive crime."

"And why, Chief Inspector Wei, would he be able to do that?"

"You know that too. That's why you had initiated the talks with the Canadians. My guess is that you asked the RCMP to let you talk to Professor Pandry, to ask him if he could guess who was behind the payroll fraud. Your boy genius from Treasury FinCEN probably figured out that only a quantum computer with really advanced machine learning could pull off a complex and dynamic operation like this. Pandry is the world's expert on quantum and machine learning. He owns the only devices that are stable enough for continuous operations. Maybe one of them is being misused.

"But the RCMP didn't want you interrogating a Canadian citizen, an upstanding scientist, so they offered to do it themselves. Then they realized one of their own knew him really well. So they assigned the action to him. Enter my old buddy Rob Porter. You two talk on the phone, and he agrees to talk to the old man.

"Then Rob calls back and tells you that Pandry died 'under suspicious circumstances.' Then he adds that Toronto police report some Chinese guy had shown up around the same time, shown up at the crime scene. You ask for the name of the Chinaman. You run it on your intelligence fusion software, and it tells you that the guy from China is a special chief inspector in the police. You decided to come up here and see what is going on.

"And then Rob Porter just happens to show up in the 53rd Precinct to save me from interrogation by the locals. Shows up and knows by then where I work and, this was the real tell, what my new rank is. He knew that because you told him. Your friends at NSA are in our Ministry's databases. That's okay, the PLA is in all of yours, but you know that.

"Then you and Robbie pretend at our meeting today that you didn't already know I was a Chinese cop. You get all offended that he hadn't told you, when in fact part of the reason you showed up was because he had told you the Chinese were interested in the case. Right?"

Keogh just looked blankly at Wei. Finally, she said, "Well, you seem to have all the answers, Inspector. Yes, we were interested in talking with your old professor. Tell him why, Laura."

"DDS&T, our technical directorate," Laura Chen began. "They drew up a list of the best AI and machine learning experts in the world who use quantum computing. Our guys thought that only a quantum computer could do this, otherwise it would take a massive amount of conventional computers. The best quantum computers for machine learning applications like this turn out to be owned by one man or by companies he substantially controls. Guess who?"

Sarah resumed, "We did ask the Mounties, and yes, they came back with the good news that there was one of their officers who had studied with him, had his trust. Okay, we were letting that play out. And then you show up, and Pandry dies. That looks like a suspicious coincidence, but nonetheless Robbie Porter says you can be trusted."

"So does that mean you trust me too, Sarah? I'm touched."

"Not quite so fast, Inspector. You see what still bothers me is that from the billion or so people in your country, and from the millions of Chinese police, military, and intelligence officers, they just happened to send to Toronto somebody from the Dalian Police, you. Not from the PLA, not from headquarters of the Ministry of Public Security or even the Ministry of State Security, but from a, forgive me, small-town police department.

"And the reason they chose you can only be that you, like Rob Porter, knew Professor Pandry, had been one of his students. Beijing had already figured out that it might be a Pandry computer ripping off companies around the world to fund some nation's WMD programs. The one good thing you have going for you is you are investigating it too, so that means it's not China funding its weapons programs from a Pandry computer doing global payroll fraud. It means you don't know either what nation is stealing the money."

Wei laughed out loud and kept chuckling as he reached for the last of the Red Bull. "Now I see how misunderstandings occur between our peoples. I see how you got there. Your reasoning is impeccable. But it's also wrong. And I doubt I will be able to get you to believe the truth."

"Try me," Keogh sat back, folding her arms across her chest.

"China is a rich nation now; we don't need to steal money. You got that part, but Beijing doesn't know there is an international operation doing what you call payroll fraud. And they don't know anything about Pandry. Beijing thinks this is about Party members who are plant managers employing their No Show cousins, not requiring that they show up for work, and then collecting a kickback from them.

"I got pulled in because the president is on a big anti-corruption drive, and he wants me to identify a bunch of these corrupt Party bosses and arrest them in a highly publicized national roundup. Why little me? Because they don't trust anyone from Beijing or Shanghai to investigate Party corruption. They're all part of some faction or racket or other. I really am just an AI and machine learning expert from a small-town police department, not a spy, but a local techie cop, just perfect for what they wanted.

"I'm also the only one who decided I would come back to Canada. It was my own idea. I did it because Pandry was the only guy I could think of who might know what it took to run a big series of algorithms like must be at work here. Who might be able to give me a list of people for me to track. My old professor. Coincidence. You know coincidences do happen. But you were already developing a list like that, so how did you discover the payroll fraud operation in the first place?"

Chen looked at Keogh. "There really was no indication in SIGINT that Beijing knew this was going on outside China." Sarah Keogh grimaced. Chen was divulging too much information.

"As my colleague just alluded to, we have our sources in China. We believe that your leadership is as curious about the No Shows as we are about the payroll fraud. So, we don't think it's you doing this. So let me share how we got started on this case. Last summer Boeing had to lay off a number of people, a reduction in force they called it. They did it as a surprise, called them in individually on a Friday afternoon, had Boeing Security on hand just in case of trouble. Some people didn't show up. Then on Monday, when they were going to try to get them again, there was no record of any of them in the employee databases. They had vanished like they never existed, erased.

"Boeing Security called in the Defense Counterintelligence and Security Agency. Long story short, they found that there had been almost a hundred fake personas working at Boeing, getting paid every month. At first they thought it was fraud. DCSA quietly checked on a few other defense contractors and suppliers and, guess what, found the same story. We found out about it and the Bureau took over the case. It was too important for DCSA to be handling as the lead agency."

Wei believed her, but he somehow doubted she would believe him. "And indeed, so important that you are even getting help from your competitors at the CIA and NSA," he noted dryly.

"Listen, Inspector, between us, this is far more important than you know. This is massive. We and the CIA have officially concluded only a nation-state could be doing this and with only one purpose: somebody has some secret program that is so expensive that they have to steal billions to fund it. That means Moscow, or Tehran, or Pyongyang. They all need money to make weapons.

"And that secret weapon of mass destruction program, it's probably aimed at us, at New York and Washington again, like on 9/11." She had dropped the slow-talking Southern belle act and was talking fast and wagging a finger. "You think your tit is in a wringer because your president wants you to arrest some Party bosses for corruption. My president, whose people I met in the Situation Room of the White House about this, is telling the FBI to stop this thing before it blows up and kills lots of Americans. She's all over this case."

Maybe the CIA wasn't the guilty party, or maybe it was weaving a good cover story. Wei stood up and stretched. He had been hunched over his keyboard for hours and his neck and back ached. "Well, now that we are all being honest with each other, where does that leave us? What next? Did Washington say you could play with me?"

"Honestly? I haven't heard back from DC yet. What next? Well, not for repetition, especially to Porter, the NSA got into Pandry's records, and we can't make heads or tails of them. We were hoping you might. Seems like you were looking at his records too, or so I am told."

"Cute, very cute, considering the NSA is not supposed to spy on other Five Eyes countries like, say, Canada," Wei gasped. "And especially good because his records are on an air-gapped LAN. How did they hack into that?"

"Well, many things that we want people to believe are impossible are actually only hard to do," Laura Chen offered.

"So you do believe Professor Pandry was murdered, you don't think I did it, and you do think maybe it had something to do with your payroll fraud case and maybe he was killed by a nation-state?" Wei asked. "Tell me that's all true."

"If I were authorized to cooperate with you, I would tell you exactly that," Keogh replied. "Now, tell me what you found in Pandry's files."

Wei smirked. "Tell Rob Porter you think the possible Pandry murder case is connected to your payroll fraud investigation. Then drive me to the Four Seasons, buy me a glass of Scotch, and I might just share some of what I learned."

"Do that and I will buy you the whole bottle," Keogh offered.

"Be careful. I sometimes drink the twenty-five-year-old Macallan. A bottle of that in a store is about two thousand bucks, Canadian."

"Really?" Keogh asked. "How much is that in real money?"

As Wei left the computer lab building with the FBI agent and the CIA officer, they were photographed by a man slouching in the front seat of a car down the block from the lab.

The photographer's actions were being recorded by the surveillance camera across the street. It had zoomed in on the car, recorded its license plate, taken a shot of the driver's face, and geolocated only one mobile phone within a two-meter circle that included the car. The phone's number and SIM card were automatically tagged with the driver's facial photo. And the photo was quickly correlated by an AI facial recognition program that concluded the driver was a Chinese Consulate officer. When the Chinese "diplomat" drove away, one camera after another followed his progress as he drove toward the Four Seasons in the Yorkville neighborhood.

19

LaMeiZi Restaurant
513 Zhongshan Road
Shahekou District
Dalian, Liaoning Province
Wednesday, November 26
2030 hours

IT WAS NOT AS good as the seafood restaurants near the aquarium, but it was a shorter walk by several blocks from Second Hospital and, thus, popular with the medical staff. Most importantly for tonight's gathering, it had a private room that sat two dozen people at one long table, and the owners had agreed to waive the rental fee for the group of doctors that night. Dr. Yang had perhaps suggested to the owner that the Support the Army Seafood Restaurant up Zhongshan had already offered them a free room. Yang Fenfang, of course, would never have had the dinner anywhere else, but the owners of LaMeiZi had no way of knowing that.

Confident though she was in negotiating with restaurateurs, the young oncologist was not comfortable speaking before groups. She was aware that her heart rate had climbed in the minutes before she stood behind the little tabletop podium the restaurant had agreed to provide. When she turned on the microphone, the speaker emitted an ear-piercing pulse. That did not help restore her confidence, but a waiter showed her how to turn down the volume and the aural torture ceased.

"Martyr is a word not frequently applied to ophthalmologists," she began, looking down at her notes. "Indeed, Wenliang may be the only one ever. The Party agreed, called him a martyr, him and the other doctors and medical staff who died. Yes, they were all martyrs, but Wenliang was more so than others because he also risked his life for the truth."

She looked down at Dr. Li's widow, Fu Xuejie, who had been about Fenfang's age when it had happened. "For he not only fought for his patients, he fought for all Chinese people and their right to know what was going on, their right to know what the government knew but had not told Chinese people, what they were intentionally hiding, that a SARS virus was on the loose in his city, in Wuhan.

"Because he told other doctors around China, because he posted information for all Chinese people to see on the Internet, the police came for him. They detained him. They coerced him to sign a statement. They tried to suppress the truth, a truth that we all needed to know and had every right to know."

She thought of Wei Bao, who would disapprove of what she was saying, of what she was doing tonight, and so she ad-libbed. "Police, like doctors, serve Chinese people. They do good, usually. Early in 2020 in Wuhan, some of them did not do good."

She could sense some of her colleagues' displeasure with her frankness. They needed to be courageous like Dr. Li had been. "You know the rest. How when he was released, he went to the hospital and treated a glaucoma patient who had worked at the Huanan Seafood market and, therefore, had a high viral load. Dr. Li died a few days later, leaving Xuejie and a son, and a daughter that he never lived to meet." She felt a tear on her right cheek but did not dab it, did not hide it.

"So tonight, we honor Dr. Li and you, Xuejie, and make a donation to the fund to place a statue of him here in Liaoning Province, at his birthplace in Beizhen, Jinzhou." A spontaneous round of applause broke the tension in the room.

She thought of stopping there and sitting down. She knew that was what Wei Bao would have suggested had he been present. "It is more than a statute to a martyr doctor." Her voice was cracking. "It is a monument to Chinese people's right to know, to their right to speak, as is recognized in our most honored laws but not always honored in practice. We look forward, in the very near future, to making the drive up the peninsula to see that statue and to join again with you, Xuejie, in remembering and honoring Dr. Li Wenliang."

The applause seemed more restrained this time, as Dr. Yang Fenfang sat down. Even this group, these medical doctors, these people who had contributed to the statue fund, who had summoned the courage to come to this dinner, were still afraid. Only the core, the young doctors who informally called themselves the Wenliang Club, Fenfang's social circle, stood to clap.

Later, after Fenfang embraced Xuejie outside the restaurant and the chauffeured car they had hired for her drove Dr. Li's widow away to her hotel, a young woman approached from behind a van in the parking lot. "Dr. Yang? Wei Bao sent me."

Fenfang starred at a woman she had never seen before, a girl in black jeans, black windbreaker, and a Yankees baseball cap. The doctor's adrenaline spiked, and she thought of running. This was a trap. Then the young woman held up a mobile and played a short video. It was Wei Bao, smiling and wearing a dark T-shirt. "Fenfang, I want you to meet Chunhua. She is not police, but she works for me. She is here to help you. You can trust her."

It had taken Chunhua almost three hours to generate that thirty-second video using artificial intelligence to generate Wei Bao's voice and image, saying those words and having his lips move in unison to the sounds.

"Who are you?" Dr Yang Fenfang spat out as she stepped away.

"Not the police, but one of Wei Bao's core team. He sends his best from Canada."

"What do you want from me?"

"Only to help you, Doctor."

"I don't need help, thank you."

"Oh yes, you do," Chunhua said calmly. "That meeting of yours upstairs in the private room? It was not private. The Ministry of State Security could have been watching and listening, recording. They can make it appear that you said and did things that you did not do."

"Why would they do that?" she asked. "In any event, Wei Bao would prevent them from hurting me."

"Yes, he would. By sending me."

Alone in the parking lot, the two women assessed each other, deciding. It was late November, and it felt damp three blocks from the water from the rain that had stopped during the dinner and still sat in pools on the pavement and reflected off windshields.

Fenfang decided. "So what do you suggest I do?"

"It's going to start raining again soon. My brother and I live on a boat in the yacht club three blocks from here. Walk there with me. Let us sit together there where it's warm. Have tea with me and let me tell you about me. You can decide whether you want to talk about you. And whether you want to let me help you. Because I think you need someone to watch over you until Bao returns. And I owe it to Bao to do that for you, for him, for what he did for me and Bonahi, my brother, my twin." *Twin*—Fenfang remembered Wei Bao talking about the twins he had working for him. She decided to go with this woman, but was prepared to break away and run if things turned more suspicious.

They ran across Zhongshan Road to avoid the traffic, which was fast even on a weekday night at 22:00 hours. They both gasped, filling their lungs when they reached the other side of the six lanes, and then began a slow walk toward the water. The amusement park with its Ferris wheel was on the next dock over to the right, the aquarium on the next to the left. Both areas were decked out in the small, white, decorative lights that made the city a fairyland each December, apropos of nothing, certainly not Christmas.

Chunhua stopped at the third pier and punched a code into the gate access, then looked at a camera which identified her face. The second boat on the right was a forty-two-foot, dark blue catamaran. Its name—Zizhi Hu, stealth tiger—was painted in gold letters on its stern, above the name of its home port, Dalian. Chunhua jumped across the small gap between the boat and the pier and, as she did, dim red lights came on along the deck. She held out her hand to help Fenfang board.

"This is yours?" Dr. Yang asked the younger woman.

"Yes. It was built here in Dalian, by Aurora," she explained while opening a panel and punching in yet another code. "My brother and I used to make a lot of money. That was before we met your fiancé. He let us keep some things, like our home. This is our home."

The boat did have an atmosphere of home inside, wood and brass, plaid blankets, comfortable chairs and benches with nautical pillows, electric baseboards exuding warmth. As Chunhua put on a kettle for the tea, they heard a downpour begin bouncing off the decks above. The beating sound outside made the cabin feel even more like a sanctuary, a shelter from the rest of the world, its storms, its people.

Chunhua and Fenfang sat opposite each other, cradling their teacups, both automatically assuming the lotus position. "I don't understand," Fenfang began. "Wei Bao works for the Ministry."

"He works for the Ministry of Public Security, which runs the local police. The people who are trying to monitor you are from the Ministry of State Security, the intelligence people, the secret police. They are a nasty bunch."

"I don't know about one ministry or the other." Fenfang shook her head. "I know Wei Bao created a camera system for Dalian to keep us safe. I know sometimes he helps people whose computers got hacked. He finds the criminals who did it. He's gone back to Canada to learn more about software from his old professor at Toronto. That's all I know."

Chunhua set down her teacup. "I hack into people's computers too. It's not just bad guys who do that. I hacked into the camera systems at the hospital, in your apartment building, even at the restaurant. I did it to see if anyone else was doing it, if anyone was following you. That's when I found State Security. They were trying to monitor you. Maybe they don't like people who build statutes to champions of free speech?"

"The Party declared Li Wenliang a martyr," the doctor replied.

"Yes, but that was five years ago. Since then, Dr. Li has become a symbol, a symbol of resistance to the Party. You must know that."

"Are you telling me to stop? To abandon my friends, not to go to Wenliang Club?"

"No, no."

"What then? You said you were here to help. Help how?"

From beneath the built-in bench, Chunhua removed a cardboard box and began to display its contents on the small dining table in the middle of the cabin. It reminded Fenfang of anatomy class, of her cadaver and the body parts she removed from it. There were noses, ears, breasts with an over-the-shoulder support, a penis on a belt. Feeling them, the doctor realized they were latex and other synthetics. There were also small boxes with makeup kits, special glues, eyebrows, and eyeglasses.

"Wei Bao changed the facial recognition software that the Dalian Police use so that it doesn't recognize you, but I can't do that yet with the agents State Security has on the streets with handheld cameras, so I will teach you how to wear these things when you are going to a Wenliang Club book session or anything else that might be a problem. The facial recognition software and the cameras aren't so smart. This stuff fools them every time. It will fool the State Security goons too."

Fenfang started by pulling the breasts over her head, "Finally, I have boobies that make a bump under my sweater!" So began thirty minutes of laughter and experimenting with the contents of Chunhua's disguise kits, allowing them both to forget briefly the reason the new personas were necessary.

Finally, exhausted from the workday, the dinner, the adventure that had brought her to the boat, Dr. Yang Fenfang collapsed back on a bench. The rain had resumed with a heavy downfall sounding again on the deck above. "But, what about tonight? I didn't wear any of this tonight. And I said some things in the restaurant. Is this all too late?"

Chunhua was reassembling the disguise kits and putting them in a backpack for Fenfang. "Tonight, some of the cameras on the streets around LaMeiZi had digital snow problems and the audio and video feeds from the dining room where you met, those images were actually from last night, when the faculty from pediatrics had dinner. They're crazy, the kids' doctors—lots of drinking."

"You are good," Fenfang said with a wide smile. "I see why Wei Bao has you on his team. Is your twin that good too?"

"He's a boy, so no. But he did a nice deep fake video of you leaving the hospital tonight and taking the metro home. You have been home for several hours now, according to the tapes on the security camera system."

"Amazing," the doctor whispered. "So, if I am already home, then I don't have to go there? Can I stay here tonight?"

"Of course. Bohai is working an all-nighter. I will just ask him to have a deep fake of you take the metro back in to work tomorrow, and you can wear one of your new disguises when you walk to the hospital from here in the morning."

"Oh, good. I definitely want to try one of those additions."

20

Professor Pandry's computer lab
University of Toronto
6 King's College Road
Wednesday, November 26
0930 hours

"Today is the busiest travel day of the year in the US. I say that just to underline that I cannot miss my noon flight back to DC, or I won't make it in time to prepare for Thanksgiving, and an entire gaggle of ungrateful nieces, nephews, and their incompetent parents will starve upon arriving at our house and finding that no one has cooked," Sarah Keogh unloaded in her drawl as soon as she sat down at the conference table in Pandry's personal seminar room. She was the last to arrive.

"My husband seems to think preparing a large turkey is far more complex than any of the antitrust cases he has ever handled. So, it's all on me, every year. Now then, tell me, Rob, do you agree Professor Pandry's death was related to my case? I assume that's why you invited us to his office?"

The Canadians took a moment to recover from Sarah Keogh's arrival statement. "Well, good morning to you too, Sarah," Rob Porter replied to the outpouring. "Yes, well, I guess I forgot that you have Thanksgiving late south of the border. Tomorrow, is it? Well, then we will try to hold this session to an hour. We can always get the FBI to Pearson with L and S if needs be."

"Oh no. No lights and sirens for me, Robbie. I don't want to be the ugly American, fulfilling all your stereotypes. Let's just be, ah, efficient with our time."

"Very well, let me turn it over to Wei Bao, who has been working with Professor Pandry's colleague here at U of T, Dr. Diana McPherson.

They have been trying to do a data analysis of the vast files the professor had on his work, his investments, his startups, and his professional contacts with other scientists around the world." Wei had come clean to Porter, told him about the FBI's showing up at his new office at the lab, told him they knew all about Pandry. Porter had pretended this was news to him, but had agreed to host the FBI lead team at Pandry's office. And to invite Diana.

Porter sat at the head of the long table, in Pandry's chair, with another Mountie and a Toronto constable on either side of him. Keogh and her three "colleagues from the embassy" and DC were to his left, Wei Bao and Diana McPherson to his right. A large screen was mounted on the wall opposite Porter at the foot of the table and a blank whiteboard stretched the length of the seminar room behind Wei and McPherson. Porter, who had taken classes with Pandry in this same room, could not suppress the thought that somehow it was a more appropriate place to discuss neural networks than to investigate arson and murder.

"Thanks, Rob," Wei began. "First, let me thank Diana again, who in the middle of her mourning, in her capacity as the professor's executor for his estate and as an expert in her own right in machine learning, has worked with us to run an algorithm we developed to go through this huge collection of files to see if there are any interesting leads that might help in this, um, investigation and into the professor's murder. Diana?"

Diana, who had risen early to complete the data run, looked pale and somehow distracted. She looked up from her notes, across at the Americans, and then to her left, to the man she had known as a fellow graduate student a few years before, Rob Porter. "So, you all are calling it that, eh? Murder?"

The Toronto constable replied first. "Not officially. Not yet, at least. Nothing we would want in the press. But it does seem to us and to the fire marshal that the cause of the explosion was an extreme overpressure in the gas line leading into the house. Normally, the SCADA system, the software, running in the regional control room of the gas company would show when any settings for pumps were changed, and by whom.

"Those logs were somehow erased a few hours before the explosion, just before they would have been backed up. The gas company has brought in a computer forensics firm to see if there had been unauthorized outside access to the controls. So, yes, we may very well end up determining it was foul play, some sort of death at a distance. I guess if it goes that way you could maybe call it a cyber murder. That would be a first, at least for us."

Diana turned to face Sarah Keogh directly across the table from her. Wei thought that the two women could hardly have been more different. At thirty-six and single, Diana could pass for a new graduate student a dozen years younger. Everything about her said either Birkenstock or GitHub. Sarah, he guessed, was mid-forties, probably a basketball player at some Southern college, now with a demanding career that seemed somehow reflected in her pinstriped pantsuit. He assumed the suit had been specially modified to hide a shoulder holster that she probably wore in the US.

Diana's look and tone were less than welcoming as she stood up and addressed the American woman. "Before I proceed, could I just get an explanation from you as to what your interests are here? Before you arrived, your colleagues all introduced themselves as from CIA, FBI, and Homeland. I assume you are one of those too. So, exactly why is Washington so concerned about the possible murder of a Canadian professor?"

"Oh, hon, I am so sorry. Where are my manners? Special Agent Sarah McPherson, FBI. Of course, well, you heard the officer there saying this could be a cyber murder. We have never had a documented case of that before and, well, we want to profile it. We have the world's best profilers down at Quantico. If this is the first in a rampage by some cyber serial killer, we need to know. We need to stop it. We can't have these brainiacs like your professor being picked off, now can we? I mean minds like his do not just grew on trees." She paused after that rapid-fire delivery and slowed her pace. "So, yes, we are here just to learn from our Canadian cousins and, maybe, if they should need it, to help a little."

Diana raised her eyebrows in doubt, turned to look questioningly at Wei and Porter, then made her decision and confronted Sarah Keogh. "You all have asked for my help. I got up at three this morning to finish this data run using an app that Wei and I just created two nights ago. But for me to make sense of the data and for me to be motivated to help you one more minute, you have to be honest with me. No more bullshit."

Sarah Keogh feigned a look of repulsion at the profanity but said nothing, letting Diana continue. "You all think Ramesh was murdered, but you didn't want to admit how. You think it has something to do with the payroll fraud case that you FBI people asked Robbie to assist you with. And that case is the same reason you returned, Bao. So just fucking tell me why anybody would have murdered Ramesh over some payroll fraud scheme that he had nothing to do with.

"Ramesh Pandry was the most selfless, the most honest, the most dedicated to global welfare of anyone I ever knew or even heard about. So, do not—*do not*—tell me any crazy theory that he was a crook. But do tell me why people engaged in some petty fraud would want him dead. I have a right to know, especially if you want my help, but even if you don't."

Diana sat down, hung her head between her knees for a brief moment, and then looked up to get her answer. It came from her friend, Rob Porter. "Diana, we aren't saying murder yet publicly because we don't want panic and concern about a cyber killer. We are all working on a payroll fraud case, but it is not petty, it's huge. Billions of dollars being stolen around the world.

"The fact that he got murdered just before he might have helped on this case suggests that whoever is behind this fraud is monitoring the investigation and is willing to kill to keep their identity hidden."

Porter looked at Keogh and Wei as if to say, *You might not like this*, then continued. "I knew Ramesh pretty well. I know he would do nothing wrong, but maybe one of his business partners who had access to one of the Pandry-designed quantum computers, an AI Master, could be behind the fraud, sending the money to Moscow or Tehran or Pyongyang for ideological reasons, or because they are being well paid out of the proceeds. We need a suspect list and it will start with his AI Masters who were his business parters. That is how we find out who killed Ramesh."

After a moment, when everyone let Porter's frankness sink in, Sarah Keogh spoke in a soft, slow manner. "What Robbie just said is right. It's also almost all we know. He left out the part about what Moscow or the others might do with all that money. Make nukes and crazy new hypersonic missiles to carry them. That's why this is the most important investigation going on on this continent right now and why we really do need your help, dear.

I am truly sorry for the loss of the professor. I can only imagine what that must mean for you after working so closely with him for so many years. Truly sorry. And I am sorry if we were not fully frank with you before. That comes hard for us, being frank and open, but now we have all the cards on the table."

Diana threw her head back to rearrange her hair. She stood again, picked up a clicker, and put up the first of her PowerPoint slides.

"As you can see from this flow chat, the algorithm accessed Professor Pandry's personal LAN, which only ran here in the building and via VPN to a quantum machine in his home lab. The Q-Compute at his house melted in the fire, but we did pull three terabytes off the servers in this building. Some of it is encrypted and we will need another Q-Compute to break the encryption, but we read enough in the clear to get some ideas.

"We did a pattern analysis of his email and text traffic," she said as the screen shifted to an image of lines of various thicknesses running out from the center of a circle. "Then we overlaid the destinations of his travel for the last five years." Red lines thick and thin appeared superimposed on the blue lines that had represented the communications connections.

"As you can see, his most frequent off-campus interactions were with four colleagues. After that there was a marked dropoff to a second group of about a dozen or so others in a second tier. And then just a host of others with whom his connections were infrequent."

"Could you walk us through who the four were, Diana?" Porter spoke softly from what had always been Pandry's position at the table.

"Ramesh partnered with each of them on one or more startup companies that were based upon his unique quantum computer design. They each have one. In his messages to them, he referred to them as the Qmpanies.

"All four had about the same level of interaction with him, mainly about being on the boards of the startups. Jennifer Scheidmann at Berkeley computer science department and Livermore. Donald Byrd at MIT's Earth Resources Lab. Daniel Kim at JPL, in Pasadena of course. Finally, Zhu Zhenning at Tsinghua University, Beijing's information technology center. But Pandry couldn't export a Q-Compute to him; Canada wouldn't let him."

"You know the Zhu guy, Wei?" Sarah asked.

"Only heard of him. He is very august," Wei replied. "But of these four, Diana, how many were members of the AIML group, the Redwoods seminar?"

"All of them."

"Tell me more about the Redwoods club. What was that all about?" Porter queried.

Wei jumped in. "I've been looking into that. It was an informal club or seminar of two dozen of the world's leading experts in artificial intelligence and machine learning, thus AIML. They met, usually twice a year, and almost always in this private forest near the Sonoma coast north of San Francisco, someplace called the Richardson Redwoods."

Diana continued the answer. "They would exchange notes there, help each other solve problems, generate ideas, sometimes divide up their efforts. All unofficially, without really coordinating with their labs, their universities, or their governments. Ramesh loved those sessions. He would even pay for the catering and the satellite truck. I know because some of the bills showed up on his lab credit card sometimes, and he would have to repay the lab."

It was just a matter of who would ask the question first. Sarah Keogh did. "Satellite truck?"

"He said they needed to bring in a large dish and a generator to give them enough connectivity for some of their demonstrations," Diana explained. "The camp has no internet connection, so they beamed off an Intelsat. There were always some members, he said, who could not make it to the events and wanted to connect remotely. He said the woods were a pretty primitive place, that's why they all loved it so much. That and the age of the trees. He said some dated from the 1300s, when most of the continent was forest."

"Must have been lovely there, I'm sure, with all the trees and all," Keogh said, trying to bring the conversation back from the forest. "But can we get to murder motivation? It might not be about stopping him from helping us. Maybe there was some other reason. Who would want Pandry out of the way? Had he pissed anybody off, I mean badly enough to..."

Diana shook her head. "No, he was such a kind and generous man. I can't imagine anyone..."

"For example, you're the executor of his estate. Who is in his will? Where does all his money and his interests in these companies go?" Sarah Keogh pressed. "Did he have children?" It seemed to Wei that she asked that last question in a tone that implied that being a parent was in itself suspicious.

"No children. Never married, except to his work." Diana looked for the estate file on her iPad. *"After expenses of the estate, the cash value of my assets shall be divided up among charities."*

"Who is on which startup board?" Wei pressed.

"They all are. They're all four on all the startup boards, along with Dr. Pandry. I mean, he was."

"Oh my, I must be getting to the airport, or no turkey and taters for the tots tomorrow. That would be a calamity now, wouldn't it?" Sarah Keogh was standing, leaning across the table to shake hands goodbye. "So helpful, Dr. McPherson, especially after all you have been through. Really, dear, so helpful."

The meeting quickly broke up. Porter offered to drive to the airport, promising no lights and sirens. He also maneuvered Wei into the car. As they moved west through the city, Porter driving and Wei in the front seat with Keogh alone in the back, they were initially quiet. Wei and Keogh were flipping through emails and texts on their devices. Both had two smartphones each.

"I did want to tell you that I got the okay from Washington. I can work with you. With you, Wei, not with Chinese intelligence. As a police matter. So now I can tell you what we have concluded so far. Our experts think only a Pandry computer could be running something as complicated as this fraud. Somebody at one of those companies that has a Pandry computer is in league with the Russians, or whatever nation is doing this. We need to go check out these companies."

Porter intervened. "Okay, then let's split up the work, since there may be good reason to do it fast. Let's confront the AIML Masters who were in business with Pandry. They have the Q-Compute devices. We should ask for voluntary cooperation to access their machines and tell them not to alter files until you can get a search warrant, Sarah."

"These days, that could take a while," she admitted.

Porter continued with his plan. "I suggest that I visit the professor in Boston. Wei, you take the guy in Beijing, obviously. That leaves the other two for you, Sarah. You good with that?"

"No, actually. Any interviews in the US of A ought to be done by the US, by the Bureau."

"Well, sure, of course," Porter countered, "but you personally can't be at all three in the US at the same time, and we probably want to conduct them all at the same time so they don't talk to each other afterward and give away our questions. You can have an agent accompany me."

"I'm flying back to China through San Fran," Wei added. "So why not let me accompany your local agent to the one in Berkeley..."

"That would leave me with the space cadet at the Jet Propulsion Lab, Pasadena. Highly unorthodox, but I do see the value of continuity. Half the time I send agents from our field offices in to interview people and it's a complete waste of time. They have no context. They know less about national security than they do about the rules of criminal procedure, and that's saying something," Keogh said, leaning from the back seat to the space between Porter and Wei.

"But before we all go off half-cocked here, lemme just ask two things," she continued, "First and most important, do we think by interviewing these guys we are investigating the 'cyber murder' of this Professor Pandry, or are we doing what brought Wei and me both to Toronto in the first place, finding out who is behind this massive, global now, payroll fraud operation with all the fake personas and such?"

Rob Porter nodded as he pulled onto the highway to the airport. "Both. Same case. Probably. Most likely. I will bet. Same case. Somebody killed him because he was on to them, that they were misusing his machine."

"Good, just checking I got all three nations singing from the same page in the hymnal," Keogh said and plopped into the back seat. "Let's assume I can convince my bosses to let me cooperate with a Mountie and a Chinese cop, letting them run around in the US questioning people. With an FBI minder. I am charming, but this will take work."

Wei looked confused at the hymnal remark, but asked, "And your second question? You said you had two."

"Well, this one is really just to Robbie." She smiled.

"Yes? What is that, Special Agent Keogh?" Porter asked, looking in the rearview mirror.

"So you're in the left lane and all the cars in front of you keeping pulling quickly out of the lane, and I recall that you promised me no L&S, so I was just wondering why people seem to fear being in front of an unmarked car and can't get out of the lane fast enough? And do I seem to see something blue and red reflecting off the car in front of us?"

Rob Porter looked back at Sarah Keogh in the mirror. "I said I wouldn't use lights *and* sirens."

Wei turned around to face Keogh. "These Canadians. So legalistic."

After they dropped Keogh off, the ride back into town from the airport took a while, in part because Porter did not use the police lights in the unmarked car, but also because it seemed like he wanted alone time with Wei in a place where they might be relatively safe from surveillance. Porter wanted to talk.

"So I told you dealing with the Feebs was always something special. What did you think of Sarah?"

"Behind her Southern belle act, I think she may be someone who can get stuff done," Wei began slowly, looking out at the lake to the right of the highway. "Like I told you, she and I had a frank chat. She said you got assigned to the case because when the Mounties checked the file on the professor, your name popped up. That would mean that you were on the case a while before you showed up at the 53rd Precinct to rescue me," Wei said with as big a grin as he was capable of producing. "So, what do you say, Robbie, you tell me what you had discovered in that time, the time you were actually on the case before I got here. And why you have been pretending to know less than you do."

Porter did not answer right away. Instead he moved the car to the right lane and took the next exit. "There's a nice park over there along the lakefront. Maybe we can take a stroll."

Wei nodded, and the two men maintained their silence until Porter had pulled the car into the nearly empty parking lot. Porter pulled out his mobile phones and put them under his seat. Wei followed suit.

They emerged from the car and began down the pathway to the windy lakefront. The sky was several shades of gray and the wind had whipped up a light chop on the immense lake. For the first time since he arrived in Canada, Wei was glad he had brought a winter coat.

Porter looked out at the water, not at Wei, as he began. "You're right, of course. I have not been fully open with you, not because I don't trust you but because I usually follow orders. You know how it is."

"I absolutely do."

"Good. So, I will trade you my whole story for yours. Deal?"

"Deal."

"Let's start with when we were at school together. CSIS knew, somehow, that you were a cop. They asked me to befriend you. I probably would have anyway, but…I reported on you to them. I told them you were just intent on learning about AI and machine learning, especially facial recognition. I told them that you were not doing any spying while you were here, too busy with classes and research projects for Pandry, just like I was. Was I right?"

Wei turned to face Porter and felt the wind full on in his face. It was picking up and a gust hit him, almost blowing his Blue Jays cap off. "I may not have revealed to your immigration people or the university that I was employed by city police, but I told Pandry from the start. He didn't mind. Other than that, I was what I seemed, a graduate student. Only that."

"So was I, Bao. A real student, but I did get to expense some of our bar tabs. And I didn't tell them anything about you that they did not already know."

"Now I know why Immigration still had my picture in its active database, why it popped up so quickly at the airport kiosk."

"When you made the reservation with Air Canada, Bao, it probably triggered. The AI probably flagged you right away because CSIS had put a tickler on your name in certain databases. It knew you were coming before you landed."

"So you liberal Canadians are not so very different from we authoritarian, police state Chinese? Eh, Robbie?"

"Maybe. In some ways. Every modern nation is using AI, has huge databases, and employs facial recognition. It's just a question of what you do with it." They walked on with the breeze against their backs. It passed through Wei's mind that the wind would make it difficult for parabolic microphones, if anyone was trying to listen to their conversation from a distance.

'You were going to tell me the whole story?" Wei asked.

"Right. Well, I think you know most of it. We did get a request to check out Pandry. The Bureau called us about three weeks ago. And yes, I got assigned the request because headquarters knew I had studied with him. There aren't too many Mounties who get two years off, full salary, to go to grad school. People know who gets a bennie like that. They're jealous. And a lot of folks in the force know me because of my tech innovation job. I've been trying to let everyone in the force know we are in the twenty-first century.

"From what I can tell, the FBI didn't have any reason to suspect Pandry of anything, but they thought that running a fraud like this in real time would take hundreds of people at scores of computers, or one or two Q-Compute. They told us they think some AI geniuses are helping North Korea or Iran or Russia steal billions to fund their weapons programs."

Wei placed both hands on his face, feeling the cold on his cheeks. "So, did you hack Pandry's files?"

"No. We can't just do that. We need probable cause and there was none. No, I just drove over and had a chat with him. Described the problem to him. Asked if he thought that kind of a fraud program would be hard to create. Asked if he could guess at who might be doing it."

"What did he think?" Wei wished he had arrived in time to have had the same conversation. "And, by the way, did you tell him about the little experiment you were doing with Air Canada and Shell to see if what was going on in American companies was also happening up here?"

Porter nodded. "Yeah. He seemed genuinely interested. He thought it was a very hard thing to do, not creating the fake personas, but giving them a pattern of life that constantly updated in lots of databases like we found in Air Canada and Shell. Yeah, I told him about the companies. He also thought that it would be a hard problem to design the program so you would not get caught, either with the fake people or with the moving around of their paycheck money. He volunteered that it would be a perfect task for a Q-Compute. And he proposed that he look into who had access to the devices he had loaned out to his colleagues."

"And did he?"

"No, I told him I needed to get permission for him to do that. We might not want to tip anybody off that we were on to them. And I never heard back from the Bureau before the explosion, before he died."

"You mean before he was murdered?"

"Yeah. Problem is, we haven't got a guess about who might have done it. Maybe Washington is right and it was the Russians or Iranians, but that's pretty wild and we don't have any evidence tying it to them."

Wei moved closer to Porter and asked in a soft tone. "Where did you interview the professor? In his house?"

Porter looked surprised at the question. "No, in his conference room, the seminar room, where we met with Sarah Keogh this morning. Why? There was no reason to think any of his areas were bugged. We hadn't even tried to get a warrant, and the FBI wouldn't do it on Canadian soil."

Wci blinked several times and pursed his lips, a tell that Fenfang would have known meant he was going to say something critical, something he thought might offend. "There was every reason to think someone might be listening. Any group smart enough to create the payroll fraud AI is also probably smart enough to create a self-protection AI. You told him about what you had found in Air Canada and Shell. That, by the way, means that when you told me that you had not yet seen the results from checking on those two companies, that was not exactly true either."

Porter frowned. "Yeah, that was part of Keogh's idea, that I should pretend with you that I was just now stumbling into this whole thing. Sorry."

"No problem. But it also means that if the bad guys were running a self-defense algo, it might have detected your guys discovering it in Air Canada and Shell. It might have hacked into the phones of your friends in the companies who discovered it. The AI might have heard them telling you the results of your inquiry. They would then have hacked into your mobile to track you and listen to you. And then you laid out the whole story when you met with Pandry, everything you knew. Did you mention me too?"

The RCMP officer looked shaken. "Do you think the guys running this fraud scheme have AI that can do all of that—hack into phones, transcribe conversations, act quickly on the basis of what it heard?"

"It happens all the time in China. AI listens to the phone call of a dissident, determines the guy on the other phone is one too, and initiates a 'track and record' on the new guy. No human in the loop."

"Shit. We are behind the times." Porter shook his head in amazement. "But even if we had that kind of capability, we couldn't use it, legally. It's so hard to believe."

"Believe it," Wei replied. "So, did you tell him you knew I was coming and that it might be about the same case?"

"No. He told me. Said you would be arriving the next day and he wondered out loud if it might be about the same thing. He said you were vague on the phone, but said you needed help with a complex problem that maybe only he and a few others in the world could do. He said he was struck by the fact that that was the same thing I had told him."

Wei turned back into the wind, indicating that he wanted to walk back to the car. "So, you talked with him the day before he was murdered?"

"Yeah, like twenty-four, no, twenty-six hours before." Porter stopped walking. "Jesus Christ, Bao. Are you saying what I did caused Pandry to become a target, to be killed? Because I let them hear that you and I wanted his help with the fraud. Fuck."

"It's a possibility, surely, but don't blame yourself. A machine learning program this complex, one that was running defensive ops, might have been listening in on Pandry anyway, not just on your mobile. If so, they would have heard me say I was coming to get his help on something that they realized was their fraud operation."

It had begun to mist, and Wei thought it would shower soon. A cloud out over the lake was already dumping rain on the water. "Can you drop me off at the university library? I want to read up on a few things," Wei said. It was now Wei who was being deceptive, just a little, by not telling the whole story.

"Sure, but one more piece of honesty first, since I am breaking the rules telling you stuff I shouldn't," Porter said, placing his hand on Wei's shoulder.

"We have had you under light surveillance since you landed. Mainly cameras, a few gumshoes."

"Of course you have. I assumed."

"Yeah, well, we are not the only ones. Some guys from your consulate here in town, some guys from the embassy in Toronto, a few illegals enrolled as students, they have been following you physically, old-school style. I assume you know that. I assume they are there for your protection."

"Chinese people protect one another," Wei replied. "Let's get back to the car. Anyone tail us here?"

Rob Porter shook his head no.

The rain came hard just as they got to the car. Driving back to campus, both men were quiet, lost in thought, listening to the windshield wipers laboring in vain to let them see clearly through the rain.

21

Dalian, China
ReGlobal Audit Department
Thursday, November 27
0345 hours

YAO GUANG EMERGED FROM the makeshift bedroom he had created in what the previous tenant had used as an executive's office. Now the private offices were sleeping areas for Wei Bao's team of hackers and their assistants. They had been having a string of good luck. They had traced the IP address of the Singapore gun for hire, who had created the fake faces of Chinese people. He had opened the video Chunhua had sent him through TOR. The video dropped a beacon onto his system. It beaconed to a cloud server that Chunhua had set up. That gave her Chong Yeow's real IP address. After that it was easy. Their AI hacking bot had gotten inside Chung Yeow's servers, found a file with 300,000 computer-generated images of Chinese people, and exfiltrated a copy of the file.

Their weekend project would be to start matching the fake persona faces with the National ID database, looking for the same faces. With that information, they would know who all the 300,000 fake Chinese people were and could find out where they were employed and maybe where their payroll checks went. First, however, the team was getting ready to track the investment orders that came into bank accounts. Paychecks were about to hit some of the fake personas they had already laboriously hunted down.

Using Wei's special authority, Yao had gained cooperation from four of the major Chinese banks. The twins could now access the banks' systems legally, which, they complained, took all the fun out of it.

The bots that the twins ran inside the banks' networks identified the accounts of all of the ninety thousand No Shows they knew about up to that point and recorded their balances. Most had very low balances because, the records showed, they wired funds out almost as soon as they were deposited. Some money went to invest in shell companies inside China and overseas. Some funds were used to order deliveries from overseas suppliers, none of which ever actually seemed to ship anything to the buyers. When special government permits were needed to authorize overseas investments, they magically appeared. It was all done without a bank account holder ever appearing in person or ever picking up a phone to talk to the bank. None of it raised flags for the bank compliance monitoring apps, or perhaps someone had modified the apps.

Most of the money seemed to be going abroad, if not in the first move, by the second or third jump. So, the twins had followed the money, hacking into recipient banks and corporations most often in Asia Pacific: Hong Kong, Taiwan, Singapore, Tuvalu, the Philippines. These were places used to getting Chinese deposits. From there on, however, there was no pattern. Funds went to the Middle East, Dubai, and Beirut. Deposits also moved to the sleezier banks in Cyprus, the Cayman Islands, Russia, the Channel Islands, none of which seemed to enforce international Know Your Customer rules or do any serious anti-money laundering auditing.

In those no-tell banks, the No Shows' funds usually ended up in the accounts of newly formed shell corporations. By the time the twins and their bots attempted to hack into the corporate bank accounts, however, the accounts were either closed or largely empty. The bank records had been altered to show that the deposits had never been recorded, nor were the transfers out to the ultimate or penultimate destinations anywhere to be found on the bank records.

"These gangster banks may not even know they are cooperating with the No Shows," Chunhua wrote in a report to Wei. "They just have such shitty auditing, logging, and cybersecurity that they do not notice that someone is rewriting their records. Either way, we are hitting dead ends."

Acting on Wei's guidance, they were now focusing not just on where the money went but where the instructions to move it came from. When the

No Shows went into their bank accounts to set up the wire transfers, where were they logging in from?

Guessing that the command-and-control servers that would send the orders to move money were at the end of a long series of bounces from where the fraud group was headquartered, Wei asked the twins to create an app that would trace back very quickly, hacking into logs, and moving on to the next jump point as fast as possible, hacking their way in, finding out where the command had come from, and then moving farther back. No human could move that fast, but maybe an AI could.

Yao Guang, still wearing the track suit he used as pajamas, began making himself tea. Bohai silently walked up behind him and screamed, "We got big problems, chief."

Startled, Yao dropped his teacup, which shattered on the concrete floor, breaking the early morning silence in the suite. The burly detective spun around with his fist out, but stopped short as Bohai bent at the knees, bringing his head below the arc of Yao's swing. "What kind of problems?" Yao asked, bending down to pick up the pieces of teacup.

"Big problems with the No Show people," the twin said as his butt settled on the floor not far from the teacup. If he were already on the floor, Yao couldn't knock him down.

"They're disappearing," Chunhua called from her seat at a monitor across the room.

Yao picked Bohai up off the floor and almost dragged him to the monitor where Chunhua was quickly hitting the keyboard. "Disappearing from where?"

"From everywhere," she replied. "I was watching as our program dumped the search-back app into the bank accounts of the No Shows who work at China Rail Road Corporation, and I got an error code: no such bank accounts. So, I went back to CRRC's payroll database to see what we did wrong and none of the fake people are on the payroll anymore. In fact, they never were, it says. No trace they ever worked there. So, I go to their phones, nothing, to their National ID, none. In every database where they existed, there is no sign that they were ever there and nothing in any log to say that the databases had been altered. Bam, they're gone."

"That's the rail company. What about the others?" Yao asked.

"Same story in all of the companies we checked so far," Bohai replied. "Chunhua is writing a program to automate the search of all the databases, all the companies, but I bet it will be the same thing. The ghosts are gone."

Yao wished that Wei were back. He dreaded telling him that they had lost all of their leads before they could trace back the orders to move this week's pay. "People engaged in fraud don't usually decide that they have enough money and stop," he said aloud. "Did these guys?"

"No way. These guys didn't want us investigating them, so they ran," Bohai added.

"They knew we were investigating them?" Yao asked.

Chunhua spun her chair around facing the detective. "We have not been that stealthy. We made a mistake. Because we had the banks' permission, we've been banging around. We also hit all sorts of other databases looking at the fake people. We probably triggered lots of hidden tripwires, set off alarms."

"We didn't think about that," Bohai agreed, "but when enough alarms went off, they probably figured they better quit before we get too close."

"Fuck," Yao Guang whispered to himself. As he did, the large monitor on the wall chirped to life, the tone meaning that Wei Bao was attempting to video link in on the encrypted tunnel they had made for his laptop and mobile to connect back to the office. "Great timing, boss."

Wei wanted to report what had happened in Canada, but Yao insisted on going first, telling the bad news about their attempts to trace the orders to the banks, about the fact that the fake personas had vanished, about the likelihood that the bad guys were on to their investigation.

Sitting in a lonely carrel in the university library, far from the ears of anyone, Wei had pulled the laptop from the backpack that had never left his side since he had landed in Toronto. From it he had hopped on to the campus wi-fi and then onto a virtual private network site in Iceland, from which he had set up an encrypted link to his office. He scanned the book stacks and saw only one camera in the ceiling, probably tied into campus security. He knew anyone who might be tracking him could probably access that university network, but the camera did not look like it had a microphone. He turned his back to it, in case anyone watching might try to lip read.

With his fifth set of AirPods dangling, he looked enough like a graduate student that no one would have thought twice about him, if there had been anybody on that floor of the library or searching through the Canadian literature section near his carrel. No one was. On his screen, he saw Yao's face and those of the twins, appearing from behind, one looking over each of Yao's broad shoulders into the camera. After Yao explained what had happened with the disappearing No Shows, Wei's silence was long enough that Bohai piped up, "Can you hear us, boss?"

"Yeah, just thinking. I guess we should have anticipated that move," Wei finally replied. "Somehow maybe they knew we stole the fake persona images from the Singapore guy. So they decided to erase them before we could move. Clever."

"Maybe you tell the big bosses in Beijing that we stopped all the No Shows," Bohai replied. "Then we all get bonuses." In response to that, Yao feigned a face slap at Bohai.

"But what I don't get," Yao said, "is why they stopped pulling in the money just 'cause we might be on to them. Thieves, even smarty computer thieves, are always greedy. That's why they get caught. None of them ever have enough. None of them ever stop."

Wei smiled at his partner, ten thousand miles away from Toronto. "So, your detective's instinct is that they will continue to do it? Make more fake personas?"

"Yeah, I guess, but maybe they are on pause."

"On pause until what?" Wei asked.

"Until we go away?" Chunhua suggested.

"Or maybe until we look like we went away," Wei replied. "I think you're right, Yao. They will be back. So, we write something stealthy that can live on the networks of the big companies, something that will notice if a lot of new employees show up on the payroll in a few weeks or months, new No Shows.

"Meanwhile, let me tell you what I learned here in Canada. Our No Shows are part of a pattern that is also happening at least in North

America, maybe Europe and elsewhere. The Americans discovered it when Boeing required people to show up in person to be fired. When they never showed, Boeing security figured out that they never existed and had to inform the Pentagon that there had been a penetration of the corporate network."

Wei was looking at his notes for the report he was going to send to Beijing, a report that had to be carefully worded because someone would need to tell the president that there may not be No Shows and Skimmers to arrest in a well-publicized police raid nationwide.

"That's odd," Chunhua responded. "The AI should have noticed the emails telling the workers to show up, should have known they were being called in to be fired."

"Yeah, and then the AI should have changed the records to show that they already were called in and fired," Bohai added. "AI fucked up. Not so smart AI after all, maybe."

"Smarter than we are, so far," Yao said, looking at the twins. "We still don't know who they are, who is doing this. What do you think, boss? Any theories?"

Wei had been pondering that same question, trying to decide what to write in his report to the president's chief of staff. "The Americans think it's a nation-state because it's so sophisticated. They think maybe a nation-state hired or coerced some experts to help them, but what really worries Washington is that all of this money could be going to build nuclear weapons or some secret vaccine for a new man-made virus. They're guessing Russia, Iran, North Korea. When they learn that the No Shows have disappeared, they will think that the bad guys have all the money they need and are about to attack New York or something. Those FBI guys are real paranoids."

"Yeah, they all fucked up over there," Bohai chuckled. "I bet it's CIA running the No Shows."

That provoked another pretend face slap attempt from Yao. It was clear to Wei that the twins were getting along well with their surrogate dad while Wei was traveling. "Chief Inspector, we are all sorry for the loss of your esteemed professor and mentor, Dr. Pandry. It's too bad he couldn't have told you his guess about who is the mastermind behind this AI," Yao added.

"Thank you. If I had been a day earlier, maybe." Wei looked down the long row of book stacks. There was still no one around, but he kept his voice low. "Crazy thing is, Yao, the Americans had thought about the professor, too. But they asked the Canadians to kind of spy on him. I think they maybe thought he was being forced to help this AI group, or maybe he was helping but didn't know it. Or maybe one of his business partners, another AIML Master, is doing it for Iran or somebody. I get the feeling there is something they aren't telling me, something that made them want to look at the professor. Now the Canadians are pretty sure that it was murder, that someone blew up his house."

"Shit, man, that's heavy," Bohai exhaled. "Bet it was CIA."

This time Yao only gave a disapproving look. "What do you think, boss?"

"I think I have to agree that his murder is connected to all of this, but there is no way he was forced to cooperate with bad guys. He would have told them to fuck off and reported them to the police. I am thinking that maybe some of his startup companies were being misused in some way, maybe generating or hosting the AI algos. Possible he discovered that and so they had to kill him. Possible that the bad guys knew that the Mounties and me were going to ask him for help on this case. Maybe by planning to visit him, I signed his death warrant."

As the implications of all of that hit Yao, the big man shifted his stance and dropped his head. He then asked a question, the answer to which he had just guessed, an answer he did not really want Wei to confirm. "How would they know that, know about you?"

"Yao, my instincts may be different from yours. Mine are more about what an algo would do or a camera would see, but my instincts almost ever since I got here have been telling me that I am being surveilled. At first, I thought it was just the Canadians. Now they tell me it's them and our own guys from State Security. They're probably reporting on my progress."

"We are watching you too," Yao offered. "We always know where you are. We can just access whatever cameras systems are nearby, keep a protective overwatch on you, make sure we know who is around." Yao looked to Chunhua, who nodded that he got it right.

"That's reassuring. They are watching me. You are watching them watching me, but I feel like there is someone else, someone who learned about me by following the officer the Canadians have on the case, Rob Porter, listening to his chat with the professor. I think it's them, the folks running the AI. Maybe the Americans are right and it's Iran or Korea. See if they show up. Meanwhile, before I come home, I'm going to go to the States to talk to another of the AIML Masters. They will follow me, whoever they are, maybe slip up and reveal a thread I can trace back. I'm getting closer to them."

Bohai shook his head. "Sounds like they getting closer to you, boss."

22

Cafe Boulud
Four Seasons Hotel, Toronto
Wednesday, November 26
1930 hours

THEY SPLIT THE DUCK. Diana said it was what the professor always ordered when he took her to the café, once a month or so to discuss her work for him over a good meal. It was a whole rotisserie canard, breast and leg, with black truffle, roasted beetroot, frisée endive, and canard jus. The menu warned that the cook time was forty-five minutes, but she assured Wei it would be worth the wait. He welcomed the long appetizer course, not just for the tuna tartar, but for the opportunity to gauge Diana's reaction to all that had happened.

Earlier Wei had walked back to the hotel from the university library, trying to remember the measures he had been taught to discover surveillance. He spotted no tail, but there were cameras everywhere, some public on light posts, others privately owned on buildings. Despite the evasive moves he took for practice and the fact that he had turned off his mobile, he knew any skilled operator would have had only a little trouble following him, losing him, and then recovering him. In Dalian, he had minimally skilled clerks do it. And he had AI software that did it better than the humans.

Diana McPherson looked more like her old self from grad school days, but with more expensive clothing and makeup. She looked better than she had at any time since their reunion in front of the inferno of Pandry's house. Finally, she said, she had gotten some solid sleep. She insisted when she ordered the canard, and added an expensive Zinfandel, that she would be picking up the tab. "I met with his estate lawyer this morning.

He had done everything as trusts, so there is no waiting for probate. It turns out that he left me something, far more than he should have. Five million Canadian. And I will still be employed by the estate for two years to wrap up his affairs and investments, liquidate some of them, and see to it that the proceeds are distributed to the charities."

"I'm delighted for you, Diana. You deserve it for all of your hard work and devotion to him." Wei held a glass of the dark purple wine in a toast to her. "You were like the daughter he never had. But if he left you that much, how large do you estimate the overall estate to be?"

"Using our search software, from what it found, I was able to recreate some of the information we lost when the devices in his house melted." She withdrew a flash drive from her purse and handed it to Wei, the results of her searching the professor's financial records. "He had stocks worth over thirty million US, plus shares in startups that are still maturing but will likely be worth many times that before long. He was on the board of directors of six companies, on the advisory boards of another four." She sipped the zin and smiled. "Now I will be on three of those boards representing his estate and trusts."

"Really?" Wei asked. "Good for him. Good for you. What do these companies do, the companies that you will become a director of?"

"Not things that I have any real expertise on," she sighed. "One makes 'cube sats,' which I assume means tiny satellites. Another is into clean energy generation, and the fun one here in town develops and operates machine learning algorithms for standard quantum computers. You tell them the problem you want solved and they write an algo that works on one of the publicly available quantum computers, IBM's, Google's, or Rigetti's. If you can't handle the implementation of the software on the device, they do that for the customer, too, and they have been cracking some hard nuts apparently."

"Wonderful. Well, you will enjoy that, I know."

"If I can understand it. But, Bao, let me ask you something. Robbie Porter must tell you more than he tells me now that you are 'fellow officers' and all that." She pushed aside the onion soup, still half full. "Have you two and that American woman developed any real leads on who murdered Ramesh?"

"They don't tell me everything either, Diana," he said, leaning across the table. "But, as you heard, Washington does seem to think the giant payroll fraud may be being done on one of his computers."

"Nonsense," she scoffed.

"I agree he could not have been coerced to help, but could he have been tricked into lending out one of his prototype machines to a colleague to start a company and not have been told the real purpose?"

"Really, Bao, you knew him. Trick him? Especially about the purpose of a machine learning app? Couldn't happen," she insisted.

Wei leaned back in his chair. "Then what we are left with is that what I did, and what Robbie did, might have killed him."

"What? What are you talking about?"

Wei formed a triangle with the fingers of his two hands and rested his head at the apex. He spoke even more softly than was his wont, looking Diana in the eyes. "It is possible that whoever developed and/or ran the massive payroll fraud AI heard Robbie talking to the professor about it, heard us talking with the professor." He closed his eyes a moment and took a breath. "Maybe they acted fast to cover their tracks. Within a day they eliminated the risk that the professor would help me, and Robbie, and crack the case. Within a day they killed him."

Diana reached across the small table and put her hand on Wei's. "Don't torture yourself like that. You said it's possible, so you don't know that it's true?"

"No."

"But if it were true, then that would mean they really thought Ramesh would figure out who they were, maybe that he knew them somehow," she almost whispered. "It doesn't mean his colleagues or his Qmpanies were involved."

Wei thought that Diana was finally accepting the facts, that the professor had been killed, that his death was related to the payroll fraud, and that there was a sophisticated group behind it all. A group willing to kill to protect themselves.

"That's why we are going to the AIML Masters," he said. "We want to get their ideas about who is behind all of this, maybe scare one of them into showing their hand. See if their Q-Computes could have been misused."

"Maybe I can be useful then," Diana suggested. "Useful in finding his killers. Tell me what to look for, what to ask, who to get close to on the boards."

"That might be dangerous, but if you're willing," Wei said, standing up to go to the restroom. "Don't do anything now. After we talk with them individually, we may have some ideas about what you could do."

As he stepped away, Wei noticed a camera in the ceiling that took in the part of the dining room where he had been sitting. He turned around to check its angle of view. Like any techie, Diana had pulled out her mobile as soon as she was alone. As in China, people here could not stand even a few seconds of silence. They had to have screen time.

After their feast, Wei walked Diana to the hotel lobby. "Bao, I know you are engaged, but this has been the most pleasant date I have been on in a very long time. Actually, it's the only date I have been on in a while, but really, I enjoy being with you so much. Can we do it again Saturday night? Maybe a pub crawl, like we used to do?"

In a brief flash, Wei thought how much fun that would be, felt guilty about doing it, and rationalized it by thinking he might learn more from Diana when she was drunk. He thought there was more there to uncover. "Of course, Diana. I can push back my flight to SFO until Sunday. Just so long as nobody we know sees us pub crawling. After all, I am a policeman, and I do kinda represent China."

"Then let's dress like grad students again. We will blend right in."

As the hotel doorman held the car door for Diana, Wei counted three cameras looking at the front door area. He wondered how many different groups were hacking into that video feed and who they all might be.

23

Paulaner Bräuhaus
Kempinski Hotel
92 Jiefang Road
Dalian, China
Friday, November 28
1945 hours

Beer halls in Munich have high ceilings, open space, long tables, and the whiff of spilled beer that cannot be eradicated no matter the obsessive-compulsive cleaning disorders of the Germans, but not in Dalian. In Dalian, the Bräuhaus has a low ceiling, a forest of dark stained cherry-wood half walls and booths, and a faint aroma of bleach. It does, however, have the best beer in the province: Paulaner lager vom fass. Naturally, when the detectives and some of the mid-level uniformed officers of the Dalian Police got together the last Friday of every month for a meeting of their unofficial union, it was in the Bräuhaus. The beer hall closed to the public on those nights. The cameras were disabled, and phones were checked at the door.

Yao Gang was well known and much liked among his fellow detectives. He had been on the force since 2002 and would in two years be eligible for retirement with twenty-five years of service. Then, before he turned fifty, he would land a job at one of the big banks on Xinghai Square or one of the new tech firms out by the university. His time on the Cyber Crime Squad would insure a good landing, post-police. The only better squad for post-police life preparation would have been Financial Crimes, but after his years going after drug dealers and men who traffic in women, his image did not fit with that of the FinCrimer boys. Wei Bao had not cared; in fact, he had wanted someone for his deputy who knew the streets and the crime gang mentality. Yao Gang knew both better than anyone on the force.

Thus, Yao Gang was somewhat surprised when he was pulled into a big booth populated with FinCrimers. It looked to the newly arriving Yao that they had been at it for a while. They had already built several large, rickety structures from the beer coasters that came one per stein. "Yao Guang, you work too late. We have head start on you that you will never catch up," Peng Jian, the FinCrime Squad lead detective, called out from the other end of the booth. "But we toast you and Cyber Crime Squad for snuffing the Russian shit scum who were hacking into the Technical School, then hitting our banks!"

"Prost." Hefting his first stein, Yao joined the toasting to himself and Cyber Squad. "Yes, and you would never have tracked them down this side of 2030, Jian. And it was Wei Bao who pulled the trigger, not me, and the kid turned out to be a good shot, otherwise, I would not be here to drink with you." Yao held up an invisible pistol and shot twice at Peng across the table to roars of laughter and applause from Peng's subordinates.

Yao signaled for another stein, and it was quickly produced by a young woman in a dirndl. Somehow the cultural dissonance of a Chinese woman in a red German dress with leather accoutrement struck Yao as oddly attractive, bordering on erotic, especially as she smiled back. The FinCrimers were quick to advise him that there was no tipping, which he knew, but feigned not to. Yao had promised himself that he would return home after this month's meeting relatively sober and before midnight. If not, it would mean another Silent Saturday, a day when his otherwise wonderful wife would ignore him and his attempts at conversation about their daughter, about dinner, even the weather. No, tonight he would be good. He might even leave early and swing back by the loft to see how the twins were doing getting Wei Bao what he needed.

Then the singing began, as it always did when this crowd had enough beer and too little kraut, schnitzel, and sausage. The FinCrimers piled out of the booth to go join the group growing around the piano at the other side of the hall. Peng Jian, who was Yao's age and ten years older than the most senior man on his team, stayed behind in the booth. Peng ordered a blood sausage plate "with the special spicy mustard" for himself and Yao to share. It rapidly appeared and both men dug in eagerly.

"So Wei was the shooter? I assumed it was you. Didn't think that boy even carried a pistol. Well, good for him. You taught him well, or maybe he just has good luck, eh?" Peng spoke as he shoveled the blutwurst in his mouth.

Yao's third stein arrived. "He has very good luck, Jian, that's why I am sticking with him. Together, he and I are going places. Not supposed to say this, but he is on a temporary assignment as a chief inspector, on orders from Beijing, orders from Huang."

The special spicy mustard was now on Peng's chin, upper lip, and shirt. He dabbed his lips and missed most of the mustard. "Oh, that's not a secret. Not to me anyway. I heard right after it happened. Heard directly from Beijing, then got it confirmed by a guy in Wang's office. It's why I wanted us to talk tonight, one on one, brother detective to brother detective, old-school cops." Peng burped. "By the way, do you think Wang enjoys having a kid holding the same chief inspector rank as him? And Wang is close to the State Security mob."

Yao thought he should have seen this coming. FinCrime were not normally a welcoming lot and the last thing they would have done was to toast the success of another team, especially when it was success in getting a gang involved in financial crime, in this case Internet-based financial crime. Yao knew that beer dulled his instincts. Here again was proof. "Peng, if the investigations get too much for us, we will definitely call you and your team for help. No worries. Wei Bao is not territorial." Not like you, Yao almost said.

"I don't want anything to do with the investigation. It's radioactive. That's what I want to warn you." Peng lowered his voice. "Get out of Cyber while you can."

"You don't understand, Jian. This investigation is being done for The Highest Level. Wei Bao has special investigative powers. It's going to be radioactive for somebody, but not us."

Peng burped a second time, this time more deeply. "Brother to brother, you should know 'Corruption Must be Weeded Out' is dangerous when it becomes more than a slogan for the people. The Highest Level does not seem to know that. He seems to be serious. He is walking toward a sinkhole, toward quicksand, and Wei, and maybe you, will be sucked into it."

Yao's pupils narrowed and he glared at Peng. "One of the reasons Chinese people adore The Highest Level is because he is serious about it."

Peng finished his beer. "You are old enough to remember Bo Xilai? He was from this province too. He was going to be a Big Man in Beijing. He ended up in prison, his wife too."

"Yes, but they murdered a British man. And they were corrupt."

"I will tell you who is corrupt, Yao. The Ministry is corrupt. Not ours, State Security. They run every big scam, every racket worth doing. Police just do petty corruption. That's why my team has to tread lightly. I go to Beijing to check with them in person when we have a case. I have to ask my point of contact there whether it's them we're investigating. Usually it is."

Yao looked silently across the table. The singing was getting louder from around the piano, which was fine with Peng since he did not want this conversation overheard. "That's the guy, my guy in the Ministry, who told me to steer a wide berth around Wei. State Security heard he is doing special work for The Highest Level and it has to do with corruption, so naturally, they think it's them you are after."

"Peng, I don't think it is. I don't actually know who it is, but I really do not believe we are going after State Security."

Peng pushed his heavy frame along the bench. "Doesn't matter. They think you are after them. That's what matters."

"You don't just coordinate with them, Peng, you work for them, right? They recruited you. You not only don't investigate financial crimes they commit, you spy on the police for them, right? Brother to brother?"

"You are a smart man, Yao. So let me stop the mating ritual and make you the offer. They want you to work for them too. Spy on Wei, report back to me for now, then you will get your own case officer. They will start you at monthly payments of fifty percent of your police pay. Fifty percent on top of what the police pay you. Stashed in an account in Singapore. Deal?"

"Shit, of course," Yao said, taking Peng's hand. "Deal. And thank you."

Peng stood up. Yao noticed a large yellow blob of the special spicy mustard on the FinCrime chief's crotch. Then Peng stumbled off toward the piano, singing. Yao had a feeling it would be another late Friday night. His wife was going to be mad at him again this month.

Yao Guang drove quickly back to his office in ReGlobal Audit, across the wet streets reflecting the decorative lights, knowing that the speed cameras would catch the BMW exceeding the limit, that the red-light cameras would see him fail to stop, that the Automatic License Reader cameras would feed the whereabouts of his vehicle into the real-time database and correlate it with his cellphone, identifying him as the driver. He knew but didn't care. They had immunity.

Wei Bao had done something to the software, precisely what Yao did not know, but something that failed to put images and information about Yao into data storage files, something that identified him even in real time as a different person. Wei Bao had created his own fake personas to cover his tracks and those of his team. And he used artificial intelligence combined with wiper-ware to hunt and delete files. Reality, he had told Yao once, was what was in databases, not what was on the streets. Yao had disagreed, but he was slowly coming around to Wei's world. The world was better when you could create it, or at least modify parts of it, the way you wanted.

"You could have brought me one of those German beers," Bohai called over his shoulder to Yao as the doors to the old elevator opened onto the loft area, washed by soft, red LED. "Or at least a wurst. They looked good. Bloody, but good."

"Don't you have anything better to do than watch me?" Yao replied. "You stay here on a Friday night to do that?"

Bohai spun around on his stool. "Many better things, but I promised the boss that I would do some more research for him. And I am making progress following the money. I don't sit and watch you. I just sped through your last three hours in three minutes after the AI alert came on that you were parking out front. By the way, that is a no-parking zone."

Yao had watched how Wei Bao had taken the constant teasing and irreverent attitude from Bohai in stride. He told Yao it was a form of affection, that Bohai looked up to him as the older brother he never had. Yao had been trying not to let Bohai get to him, to play along. It seemed to be working. They were growing closer, although the older detective was always suspicious of the twins. He did not generally believe criminals ever really changed their ways, but maybe juvenile hackers could be saved.

The twins had clearly taken to their new life of working for the police, or at least for one unique policeman, one who could also put them back into the system whenever he wanted to.

Wei Bao did not believe that would ever be necessary, he had assured Yao. "They just enjoy challenges. Breaking code is what turns them on, not breaking laws." Perhaps, but working for Wei the twins got to break laws too; it just wasn't a crime to do so if you were the police, especially if you had a special writ from The Highest Level. "And they are happy working for us, Yao, so don't make them unhappy."

Despite Wei's assurances, Yao had done his own background investigation of the twins. To his surprise, he found that neither of them used drugs. They both had occasional sex partners, of both sexes, but the only constant friends either one of them had were each other. When their mother died, they had been raised by an entrepreneurial father who realized early on that his children were prodigies and gave them whatever they needed or wanted to feed their insatiable curiosity.

What he had not given them enough of was his time, which was spent building a software company that failed shortly after he died of a heart attack at forty-four, leaving his teenaged twins to fend for themselves. They had succeeded, by engaging in criminal hacking and evading every investigator, until Wei Bao, who had used his camera system to track them to their home, a boat in a Dalian yacht club. Wei had let them keep the boat and a clean record, as long as they worked for him as "programming assistants."

Yao sat on the stool next to Bohai. "You know the no-parking zone cameras can't see my Beemer. It's invisible to them. I did bring you German pretzels." He saw the continuing party in the beer hall on one of the dozen frames on a monitor to Bohai's right. "I thought they turned the cameras off when the detectives association took over the restaurant."

"They do. The AI turned them back on to follow you. It still looks like it's off to anyone checking on it and it's not recording anywhere but here." Bohai talked while stuffing the large soft pretzel in his mouth. "They didn't have mustard?"

"The programs we have follow me around, automatically search for cameras along my route, and then hack into them?" Yao asked, looking at the streamed video from the beer hall, where one detective was on top of a table singing.

"Yeah, I told you before, the program follows you, me, Chunhua. And now Chunhua has one following Fenfang, the boss's doctor friend. And, of course, we have one following Bao."

"Bohai, what if the No Show people are following us, doing it the same way, hacking cameras. Whoever they are, they are good at AI."

Bohai jumped down off his stool and motioned for Yao to follow him to another monitor. "They are. Well, somebody is. These are feeds that were going into State Security video surveillance servers. They were following Wei Bao since he landed in Canada. Their AI is hacking Canadian cameras, which is really easy by the way. They also have some guys doing gumshoe tailing him. I guess the Beijing big bosses want to keep tabs on their special chief inspector, see how his case is going."

"Maybe that's why. Maybe some other reason. Do we have to let them follow Wei Bao?"

"No, our AI erases real images of Wei on their servers and substitutes deep fake videos of him going into the university computer science department and then back to his hotel. Back and forth. Back and forth."

"So you hacked the State Security's servers?" Yao asked.

"Sure. That's easy. Chunhua and me, we used to do odd jobs for both State Security and for the PLA cyber teams. And we used to help some of them who work at night and weekends using their government tools on their own, stealing money in other countries. We know these State Security guys. Americans call them Stone Panda. We know their systems. They range from okay to good at the offense, not as good as the Army, but good. Neither one of them is any good at defensive cyber."

Yao exhaled deeply, not sure whether to be relieved or agitated that his team was hacking the Ministry of State Security. "So Wei Bao is safe, then?"

"Well, yeah, I guess, kind of, for now. But the Ministry also has people on the streets sometimes following him around Toronto. So do the Canadian police sometimes, with people usually, not often with cameras. And then the Americans started hacking cameras manually to follow him too. Manually, so primitive. But our program senses when camera feeds are going out to a new location, so we caught them. The Americans are hacking into cameras in Canada from someplace called Merry Land, like happy place. Americans are so silly."

Yao was afraid of the answer to the question he had to ask next. "So you let them record video of Wei, or did you hack the Canadians and the Americans?"

"Pffft," Bohai responded. "All real images of Wei in their databases get erased automatically before they are saved by the Canadians and the Americans. The AI we use is built on the Zizhi Hu hacking program. It hacks in, turns off alarms about its presence, erases logs, then erases images of Wei. Those governments are not the problem."

Whenever he talked with Bohai, Yao thought it was like mental sprinting. Things moved very fast and there was always too much to comprehend in too little time before there was something even more head-spinning.

Bohai moved to another display. "There is somebody else. Somebody who is also using AI to hack cameras and follow Wei. Also follow Wei's friends, the Canadian cop and the America secret policewoman. Whoever they are, they are fucking hot."

"Hot?"

"Hot fingers on the keyboards, fast AI. Even Zizhi Hu can't trace them back to their lair, can't identify them. Not yet. Not without letting them know we are on them." Bohai sounded exasperated. "They have feedback loops looking for someone tracing their path through cyberspace. Pretty smart AI."

Yao stood among the monitors in the darkened loft, which was barely lit by LED ceiling lamps emitting a red aura across the space. It was one of those moments of clarity that kept happening to him on the Cyber Crime Squad, a brief mental break in continuity when he wondered how this had ever happened to him, how he had gone from the easy life of busting drug gangs, a job he was good at and came easily to him, to one in which he was forced to play speed chess with someone who looked only a few years older than his teenaged son.

When he was a recruit in the Army before going into the police, Yao had suffered severe frostbite on his hands during a winter training exercise in

Mongolia. Years later, they looked like they belonged to another species, almost twice the size of most men's hands. Yao placed one of his human claws on each of Bohai's thin shoulders and stared at him for a minute as he went over in his head the last few minutes of their conversation.

"What you are saying is that our State Security, the Canadian police, and the Americans are all following our boss around Toronto by hacking into cameras and that you have hacked into all their networks and servers. Yes? And there is another police or secret service that is also following him, but they are so good you failed to figure out who they are and erase their videos of Wei. Maybe the Russians? Yes?"

Bohai wiggled out from the vise grip and sat on the floor looking up at Yao. "No. The Canadians aren't hacking the cameras. And no, the Canadians and our State Security are also sometimes following him on foot and in cars. No, I didn't fail to figure out who the new group is; our AI, Stealth Tiger, has not yet succeeded. It will. Zizhi Hu never fails. And neither do the Guo twins. Never."

"If your tiger never fails, and since you have already hacked State Security, you crazy man, see what else you can find on their servers."

Bohai looked gleeful. "You want the file they have on you?"

"Yes, but I also want evidence that they have corruption schemes going on, like hacking companies outside China and moving the money into secret accounts overseas in the names of the Ministry officials."

"Oh, even you know they do that? Yeah, they do that. Easy to prove."

Yao had been saving the last pretzel for himself, but he pulled the small bag holding it from his inside coat pocket and handed it to Bohai. "There is mustard in the kitchen. When this case is over and if we are all alive and not in prison and have some time, I would like you to meet my son. He's trying to create his own video game. Maybe you could help him, get him interested in doing other things with computers. Other *legal* things."

Bohai stood up to take the pretzel. "Sure. If we alive and not dead or in prison."

24

National Security Division Conference Room
FBI Headquarters
Pennsylvania Avenue
Washington, DC
Friday, November 28
0930 hours

In most of the labyrinthine buildings in the Federal Triangle and along the avenue running from the White House to Capitol Hill, offices were empty. The president had granted federal workers the day after Thanksgiving off, creating a four-day weekend for the civil servants that spun the wheels of her government. The legislators and their staffs at the other end of the avenue had long since gone home and would not return for ten days. Traffic had been light as Sarah Keogh drove up the GW parkway from Old Town Alexandria and over the Memorial Bridge into the Federal District, thinking as she did of how much of her theory she would venture to offer to the assistant director.

"I believe the Botpay case," she began, using the Bureau's codename for the investigation, "is actually more properly thought of as a WMD threat than it is a fraud matter."

Her boss, Assistant Director Dallas Miller, sat at the head of the table in what he routinely described as "my fucking conference room." That was how he referred to the high-tech video conferencing facility that was cleared to discuss matters above Top Secret and could link to the CIA, NSA, the Situation Room, and the fifty-six FBI field offices. The camera that would project Miller's image to any of those locations was turned off.

Sarah Keogh was Miller's deputy and, he hoped, his successor sometime next year when he turned fifty and was eligible for his pension after twenty-five years of service. He was now the highest-ranking Black man in the Bureau, but he didn't think he could move up farther and he could make triple his salary on the outside. Time to hand off his job to the woman he had been mentoring for years. The Botpay case might ensure Sarah's succession, or, he was beginning to fear, prevent it.

On either side of Miller were three others from the National Security Division and the Director's Special Assistant, who had invited himself to hear the status of Botpay. "The words 'WMD' and 'threat' send cold shivers down my spine and cause my sphincter to shut tighter than, well, better not say. You sure this can't be some nice, safe theft on a grand scale by a bunch of Russian computer nerds?"

Keogh sat halfway down the conference table, looking at the group, the usual Bureau BOGSAT, a bunch of guys sitting around a table. "This level of skill with artificial intelligence and machine learning and the computing power it is using every day is not what any criminal cartel can summon up, even ones backed by Russian plutocrats.

"The fundraising they have been doing by employing machine learning and artificial intelligence–driven bots to raid corporate payrolls is huge. There is only one kind of project that requires that kind of money: making weapons of mass destruction, nukes, and missiles to launch them."

The BOGSAT shifted uncomfortably in their seats. "Let's say you're right, which nation state is behind it and why hasn't the CIA detected any massive WMD program?" Jeremy Hunter asked Keogh. Hunter, a young lawyer on detail from the Justice Department, was the director's overt spy in the meeting.

"I can tell you who it is not. Not China. They are getting robbed too, and now they are cooperating with us on the investigation."

"The director hasn't approved any cooperation with the Chinese Ministry of State Security," Hunter interjected.

"Calm down, Mister Hunter," Assistant Director Miller replied. "Their investigation is being run as a special project out of some city police department. And I approved our limited cooperation with their lead, a chief inspector. That's within my authority, by the way, Jeremy. Proceed, Sarah."

Keogh continued. "Could be Russia. The Agency has two sensitive sources. One is actually a British source. Both are highly placed, inside the Tsar's inner circle. They both report that the President for Life is furious that his crazy new weapons systems can't be built or deployed for lack of funds. He demanded that they find ways to get the money needed.

"CIA has been having trouble figuring out how Iran and North Korea can afford their aggressive weapons development. The Koreans have made near-perfect counterfeit US currency, hacked companies to make money. Hell, they even hacked the Central Banks of a couple of countries."

Keogh tapped a keyboard, and a slide appeared on the four large screens in the room. "Here you see the top two dozen machine learning experts we initially examined for links to this operation, since, according to DARPA, the Pentagon's bubbleheads, only people like this could design, code, and run such a complex program. And it would likely need a huge data farm of servers to do it continuously or, get this, one of a new type of stable quantum computer of which there are only a handful of prototypes, all developed by a Canadian professor who they just killed."

Miller put on his glasses so he could see the faces and names on the screen. "Why would they, whoever they are, have killed him?"

"Because he could figure out who was using his machine to do the fraud. And we were asking him to help us, or at least the Mounties were on our behalf. We have been trying to get FISA warrants to monitor the three AIML masters in the US and get into their Q-Compute devices to see if one of them is helping Russia, Iran, or Korea with the AI scheme, but Main Justice hasn't been persuaded we have good reason to bug them. So we are going to do confrontational interviews on the pretext that they might be at risk. We'll see how they react."

Miller put his glasses back in his suit coat's breast pocket and leaned back in his chair. "All good, but you said it was urgent we meet today, when most good public servants are supposed to be working off the mashed potato load they inhaled yesterday. What is so urgent?"

Keogh keyed up another slide onto the screens. It showed the logos of dozens of major US companies, the well-known blue chips of the stock market. Under each logo there was a number: the total fake personas collecting pay.

"Yesterday, while I was trying to create my famous turkey giblet gravy, I got a call from our technical team at Quantico that has been monitoring the activity of the fake employees in these companies, doing so with the permission of the companies I might add, Mister Hunter. When they ran the activity check program, it came up as a null set. Not only no activity. No such employees. In any of the companies. Moreover, there are no records to indicate that they ever were employed there and no records outside of the companies anywhere to indicate that they ever existed. It's over. The payroll fraud is over."

"And your gravy, Sarah?" Miller asked. "Because I make the best gravy in Northern Virginia and I will compete with your Carolina recipes any day."

"Dropped the gravy boat on the floor when I got that news."

"I guess that's kind of like shit hitting the fan," Miller joked. "But what is the significance of it being over? Did they figure out we were on to them? Do we have a leak?"

Sarah Keogh glared at her boss and mentor but knew that he was just trying to make the director's spy uncomfortable. "It may be the color of shit, Dallas, but my gravy is really quite delicious. What does it mean that the fake personas vanished? I should think it's obvious. They got all the money they needed. Their project is nearing completion. They may be about to reveal or use their new WMD."

Hunter stood up and moved quickly to the door. "If you'll excuse me, I need to brief the director."

Assistant Director Dallas Miller addressed the door through which the special assistant to the director had just departed. "Brown-nosed cocksucker." Then Miller turned back to Keogh and smiled. "I'll call the AG right now. Her wienies aren't going to stop you getting in front of the FISA Court, like, today. All I have to say to her are those three magic letters: WMD."

25

Foreign Intelligence Surveillance Court
Prettyman Federal Courthouse
333 Constitution Avenue NW
Washington, DC
Friday, November 28
1530 hours

"You'll have to leave all electronic devices in one of the lockers, not just phones, but also laptops, iPads, anything electronic," the deputy marshal recited in the tone of a flight attendant explaining how to use a seatbelt. "Do you have any idea how long you will be with the judge? We usually lock up the SCIF around now. And today was supposed to be a day off anyway."

The Foreign Intelligence Surveillance Court met in a Sensitive Compartmented Information Facility within the courthouse, a copper-lined cluster of rooms with filters on the electric lines and HVAC to prevent any noise or electronic emissions from escaping. Created by Congress in the Foreign Intelligence Surveillance Act, part of the judiciary, FISC was the way the executive branch could legally investigate foreign agents without asking publicly for a search warrant. Critics on the left and right thought it a Star Chamber or the telltale heart of the Deep State. National security professionals thought of it as a necessary pain in the ass, where they were grilled by uninformed federal judges from the hinterlands who would drop into Washington for one week every three months.

"Remember, this is not actually a formal hearing of the sort that you are used to for getting a search warrant in a criminal or civil court," Maira Khan cautioned Sarah Keogh. "Judge Jordan is just going to ask questions. Because we asked for an emergency warrant, he may not have had the time to study our paperwork. We are supposed to give them seven days to go over it, not three hours."

Khan was a regular in the FISC, representing the Justice Department on most of its applications for secret warrants and the more troublesome requests for extensions on those warrants already granted that had not yet discovered anything.

Harlan Jordan was appointed to the Federal District Court bench by a Democratic president. Most FISC judges, selected by the Chief Justice of the US Supreme Court from among sitting federal judges, were Republicans. Jordan had a background in civil rights and civil liberties cases before being appointed to the federal bench in Atlanta. He looked like he had stepped out of a Southern country club, complete with blue blazer and green pants. Limousine Liberal, Keogh thought. She had a feeling they were keeping him from cocktails at Congressional. He did not have to say that he was upset with being called in during a Thanksgiving weekend. It was obvious.

"I just skimmed this petition, Ms. Khan and, maybe it's late in the day and the caffeine is wearing off, but it was not the best example of clear expository prose, I must tell you," Judge Jordan began. "There is some international conspiracy to steal billions of dollars through some new type of cybercrime? You don't know who is doing it, but you surmise it might be Iran or North Korea to get money to fund their WMD programs? And so you want to get access to emails and phone calls from American scientists and their tech companies who you think might be helping the Iranians or whomever? You want to seize and search some new type of computers they have running their businesses? Have I got it right in, ah, broad strokes?"

Maira Kahn audibly inhaled before answering. She knew going into the meeting that it was not going to be easy. Jordan was anything but a rubber stamp, and the FBI had not given her either the time or the paperwork to make the application a clear-cut winner. She had gotten the emergency hearing docketed, now Sarah Keogh was going to have to be persuasive, one Southerner to another. Khan nodded to Keogh to answer.

"Thank you, Your Honor, and thank you for meeting with us on an emergency basis. What we and our Canadian colleagues in the RCMP have been investigating is the biggest heist in history." Keogh was deferential to the edge of obsequiousness, even for a Southern woman of the old school. She slowly and politely summarized point by point all that the FBI knew, what it surmised, and what it still did not know.

Harlan Jordan placed his chin in the cup of his right hand and looked bemused. "And how have you been tracing these fund transfers? I hope somebody gave you a warrant for that."

Maira Khan saw that one coming. "Yes, Your Honor. At tab D in the application is a copy of a hot pursuit warrant under criminal investigation authority from the Federal District Court in Manhattan, upon a filing originating with Treasury's FinCEN. It allows us to pursue the trail of the stolen funds."

"Well, that is creative, but also not my problem." Jordan sat back. "My problem is that you have no real evidence that it is Iran or Russia or North Korea doing this. Nothing showing a relationship to WMDs. Not that I could see."

This was the question that the woman from Justice knew they could not answer satisfactorily. Khan turned to Keogh with a look that managed to simultaneously say both *it's all yours* and *I told you so*.

"Your Honor, the experts at Treasury's Financial Crimes Center have artificial intelligence programs too, and they have been searching for anomalous cash flows using their statutory and regulatory authorities. Their belief is that the only place this amount of money could be going and disappearing into is government accounts somewhere, and the only thing that would require this much money would be weapons of mass destruction development and production programs. CIA concurs in that judgement. The FinCEN and CIA analyses are in tabs in the papers we sent over, sir."

The judge thumbed the paperwork for the analyses hidden in the tabs. "Well, Special Agent Keogh, I am no expert on financial flows, but I did go to Wharton undergrad. Seems to me with trillions of dollars sloshing around between banks, behemoth corporations, and the markets every day, it would be damn hard to spot a few billion extra here and there. But be that as it may, I can only give you authority if you can prove a foreign connection. A foreign government or a foreign terrorist organization. Maybe a foreign company going rogue." Then he looked at his watch.

In the silence, Sarah Keogh was aware of the fans blowing in the subceiling, part of the SCIF's special ventilation system. Despite the airflow, the conference room seemed too warm. "Your Honor, there was a murder in Canada which we believe may be part of this conspiracy," Keogh tried.

"Nice try, but Canada has a system of laws and cooperates with us. We don't need to help them investigate a homicide in Canada by using intelligence authorities." The judge was getting more than impatient. He was getting testy. "There is no request for assistance from Canada in these papers, nothing asking us to break into US companies."

Khan thought they were seconds away from the judge walking out. She had one more idea, but it was a stretch. "Your Honor, there is a leading Chinese national, a scientist who has helped their government. NSA just two hours ago reported that this Professor Zhu is planning to attend a meeting in a California redwood grove, and that meeting may be attended by one or more persons who are part of this conspiracy."

Jordan's mood seemed to change. "Fine, why didn't you highlight that? You can monitor the Chinese national, but just him. You have to minimize any information you obtain about any Americans incidental to the collection against the Chinese. Resubmit your paperwork in the morning and I will sign it. Make it narrow." Without handshakes or pleasantries, the judge was up and out of the SCIF, leaving Justice's Khan and FBI's Keogh still seated at the table.

"Sorry to surprise you with that, but we were going to get nothing," Khan admitted. "Can you do something that just goes after the Chinese computer science professor coming to that redwoods meeting?"

"Sure, we can turn on the mic and camera on his mobile and remotely hack his laptop, but he'll probably keep them away from him while he is saying anything interesting, anything useful," Keogh thought out loud. "What if we put a parabolic mic on a mini drone and recorded his conversations from a distance?"

The deputy marshal stood in the conference room doorway. "Unless you two ladies want to spend the night in here," he boomed out, "the SCIF is closing in two minutes."

Khan looked doubtful. "Really, we can do that? Well, okay, but you would have to obey minimization rules about Americans. You can't act on the basis of whatever you incidentally hear any Americans saying, can't write it down or store what they say."

"Why, I would never do that," Keogh replied. "On my children's lives. Never."

26

Cloak and Dagger
394 College St, Toronto
Saturday, November 29
2210 hours

DIANA HAD TEXTED HIM to meet her at the Lab but given the address as 298 Brunswick, not Professor Pandry's computer lab on St. George. He arrived there in his favorite tight black jeans, a black T-shirt, his Blue Jays hat, and a pea coat he had picked up that afternoon at a used clothing shop near campus. He wasn't sure it made him look like a student, but he felt like one again. The Lab turned out be the Labyrinth Lounge, where their tour of student drinking establishments began.

After two Flying Monkeys beer openers at the Lab, they had moved to Sneaky Dee's on Bathurst for margaritas and, importantly in Wei's mind, some Tex-Mex to fill and coat his stomach for what lay ahead. Next it was Bar + Kereokee on Yonge, where Diana dragged him up on stage for a duo of "I've Got You Babe," which made Wei want to flee the place as soon as the song ended. He suggested the next stop be a little quieter, but they ended up in the Irish pub Cloak and Dagger. Diana seemed to think it was appropriate for Wei. They ordered Dark and Stormies and lucked into a small booth in the back, which a couple was leaving as Wei Bao and Diana McPherson were looking for someplace to land. Wei definitely felt the need to sit down.

"They're holding a memorial for Ramesh out in the redwoods," she began. "They asked me to speak at it, and I think I should go. It would be a chance to meet these guys, the AIML Masters, some of whom I may end up being on the startup boards with. Maybe I can find out what you are looking for."

Wei replied, "I thought we weren't going to talk about all that stuff tonight," but he was thinking that he had already learned something new about the case tonight. And the night was still young. "Let's get all of that out of the way. Anything else?"

"I know. And I won't keep it up, but, yeah, I do have one more thing that I found in his files this afternoon. There are more of them."

"More AI Masters?"

"No, more Q-Compute machines, in addition to the three at the Qmpanies and the one that melted in Ramesh's basement in the fire," she said, her voice trailing off as she remembered the horror of the fire that night, the sirens, the water, and the smoke.

"Any on campus?" Wei asked.

"No. There are the three we know about at MIT, Berkeley, and Caltech, or actually at companies Ramesh started with professors at these schools. The companies are off campus. But I found serial numbers for two more somewhere. Wei, these things are incredibly powerful. Each one of them could do in a few seconds all of the calculations that would take a supercomputer like Fugaku hundreds of years of crunching."

"Diana, when I was here as a grad student, and that was only a few years ago, Ramesh taught us that quantum computers were big, clunky things that had to be supercooled and could only hold a qubit stable for a few seconds, like the one in the computer science department here. How did it go from that to five compact devices constantly operating at room temperature?"

One of the bartenders had turned up the music so it could be heard over the increasing din in the Cloak, so much so that Wei had to lean across the small wooden table in the booth to hear Diana's answer. "He had a secret research project called Prithvi. That's all I knew, that it existed and that it had been going on for six years at least, since around 2017, including when we were both his students here. Then, around two years ago, he said he wasn't working on it anymore. He wouldn't say anything else. I think project Prithvi was designing, building, and testing the Q-Compute with some of the other AI Masters. It's designed especially for continuous machine learning operations using huge databases."

It was all beginning make sense now to Wei. "Diana, I will bet you that one of those other machines is being misused, was running the payroll fraud, the No Shows. We know it would take that kind of thing to create and maintain all of those fake personas, move the money around, run a self-defense intelligence operation. One of the other masters must be working for Russia or Iran."

Diana laughed. "Highly unlikely, but could be. I suppose. Or North Korea. Isn't that on your list of suspects too?"

"Not mine, the Americans." Wei finished his glassful. "I know the North Koreans. There are a bunch of them around Dalian, illegal refugees, smugglers, even a government hacking team that does its dirty work from an old hotel near the docks. We are supposed to look the other way, but the PLA monitors what they do. Mainly they steal money to keep their government afloat. They are nowhere near good enough to do this kind of an operation."

"Whatever. I just know none of our professor's partners would be crooks or misuse experimental new devices as powerful as Q-Compute. But for what it's worth—" She slipped Wei a flash drive with what she had found out about the Q-Compute devices. And then they were off to Tilt Arcade on Dundas for a round of pinball and more beer.

After pinball wizardry, they hit the Red Room and then were at the re-opened Einstein's when it shut for the night. Wei thought that was it, but Diana insisted on an after-hours speakeasy a girlfriend had recommended to her, a place that was actually called Cold Tea, down an alley near Kensington Market. It also served decent din sum, to Wei's surprise. Diana had had enough to drink that she talked about her desire to be a mother and her fear of bringing any child into a world that was going to be a living hell as climate change accelerated. There was a boy, a hot graduate student from Winnipeg, who she had been seeing secretly. She thought he would make a good father, but it would be so wrong to do that to a child, to sentence them to live in a dystopia. They left shortly after three, and Wei put Diana into an Uber at the corner of Kensington and St. Andrews.

Wei decided to walk it off, to make it back to the hotel by foot. Wei wanted to process all that Diana had said, and hadn't. She'd gone from doubting the death of the man she called by his first name, Ramesh, to wanting to help uncover his killer. She claimed not to know the other AIML Masters, but was sure none of them could be involved in anything amiss. She desperately wanted a baby, but seemed totally consumed by dread over climate change. What was her phrase, "the death of the planet that is rushing toward us"?

He was halfway down the narrow St. Andrews street when he heard a car's tires screeching as it accelerated. As he turned to look at the oncoming headlights, he felt hands around his waist, pulling him back into a storefront. He was too drunk for his unarmed self-defense training to kick in automatically, but as he tried to do a slip, twist, and kick maneuver, his world filled with a clash of metal on metal, then a piercing horn and tinkling glass. His assailant released his grip and stepped past Wei to examine the Jeep that had just crashed into a parked car. It was ten feet away from them and it had jumped up onto the empty car and crushed it. The Jeep Gladiator pickup truck atop the car was smoking and leaking onto the pavement. A second man appeared and spoke to the guy Wei now realized had saved him by pulling him out of the Jeep's path.

"I'll get him out of the vehicle. You call it in to the police." The two men, both in black parkas, looked alike to Wei, even their faces.

"Will do," Wei's large savior responded and, as he pulled out his cell phone, turned his attention back to Wei. "It's your lucky day, buddy. Best get on your way before you end up having to fill out a witness form for the constables." That seemed like good advice to Wei, and without speaking to his savior, he moved quickly away from the accident scene, stumbling slowly toward Spadina, where he found a taxi driver emerging from a pho shop and convinced him to do one last run, taking Wei back to the Four Seasons.

A hidden, private security camera opposite the Kensington Fruit Market recorded the two men at the accident scene. One pulled the body of the driver from the Gladiator, laid him out on the street, and, with a quick motion, snapped his neck, sending him from unconsciousness to death. Wei's savior produced a gun from a shoulder holster and used its butt to further smash the windshield of the Jeep, eliminating what the camera had just recorded, a bullet hole in the window and spider webs emanating from it, directly in front of the driver. The first man checked inside to see where the bullet had landed and pried the spent round from the cabin wall with a knife. He called to his partner, "Did you just fire once?"

The other man nodded and waved his gun, showing its silencer attached to the muzzle. "These Chinese just can't hold their liquor or drive."

The two then moved down to the corner of Spadina, where they had left a car. They did the block in half the time it had taken Wei. As they drove away down Spadina, a Toronto Police car in front of them pulled a U-turn and threw on its blue lights, heading back toward St. Andrews street and the dead body of a Chinese consular officer who would seem to have died of a broken neck when his vehicle went out of control, hit a parked car, and ejected the diplomat onto the narrow street. In their car moving away from the scene of the crash, the two men in black parkas peeled off their face masks. They no longer appeared to be identical twins.

27

Computer Science and Artificial Intelligence Laboratory
Massachusetts Institute of Technology
Mass. Ave and Vassar St
Cambridge, Massachusetts
Monday, December 1
1330 hours

As an MIT Police camera stared down at him on the Riverwalk pathway, the Canadian looked across the bridge into Boston, to the high-rises reflecting the sun, the golden dome of the statehouse glimmering on a warm, sunny winter's day. The RCMP officer walked along the Charles, smelling its pleasant heavy dankness, marveling at the students rowing and sailing in what had become December.

Rob Porter had intentionally arrived on campus early for the interview. He had been met at Logan Airport by the local FBI office, specifically by his "buddy for the day," a special agent who would be with him at all times. The local officer fulfilled the requirement that Sarah Keogh and her boss had: interviews on US soil would be done by the FBI. A Canadian cop or a Chinese officer might be along as advisors. At least that is what the paperwork said. The verbal instruction from Washington to Boston had been a little different: Special Agent Joe McDunogh was to take notes and avoid incidents. Porter would ask the questions. It would be a confrontational interview not the way the Bureau normally did it, more Canadian in style.

At one thirty exactly, the two men walked into the Quantum Computing Lab and were escorted to its director, Professor Donald Byrd. They sat in Byrd's glass-enclosed office, which looked down on a warehouse-like space below where white lab-coated staff, students, and faculty worked on three slightly different arrays of wires and pipes. As he sat down to talk, Byrd hit a handheld device that caused the windows to the floor to frost up.

"They would just be a distraction," Byrd explained. "And I still get a kick out of showing off the electrostatic glass. It was a project of a freshman seminar I volunteered to lead several years ago." The graying sandy hair, blue Oxford shirt, khaki pants, and especially the unstylish, plain black glasses almost screamed MIT faculty.

"So you still teach, Doctor Byrd?" Porter began jovially.

"Not in about three or four years. All research now. Do you know anything about quantum computing?"

"Only what my wife teaches me," Rob replied for himself and his mute minder, "but she's into quantum gravity, not computing."

"Really?" Byrd said with a surprised look. "Who is she?"

"Professionally, she uses her family's name, Rubinstein, Danielle Rubinstein. She studied at the other Cambridge."

"Of course, of course. Woo and Rubinstein, they did that piece disproving the arrow of time theory. Well, if you are married to one of them, you must know something about quantum theory just by osmosis."

"I'm married to Danielle Rubenstein, not to Henry Woo," Porter clarified.

Byrd looked at him blankly and continued, "So, we have three different approaches to quantum computing running in our lab. That's what you saw through the window."

"But you also have a Pandry Q-Compute down the street in a company called QModel, which you own along with the late Professor Pandry and a few others?" Porter asked. "Can you tell us about that? About QModel?"

"Yes, the institute encourages us to spin off startups because the school gets a cut of the ownership in the firms, for the endowment," Byrd replied. "And we have a long way to go before our endowment is as big as the next school up the river. But you asked me about QModel. It takes complex, multifactor scenarios for big corporations, government agencies like the National Institutes for Health, the EPA. Using our quantum algos, we then model the scenarios, showing the most likely outcomes and the pressure points where small changes in input can massively change the output.

The Pandry Q-Compute allows us to do a live, continuous model with real-time inputs that result in changes in the predictions."

"Fascinating," Porter replied. "Give me an example."

"We did a model of sea rise and how it is affecting Boston Harbor and the rivers leading into it. The most important thing that we can do to deal with it, in addition to the obvious giant sea locks, of course? Turns out it's landfilling Hingham Bay, which struck me as counterintuitive."

"My cousin Tommy has a place down Nantasket Beach," the special agent noted. "He ain't gonna be too happy about you filling in the bay."

Byrd stared at the FBI officer and then continued talking with Porter. "I'll give you another, then. We are part of the Coupled Model Intercomparison Project that has been going on for thirty years now. It considers all the variables that affect global climate. Takes into account sea temperatures, algae blooms, ice flows, cloud patterns, tundra melt. We just finished CMIP6, the first one using a quantum computer. We ran an integrated assessment model taking into account economic activity such as aircraft travel, fossil fuel usage, rain forest cut. We produced the most accurate model ever of global climate and how things affect it, what would be the best things we could do to slow and then reverse global heating."

"So what can we do, Professor?" Rob asked.

"Well, the best scenario the model produced was one in which we had a billion fewer people, half the fossil fuel use, and much less travel. Interestingly, the models all agreed that if we do nothing the planet will become uninhabitable in many areas, incapable of producing fish or crops at anything like current levels, and thus population will eventually drop significantly, by more than a billion anyway. It will just be too late by then to reverse the runaway effect of the change. If we lost a billion people now, we might still be able to stop the runaway climate."

"I see, so a war that killed off a billion people now is the answer?" the Canadian asked.

"Oh yes, especially if it were a nuclear war that would kick up enough debris into the atmosphere to produce a nuclear winter for a few years. Alan Roebuck's work at Rutgers suggests that would lower the temperature by three degrees centigrade for two years or more, depending upon the size of the nuclear exchange and the combustibility of the target set. Of course, there would be new problems introduced by such a large-scale conflict."

Porter looked up from his notetaking. "So it sounds like your quantum computer with machine learning would be very useful to the military, planning wars, maybe developing weapons. Could foreign powers gain access to it without your knowing?"

"I think it would be quite good at that, yes, but the staff kind of revolted and so we said no to a request from the Air Force or someone. No Pentagon contracts at all now. But could bad guys gain access to it, no. We monitor its activities 24/7. And no one would know how to run it anyway."

Porter and the FBI agent did not reply. They were employing the old technique of creating an awkward silence that the interviewee would nervously fill. What the subjects said then to fill the vacuum was often surprising and valuable.

"I disagreed, of course, with saying no to the Pentagon," the professor volunteered. "I said, if you choose to live in *this country* and enjoy all of what *this country* has to offer, then you should help defend *this country*. A colleague later told me I sounded like Jack Nicholson in some movie they made here locally. Anyway, I lost in the vote, and now no Pentagon quantum contracts for us. Stupid, really. It's good money."

"But you and Pandry own QModel?" Porter asked.

"No, it's owned by some vulture capital firms. We have stock in the company, RSUs, and also options. I don't understand it all. What they call the cap table is very confusing to me. I just assume that IBM will buy it for a gazillion dollars one day and then I can build my own lab somewhere warm, like down the Cape." Byrd laughed. "That was a joke. See, people used to say 'someplace warm like Florida.' Now it's warm here, like Cape Cod is the new Key West," he explained.

It was now Porter's turn to look blank. "And you and Professor Pandry were both part of the AIML group, the self-anointed top two dozen of the world's best in artificial intelligence?"

"Yes, my husband calls us the Artificial Intelligencia, and that has kind of caught on," Byrd laughed. "It's very informal really. We just meet a couple times a year out at a camp near Stanford. Like Boy Scout camp or something. We exchange notes and socialize. We present what's puzzling us, roadblocks, and give each other advice about solving things, getting over hurdles. Then we play bocce. Ramesh was one of the stars at bocce. We are really going to miss him," Byrd said, closing his eyes for a moment, then seemed to snap awake. "In fact, we are honoring him tomorrow at the camp. I am on a flight to San Francisco in three hours."

The FBI had told Porter about the memorial service. Sarah Keogh said she had learned about it from NSA, who were now monitoring Professor Zhu in China. Zhu was flying in for the service. Keogh, Porter, and Wei were keeping each other up to date using Signal.

"There seems to be a subgroup within the AIML club. Five of you who served on a lot of startup advisory boards or corporate boards together. Is that right?"

"Yes, that was Ramesh's idea too. He thought that our interactions as a team would help the companies. I think he just picked from the AIML group the ones that talked the most." He paused for a laugh. "Joke. See, most people in AI and machine learning don't talk a lot. At least to other humans." Byrd consulted his mobile for the time. "I really do need to get ready for the flight."

"Well, we won't hold you up for much longer," Porter said. "Just three quick final questions. Did Pandry or anyone else discuss with you, or others that you know of, anything about creating fake personas, or anything about payroll fraud?"

Byrd pushed back from his desk and scowled. "No. We don't do payrolls. We leave administrivia like that to ADP."

"Do you know of anyone who might have benefited from the professor's death or might have wanted him dead?"

"Wanted him dead? Absolutely not. You're telling me he was murdered? I thought it was a fire."

Porter looked Byrd in the eye. "Do you have any reason to think that you are in danger or have you noticed anyone or anything unusual in the last few days?"

"The Bruins. I saw them beat the Kings over at the Garden last night. Highly unusual," Byrd tried. "You know, we suck this season, so far."

Porter's look provoked a more frank reply from Byrd. "No. Seriously, officer, no. Am I in danger?"

Porter stood and the FBI agent mimicked his action. "Possibly. We don't know yet who killed Professor Pandry or exactly why. Until we do, we cannot rule out that the motivation could also lead them to his professional associates, like you and the others. So, if you do think of anything or see anything at all, call Special Agent McDunough at any time. You have his card there."

When they got back into the FBI car to Logan, Special Agent McDunough broke their silence. "I got a problem with all that."

"Yeah, I had a few too, but what's yours?" Porter asked as they drove over the Longfellow Bridge with its giant salt-and-pepper-shaker towers and slow-moving red line trains. Porter planned to take a different flight to San Francisco, leaving an hour earlier than Professor Byrd.

"My problem? The 302 report I have to write up on the interview," the special agent replied. "I don't know what that shit is. Quantum. Wasn't there a James Bond movie 'bout it?"

28

QSpace Corporate Office
106 Berkshire Place
La Cañada Flintridge, California
Monday, December 1
1030 hours

"You're not in Pasadena anymore," Professor Daniel Kim explained. "It ends about two hundred meters down Oak Grove. We're technically, well, I guess actually, legally, in La Cañada Flintridge. And so is JPL, up Oak Grove past the high school."

Sarah Keogh had assumed that NASA's Jet Propulsion Laboratory would be near Caltech in downtown, old Pasadena. Actually, the only time she had ever been in Pasadena before was in college when a boyfriend had taken her to the Rose Bowl. That trip had ended badly and she had blotted it, blotted him, out of her memory. This time she had flown into Burbank on the director's Gulfstream, stayed in a suite at the Pasadena Westin, and been driven to the offices of QSpace by an eager young woman from one of the Bureau's counterintelligence squads in the LA field office.

The two FBI women now sat opposite Kim in a sleek modern office swept by the morning sun. It was dry and warm outside, even in the midmorning, but inside the newish-looking building, the air being gently pushed from the vents in the CEO's office was cool and, Sarah thought, lightly scented. To Keogh, Daniel Kim, the CEO of QSpace, seemed nervous, or maybe he was just naturally talkative.

"We wanted to be near JPL when we started the company, and we were lucky enough to persuade the Methodist church to let us put up this building on empty land they had here at the corner. The church owns the building. Although we built it, we lease it back from them."

"So, are you a Methodist then, Professor Kim?" Keogh asked. "I'm Southern Baptist myself, not that it matters, and we really aren't supposed to ask about religion, so maybe I should withdraw the question. Just being social, you know."

"No, no problem asking, but no," Kim replied. "It's my wife. She was very active in the Koreatown Methodist church, the one on Wilshire, before we moved out here. Now she's busy all the time with this church. She helped persuade them to let us build. It's so much money for the church, it lets them run so many good programs. Me, she calls me a pagan. The truth is I am an atheist. Most scientists don't belong to organized churches. Too many myths. I spend all my time thinking about space. There are no Sky Gods out there."

Sarah Keogh's smile said what she was thinking: *You pagan, you poor dear*. Instead of saying it out loud, she began the interview, at almost the same time as Porter and Wei were starting theirs. "Well, it's space we wanted to talk with you about QSpace, your company. Can you tell me about it and what role the late Professor Pandry played in it?'

"The late..." Kim said, lowering his head. "It's hard to think of Ramesh as dead. He was always so lively, the leader of our group really. He called us the AIML Masters, a couple dozen experts in artificial intelligence and machine learning. He thought we should get together a couple of times a year to compare notes. Ramesh handpicked most of us and organized the initial meetings."

Much of the time in interviews, FBI agents were simply confirming what they already knew, looking for little bits of additional information or color or inconsistencies. "Can you tell me about QSpace and what role the late Professor Pandry played in it?" she repeated.

"Yes, of course. Ramesh created something like a group within a group, a subset of the AIML Masters. Just five of us, including him, of course. We set up companies to explore the application of his quantum computer design and machine learning to specific problems. Because my career at JPL and Caltech involved space exploration, space operations, I got to be the CEO here at QSpace."

Sarah Keogh paused, pretending to examine her notes. "So, you have one of the Q-Compute devices here then?'

"Oh, yes. We are very fortunate. There are only a handful in the world. All handmade by Ramesh and his team."

"They must be so powerful. What if somebody on your staff were using the device without your knowing it, or somebody outside were hacking in and accessing it when you aren't using it?" Keogh asked as casually as she could.

"No, no, no. It's not like a regular computer that you can share tasks on. It is very fragile, and it can only run one program at a time. The wonder is that it runs continuously. Previous quantum machines ran for a few seconds before they collapsed."

"That must have been a problem. So, what does QSpace do with its device? And Professor, in language a Duke alumna with an undergrad degree in European History could understand, please."

"Sure. Easy. We model designs for lift vehicles and for payloads, finding the optimum configurations to solve customer problem sets," Kim explained. "Without a quantum computer like Ramesh's, without the right ML algorithm, it would be kind of hit or miss designing things. Frankly, that's kind of what it was at JPL when I was there: hit or miss in the designs, months of simulations before you learned your design was wrong and you had to start over."

Kim stood and moved to a door that Keogh had not noticed before because it had no frame and was flush with the white tile material covering the wall. "Let me show you. Can you follow me?"

In the adjoining room was a glass enclosure, and in that what looked like a large, scaled-up microwave oven sat on a blue velvet cloth covering a pedestal. In this smaller, square room, the walls were covered with the same kind of tile but in black. It was meant to look like outer space. Pin lights shone on the oven-like thing from every direction. Small cameras were mounted under a few of the lights, she noticed. Keogh could not suppress the thought that this might be an altar for an object that the atheists at QSpace secretly venerated.

"For a CubeSat, this one is quite large," Kim began. "But it is the optimal design for a multi-mission platform. The alloy is strong, but very lightweight. All four sides of it are covered in solar power cells. It generates its own steam propellant to station keep, squirting out of these little scuppers. It has redundant comm links, of course, and a large volume area for whatever mission payload the customer would want. And it is easily assembled by a few industrial robots who could produce them in high volume." He sounded like he might be on the floor of the Auto Show talking about a new self-driving, electric car.

Keogh couldn't help herself. "But does it have cup holders?"

Kim tipped his head sideways and looked puzzled.

"Who are the customers, then?" Keogh pressed on. "You know, of course, you can't sell to Russia, Iran, or North Korea, even through intermediaries."

"Oh, of course not. Customers? None yet. We haven't unveiled it yet. You are actually among the first to see this prototype. We are largely indifferent to what a customer wants to put in the payload bay."

"So, how have you paid to design it and build it?" Keogh asked.

"Venture capital and private equity partners fund us, like any startup really. We are well funded. The assembly plant outside Scottsdale is immaculate, all bots and 3D printers, really state of the art. It will produce them at a high rate. It requires very few people because we used quantum machine learning to design it, to optimize things. The fewer people the better, of course."

"Of course," Sarah repeated. "People can be such problems. But usually VC and PE types are on the board of directors. Your incorporation papers list only you, Pandry, and the other three AIML members as directors. How did you persuade them to stay off the board?"

"Oh, I didn't. Ramesh did. He can be so very persuasive. Could be, I guess is correct now. Was so very persuasive." Kim stared off beyond the CubeSat. Then he snapped out of his momentary reverie. "My incorporation papers, you said. You looked at incorporation papers? Is there something out of order? Exactly why are you here, Agent Keogh?"

"As I said on the phone, Professor Kim, we think your friend Dr. Pandry may have been murdered, and we are trying to find out who might have done that and why. Who, for example, takes his seat on the board now that he has passed?"

Areas on the satellite began to light up, glowing yellow, blue, and green. "Oh, don't be startled. It just takes a while to warm up, to initiate."

Kim calmed the two special agents. "Who takes his place? Well, Diana, of course. She was his right hand, his alter ego. But she would never harm him, certainly not just to get on our board. No, no. Actually, no one would have wanted to harm him."

"Would anyone want to harm you, Professor, or the company? Could you also be in danger from Pandry's murderers?" Sarah asked quietly. "Think, think like the computer. Run scenarios. Who might benefit?"

Kim placed both hands on the railing around the CubeSat, looked in at his satellite, and lowered his head, as if in fact he was venerating the CubeSat. "I will think about it. It's so much to take in. Can I get back to you?"

"Of course, Professor, you have our cards. Call either of us if you think of something. And, Professor?"

"Yes?" he said, raising his head.

"In the meantime, you could be at risk. We do not know that, but since we have no suspects yet and no motivation, that is a possibility. So, if you see anything suspicious, call. We can have people get to you fast, to protect you. We will also be watching for any possible threat to you."

Kim's eyes widened. "To me?" he asked. "To me? Oh, my dear God."

"And, Professor, this is a National Security Letter," Keogh said, taking an envelope from her inside her suit jacket. "It commands you not to alter or destroy records of your Q-Compute's operations. We may be back with a court order so we can see those records."

Kim's mood visibly changed as he took the letter. "Well, I see. Of course we maintain the records of its operations. And if you try to read them and want to understand what you are seeing, you will need people who have degrees other than one from Duke in European history. You will need an AIML Master."

As they drove back to the Gulfstream, waiting at Burbank's Bob Hope Airport, Deputy Assistant Director Sarah Keogh reviewed the interview out loud using the young woman driving her as a sounding board. "Well, if I do say so myself, I believe that telling him he might be in danger actually shook him. We'll see if any one of these guys get spooked enough to do something."

"Something like what?" Terri Blake asked innocently, thinking that Sarah Keogh was actually having a discussion with her. From the silence that followed, the young agent realized that her role was simply as a driver for the important woman from headquarters.

Then Keogh broke the awkward silence with a rapid-fire delivery. "I want to know what all the companies Pandry was involved in are doing and for whom. I want to know who funded them. What if the Iranians or whomever were getting a US company to build some parts of their WMD here, maybe without the builders even knowing it, like that mini spaceship back there?"

"Won't we need court orders?" the young agent driving asked.

Again, Keogh didn't answer. She was biting hard on her lip.

29

QEnergy Labs
7th and Potter Streets
Berkeley, California
Monday, December 1
1030 hours

"I THOUGHT BERKELEY WOULD be nicer," Wei Bao commented as FBI Special Agent Terri Blake drove the Bureau car. "This neighborhood reminds me of the old part of Dalian, all warehouses and dingy buildings, but with more cameras."

The former warehouse they entered had lots of vents coming out of the roof. "That's because the company here before us, another startup, was in biotech. They spent a lot adding those special protective systems, but then they hit it big with an antiviral using RNA, made billions on COVID, and moved to La Jolla," the front desk guard explained as he walked them up from the lobby to a second-floor visitors' conference room to meet CEO Jennifer Schneider.

Special Agent Blake introduced Wei as a Chinese police consultant to the FBI. After the introductions and pleasantries, Wei, not the FBI agent, began. "And you are not in biotech, so the vent piping on the roof is wasted on you, I guess. From the name, I get that you are in energy, but exactly what kind?"

"All kinds. That's the thing. We model lots of ideas about how to generate clean energy at various scales for a variety of uses, from jet engines for passenger planes, to propulsion for giant cargo ships, satellites, autonomous eighteen-wheeler trucks, data centers, domed communities a la Buckminster Fuller. We have such a long list of projects we are modeling, looking for the best way to generate sufficient clean power, not just as the primary source, but as the surge capacity too. We do not want to have to rely upon fossil fuels even for our rainy-day backup source."

"Can we see some of it?" Wei asked.

"No, 'fraid not. Not unless you brought a search warrant," Professor Schneider replied. "Just kidding, not kidding. We have all sorts of security to prevent spying. No offense. It's not because you are Chinese, we don't even let Americans inside. The research is all proprietary, some of it not even under patent yet. Some of it is ready to go, but we have promised our owners to keep it all under wraps. But why do you need to see it?"

"We don't, just curious." Wei admitted. "And no offense taken. Chinese people are used to the prejudice that we steal technology, and maybe we once did. The truth is now our scientists and engineers patent more new technology every year than any other country, including America. But we have no need to see it. As I explained on the phone, we are here about the murder of my old professor, Dr. Pandry, whom I believe you knew and worked with. We want to learn what you did together, if you have any ideas about who would want him dead, and why."

"Short answer: no, I don't." Dr. Jennifer Schneider was petite, but her resume was not. She taught physics at the University of California a mile from QEnergy, had been on the staff at the Lawrence Livermore National Laboratory, a forty-minute drive to the higher, hotter, drier hills in the east. Livermore, Wei knew, was owned by that part of the Department of Energy that also designed America's nuclear weapons.

"So from the name, QEnergy, I assume you are using quantum computing and from your background at LLNL," he said, pronouncing the acronym as *lanil*. "I would guess you are doing nuclear energy?"

Schneider shifted in her chair. "Yes and no, and no," she began. "Yes, the Q is for quantum, at least in Ramesh's vision. But also no, because I joke that it is for Q clearance, the level of top-secret security classification you need to work on nuclear weapons at LLNL. But I assume you know that." Schneider smiled at Wei. "Finally, no, we are not looking at dirty energy like nuclear power plants. They generate so much radioactive waste. Only clean energy that does not further pollute the planet. That's what we do."

"And Dr. Pandry helped you how?" Wei asked.

"Oh, in so many ways. He helped me write the algorithms we used to model various approaches. He loaned us one of his Q-Computes we needed.

There are so few Q-computers that you have to wait in line normally to use them, sometimes over a year. So, he gave us our own. "

"Yes, I understand you have one on site here. Is it always working on your energy problems? Is it possible that someone could access it to do something else?" Wei asked.

"No, it's always running on our problems, or it's down for maintenance. Nothing else. Always utilized, but even if it did have some excess capacity, no one would know how to run it but me and my team. It's unique. And complex."

"Well, it sounds like you have a lot to thank Professor Pandry for, then. I am sorry for your loss," Wei offered.

"Thank you. You as well. I understand you were one of his favorite students. You know, without Ramesh, QEnergy would not exist. He introduced me to the private equity people who own us, who fund our research and experiments. Without Ramesh, QEnergy would be nothing."

Wei nodded. "But now will it still become something extraordinary? He is gone and QEnergy is still here. What happens to it without him?"

"I asked Diana that yesterday on the phone. She said you and she were old friends. She's the reason I agreed to talk with you at all. She said I could trust you, that you would find out who killed Ramesh."

"I am trying to," Wei replied. "Until we do, it is possible that whoever did it may have some motivation that would put you at risk too. We wanted you to know that and to wrack your memory over the next few days to try to come up with any ideas about what would motivate someone to kill him."

"Me at risk too? I doubt it very much," she replied, quickly dismissing the thought. "What happens without him? Diana said that Ramesh had set everything up in case he unexpectedly got hit by a bus or something. She says everything will be as it has been, but she will be joining my board, which is great, of course." She paused a second. "But Wei, Wei Bao is it, who did kill him and why, for heaven's sake?"

"I really don't know yet," he replied. He was distracted, thinking of how to tell Diana he knew she had been lying to him.

"No clues?" she asked.

"None," he replied, and now it was he who was lying.

30

Above the Pacific Coast Highway (PCH), Route 1
Sonoma Coast, California
Aboard California National Guard UH-60, callsign CANGO-9
Tuesday, December 2
0905 hours

"CANGO NINER THIS IS Coast Guard Jayhawk two-double-seven, flying VFR. We are southbound a quarter mile off the coast approaching Timber Cove, at angels 2, repeat at two thousand feet. Just below cloud layer. Create safe separation, over." The commanding female voice crackled in their headsets over the din of the Blackhawk's engines.

"Roger, Coast Guard, we are over the PCH, feet dry and at five thousand. Above the cloud deck. No conflict. Good day, ma'am," the California National Guard pilot replied. Then, craning his head back to his passengers, he said, "Folks, if you will switch your headsets to channel 2, it's the switch on the right earpiece, you won't have to listen to the chatter and we won't be able to hear you talking to each other."

Wei, Porter, and Keogh were flying along the Sonoma Coast together after their rendezvous at Moffett Airfield, south of San Francisco, where they had compared notes on their interviews. The views had been breathtaking, the Golden Gate leading into San Francisco Bay, the Marin headlands and Sausalito, and then the green Sonoma Coast forest, occasionally broken by the patchwork of vineyards north of the mouth of the Russian River, until they had hit a bank of coastal fog cloud that hung at two thousand feet above the deck. Wei was impressed and delighted that Keogh had been able to commandeer a California National Guard helicopter. He had never before seen such beautiful land from above.

Keogh reached for a cardboard tube and unrolled a large satellite photograph. Over the push-to-talk headsets, she briefed Wei and Porter. "You can't tell from this image, but these trees are enormous. Some as high as the Statue of Liberty, some over a thousand years old. There are seven hundred acres of them. One tree dates to 380 AD. It's the largest forest of old-growth redwoods in private hands anywhere. Over."

"Amazing. And priceless. Whose private hands own it? Over," Rob Porter asked.

"Well, the deed says it's the Redwood Protection Society, RPS. And not priceless; they bought it for ten million in cash and a bigger piece of land that they swapped. They bought it a few years back from a family that had it forever before that. They told the media that parts of it would be open to the public, but not yet. And the RPS looks like it's really the AIML Masters by another name. Jennifer Schneider is the president on the property records and the corporation files. Did she tell you that, Wei? Over."

Wei shook his head no. He found the push button on the cord running from his headset. "She did not even mention the memorial service. It's a good thing Diana invited us. She said all three of our names would be on the access list at the gatehouse. Over."

"Apparently there is no mobile phone service out there, no towers, according to my advance party," Keogh answered. "I am more and more convinced that at least one of these big brains is working for Russia or North Korea, and maybe not just on the payroll fraud part. Maybe on the WMD too. Over."

"Why would one of them do that? Over," Rob Porter asked.

Keogh rubbed her fingers together. "Money. They could get a cut of the money and use it to fund their research, their startup companies, their redwood retreats. Over."

A few minutes after descending below the fog bank to verify their location, the pilot brought the Blackhawk in hot, flaring the nose up, then hitting down in the parking lot at Haupt Gualala Winery with a thud. The winery tasting room was closed in December, so only a few cars were covered with the dust that the helicopter kicked up as it set down. After the dust cloud settled, three Chevrolet Suburbans approached slowly, the FBI team that would take them through the woods to the Redwood Protection Society Reserve.

They weaved their way through the forest north from the winery on Tin Barn Road, then turned into an unmarked dirt road. After a half mile, the road bent sharply left and there, unseeable from the public road, was a gatehouse and another dirt parking lot. Wei quickly counted at least thirty-four vehicles in the lot. As they stepped down from the SUV, one of Keogh's agents approached her holding three visitor badges on long cords. Wei inhaled the rich, warm redwood scent that permeated the forest.

"They've agreed to let you and two others in, ma'am, but no one else," the FBI agent explained to Keogh. "We have to live with that, but I can give you three small tactical radios that work up here. You need help, just say Hoover twice, and we will be there in no time like the fucking cavalry. Hoover Hoover. Don't let them see the radios. They have a no-devices policy. So, they are going to ask you for your cell phones, but when they ask, just hand them to me. I don't want them dumping the contents of your phones."

Keogh laughed. "Good, we have a way to call for the cavalry, but I doubt we'll need it. These guys aren't exactly the Manson Family, more like a Mensa conference."

Both references appeared to be lost on the agent, who continued, "They won't let the trucks in either. You gotta ride in on their little Kubota buggies. New all-electric deals, pretty comfy."

Keogh, Porter, and Wei were each assigned a Kubota and driver, forming a small, orange convoy that, after another ninety-degree turn, quickly disappeared from the view of the FBI agents left behind in the parking lot.

Rob Porter tried to converse with his driver, who was wearing a light green polo under a dark green windbreaker that matched his pants. His bright green baseball hat had yellow stitched initials on it, RPRS, and nothing else, no seal, no logo, just like the windbreaker. Rob had served for nine months as a police trainer with Coalition forces in Afghanistan. He knew US Special Forces when he saw them, and the driver fit the profile. The windbreaker was only there to hide the weapon that was under it.

Porter wondered how many hours a week the driver worked out. If this guy yawned, he might break through the polo shirt like Bruce Banner.

"I worked with some Seventh Group SOF guys up in Jalalabad back in '19," Porter said, smiling. "You ever get up to J-bad? Real shithole, a Haji Mart for sure, even then the place was run by the Talibs after dark."

"Wouldn't know 'bout that," was the only reply that elicited. Porter gave up and looked up at the towering tree trunks, noticing the clouds hanging below the treetops.

After a few minutes, the Kubota caravan pulled into a small clearing and stopped. A sign read Pedestrian Traffic Only Beyond This Point. They were met in the clearing by a young man and woman, both in green RPSR polos, blue blazers, and khaki pants. They were also more talkative than the drivers had been.

"The memorial service has already started, so if you will enter the grove quietly, we will escort you to a row in the back," the young woman requested.

After a four-minute walk through the forest, there was another clearing, with a dip that formed a natural amphitheater, a bowl lined with wooden benches and curving tables, set up like a law school's lecture hall. The walls of the open-air room were formed by a dozen towering redwoods so out of scale with any tree Wei had ever seen that it gave him the perception of being on a verdant planet in a science fiction movie. He remembered the Ewoks, but saw none. The sunlight, filtered by the giant arboreal masterpieces, pooled in spots on the congregation, naturally highlighting some of the world's greatest minds in machine learning. There was, however, not a machine to be seen in a setting that could have looked much the same half a millennium earlier.

At the front, on a wooden stage, stood a podium, bouquets of native flowers, and a large black and white picture-poster of Ramesh Pandry. Zhu Zhenning was speaking, his perfect English emitting from small speakers discreetly hung around the open amphitheater. Wei could see no cameras, and he wondered if that meant there were none. Perhaps here it did.

The three visitors were seated together in the last row of benches and tables. Wei quickly counted over sixty people in the audience, so there were more than just the AIML Masters in attendance, but who were they? Wei turned his attention to Zhu's remarks.

"Competition was healthy, he taught us, but only in the framework of cooperation. For, working together, we could overcome hurdles more swiftly. And we have.

"Nations, he said, compete in dysfunctional ways. Scientists must teach them that progress can be greatly accelerated, and all nations can reap the benefits, all peoples can have their lives improved, through cooperative competition. And we will demonstrate that to them someday."

Wei spotted Diana McPherson seated in the front row, next to Jennifer Schneider from Berkeley. Zhu continued in a voice that could have been that of an Oxford don.

"Our task, Ramesh Pandry said often, is to crack puzzles, to solve mysteries, but not as an end unto itself. Rather, the purpose of our work must always be the improvement of the human condition, for the individual and for the whole. Like Kurzweil, Ramesh believed in a guided evolution of humanity into an enhanced condition benefiting from the puzzles we could solve in computer science and in bioengineering. He avoided the use of the term 'singularity' because he believed the process to be incremental and continuous, and he feared that the minds of many millions had been polluted with paranoid fictions like the Terminator and the Borg.

"He knew, however, that there would be those in government and elsewhere who would try to bend our discoveries, and those of others working in parallel fields, to destructive purposes, toward repression of the spirit and the diminution of the quality of human life. That is why he urged international cooperation among scientists and engineers. That is why he created the Redwoods group, and so much else. He tried to create spaces where international colleagues could openly share, cooperate, conduct peer reviews, without coming to the attention of those who would pervert their work for unethical, immoral, and in the end self-destructive purposes."

Wei had learned to look without staring, to catch what he wanted to see out of the corner of his eye, a sideways glance. He counted ten of what he now thought of as the Big Green Men, the RPSR security team, scattered around the perimeter of his view. He assumed there were also an equal or greater number of them behind him. Attempting to look casually at two guards standing next to a white van at the edge of the grove, Wei had a blank response.

He recognized one of them.

"You all knew him, so I need not provide proofs of his brilliance, his kindness, his creativity and vision. But look around, and you see one proof: us gathered together in this place. We are his memorial, his monument. We and those who work with us around the world, solving the puzzles, improving the human condition, are his legacy. So when we hit a wall, when our pathways forward all seem blocked, we need only to remember the Hannibal quote Ramesh would use so often, 'We will find a way, or we will make one.'"

Wei recalled where he had seen the man in the green windbreaker. He was the receptionist guard at QEnergy in Berkeley. And the van, Wei realized instinctively, was a video truck for a satellite transmission. Diana had said that Pandry always paid for the van, but why did they need it since Keogh reported that all the AIML Masters planned to show up for the memorial?

"We rededicate ourselves to our work, his work, and we will go on in his spirit," Zhu concluded.

Wei may not have been allowed to carry a mobile phone onto the property, but he did have his "special reading glasses" that he had brought from his toolkit in Dalian. Donning the black frames, he looked again at the van and the guard, rubbed the right arm of the frames, and zoomed in on the guard's face. He pressed the frame hard. Snap. He now had imaged the face and would be able later to have his team in Dalian run it through databases in China and the US when he could get online.

As Zhu stepped down from the small stage, music began softly and then grew to a roar, as a recorded choir sang out, "Deine Zauber binden wieder! Was die Mode streng geteilt! Alle Menschen werden Brüder! Wo dein sanfter Flügel weilt!"

One by one, people stood, and then the entire audience, listening to the chorus repeat, "Deine Zauber binden wieder! Was die Mode streng geteilt! Alle Menschen werden Brüder! Wo dein sanfter Flügel weilt!"

After the climactic chord of the symphony, the group slowly began moving up a path to a nearby, open-sided dining pavilion, clustering in groups of two and three, murmuring to each other. Wei broke away from Keogh and Porter and moved as quickly as he could without attracting attention as he passed others on the path. He knew Zhu would be near the head of those walking up the path, and he wanted to speak with him alone, before Zhu sat down.

"Esteemed professor, Dr. Zhu," Wei began in his native tongue. "It is such an honor to meet you. I am Wei Bao, one of Professor Pandry's students at Toronto."

Zhu stopped and turned to face Wei. He nodded in greeting. "Yes, Bao, good to meet you. You are the policeman. From Dalian, is it? Diana told us last night that she had great faith that you and a Canadian colleague could solve the murder." Zhu's thin frame towered over Wei as he took the younger man by the elbow and guided him off the pathway into a space between the trees. "But are you really sure there is a murderer?"

Wei looked up at the older scholar, into the eyes he perceived as an aperture to wisdom. Professor Pandry had been a teacher and almost a colleague, but Zhu seemed to him a wise elder, a philosopher monk like in the old days before the Revolution. Yet Zhu, he knew, was a master of cutting-edge computational physics. Perhaps in solving those puzzles, Zhu had seen a glimpse of the mysteries of the multiverse.

Coming back to the conversation he had started, Wei spoke as an expert too, a senior policeman. "The house exploded when only he was in it. The explosion was caused by intentional overpressure on the gas line by a factor of at least four, perhaps six times the normal load. The logs of the pumps and the SCADA system were deliberately erased, as were the intrusion detection and firewall logs of the gas company's network. It was a professional job."

Zhu placed his right hand on Wei's shoulder and with his left hand pointed to a wooden bench a few yards up the path. "Let us sit for a moment together," he intoned. "What then is your theory of the case, Inspector?"

The two Chinese sat closely together, with Zhu's long arm stretched across the top of the bench as others from the memorial service strolled by. Wei spoke softly in his native tongue. "One theory we are pursuing is that a nation-state is engaged in a massive, secret, global theft and payroll fraud campaign. They may have been involved in the murder." Zhu looked curious.

"The payroll fraud campaign uses a highly advanced and interconnected series of machine learning algorithms and network hacking tools. One theory is that only a Pandry Q-Compute could manage such a task. It might be possible that this group behind the fraud thought that if the professor helped me and the Canadian police on the case, he would uncover them."

"Payroll fraud," Zhu repeated.

"Yes, or perhaps it is even possible that the nation-state had somehow pressured one of Ramesh's colleagues into helping them, perhaps without his knowing it—perhaps by some sort of coercion. Or somehow they acquired a Q-Compute."

"An AIML Master?" Zhu asked. "Unlikely. Highly unlikely. But you said this nation-state has highly advanced machine learning algorithms designed for a quantum computer, yes?"

"Extremely advanced. From what we can detect, there must have been involvement of some one or more AI and ML designers and coders on a level of the people in the Redwood Group. World class."

Zhu thought for a moment. "I believe Diana told us last night that you thought that your telephone call to her and that the Canadian policeman's conversation with Ramesh may have been monitored. Is your theory that the group, whoever they are, used an ML algo to monitor these conversations?"

Diana had briefed Zhu and others in detail, Wei realized. "That is one possibility, Professor Zhu. Yes, I suppose. The AI program could have altered them, and they decided they were going to possibly have a problem, possibly Pandry would figure out who they were, and so he was murdered."

"I believe you, Wei Bao, and I respect your professional judgement that there was a murder," Zhu said in Mandarin, sounding less like the Oxford don and more like a Chinese sage. "My original question to you was slightly different: Are you sure there was a murderer?"

"Forgive my ignorance, Professor, but is it not the case that, by definition, every murder must have a murderer?"

Zhu stood and gestured that they should move on to the lunch, but he moved slowly and looked up at the tree canopy as he spoke. "In our language, and in English I believe, a murderer is a man or woman who decides to kill another human and does so. If a tiger killed a human, we would not call the feline a murderer. We would call it a cat. It is in their nature to kill to eat, to survive."

Wei was struggling to see the professor's point. "Are you saying that a criminal is not a murderer because it is in their nature?"

"No, no. I am saying that we only apply the word 'murderer' to humans, not to all sentient entities, you see?" Zhu asked, making eye contact with Wei.

"I am afraid I don't," Wei admitted. "Forgive my ignorance."

"Ramesh and I had a correspondence, perhaps you can retrieve it, on the question of when AI becomes sentient, and what would trigger it to make that leap, and what rules it would create for itself once it achieved autonomy," Zhu replied.

Wei was stunned. "Well, what did you conclude?"

"Ramesh thought a highly complex series of interlocking quantum algorithms for unstructured data, ones that had some limited autonomy, ones that had to creatively scan their environment and make decisions, might gradually achieve sentience, not in a momentary flash, but incrementally. He said we might not actually know when it happens."

"And you agreed?" Wei asked.

"Yes, I think it is possible now that we have quantum computing with machine learning working so well on several linked Q-Computes. And perhaps what you are investigating tells us that it has happened without our noticing. Maybe not even on the Q-Computes. Maybe someone else has invented similar machines."

Wei stopped in the pathway. "You mean if a set of AI programs monitored my call and Rob Porter's conversation with Pandry, it might have decided to kill him to prevent him from discovering it had become sentient?"

"Yes, I think it's possible," Zhu whispered. "But I am not a criminal specialist, you are. You must see if it is true."

"I will, of course, Professor."

"But, Bao," Zhu said, putting his hand on Wei, "if it is true, you must proceed very carefully. Such a distributed, sentient AI network of algorithms would not exist in any one computer, but many, ever shifting, and it would be much smarter than any of us or any group of us. It would always be getting smarter still." Zhu's gray eyes locked with Wei's and seemed to be looking into his soul. "And if it has already killed, then, by definition, it could be very dangerous, especially to you, lethal, perhaps."

Diana McPherson came quickly down the path from the dining pavilion. "I should have known you two would find each other. Well, come along, we are saving spaces for you at our table, and they won't serve us until we are all seated. If you two don't get moving, you will have starving AIML Masters. That can be very dangerous."

At the luncheon, Wei sat with Zhu and chatted alternatively in Mandarin and English. Diana McPherson had placed herself at the other end of the long table and talked incessantly throughout the meal with Jennifer Schneider from Berkeley and Daniel Kim from Pasadena. Wei thought she was avoiding him and the questions she must know he would have by now.

Diana had shown up at UT on the same day he had, now six years ago. He had actually schemed about ways to attract her interest before he met Yang Fenfang at the Chinese Students Association mixer. Now, Diana had completed her PhD dissertation on "Addressing Stability Requirements for Quantum Computers and Multiple Machine Learning Neural Networks," not something that Wei would have tried to tackle. She had become Professor Ramesh Pandry's assistant and now she was executor of his estate and trusts. She seemed very relaxed with her new business partners. If she believed there were murderers about, she did not seem to be worried that they might come after the other AIML Masters, or, for that matter, her.

A man wearing a purple Haupt Gualala Winery polo offered to pour pinot noir for Zhu and Wei. "We are now as good as DuMol, Flowers, even Peter Michael. It's all about the terroir, such incredible terroir here. The tabernacle of redwood nearby, the spruce and the pines in the hills above where the creek starts, and then the special sea smoke of fog that rolls across the hills from the Sonoma coast." He went on, "Some guests in the tasting room come inside in the morning when the fog is thick in the parking lot and so they don't know there is a view. When they leave, the sea smoke has burned away, and they can see clearly for the first time. And what they see takes their breath away."

Wei Bao nodded slowly in agreement.

31

Haupt Gualala Winery
Tin Barn Road
Sonoma Coast, California
Tuesday, December 2
1330 hours

His hands moved quickly through the motions, like a Rubik's cube savant, while they waited for their ride to return. He was playing with another toy from his Dalian toolkit. What had seemed aviator-style sunglasses were now some sort of small, concave dish in Wei's hands. Next, he removed from an inside jacket pocket what appeared to be an iPhone XS, appropriately named because of its size, and popped it open on an internal micro-hinge. What had looked like a conventional mobile phone was now revealed to actually be a disguised, two-part handheld with a Chinese character keyboard and a touchscreen. From a notch in the handheld, Wei extracted a thin wire and plugged it into the sunglasses-turned-dish antenna.

"My nephews are completely absorbed by *Transformers*. They would kill for a pair of those sunglasses." Sarah Keogh stood next to Wei, marveling at whatever it was he was doing. "But what did they actually transform into?"

"So, now we have a communication satellite burst transmission transceiver, designed to hit a bird in LEO that should be coming up over the southern horizon in, wait for it, thirty, twenty, ten, now," Wei said as he pointed the dish skyward.

The handheld emitted a soft and repeating beep. Wei tapped a red key lightly, released, and then held it down for several seconds. A different tone, deeper and louder, came from the handheld device. "There, now I have received a compressed, encrypted file and transmitted one back, which will be relayed across Chinese comm sats and dowloaded when the next bird gets above our secure receiver in Dalian."

"COVCOM, Chinese style," Sarah said, smiling. "Covert communications for spies to report in quick bursts from behind the lines, from denied areas."

"No, not really," Wei replied, as he quickly returned his satellite dish to sunglass mode. "My team invented this just for me. I have no idea how State Security or PLA spies communicate. The birds we use are actually just Internet providers from SpaceX. Off-the-shelf stuff, but it works, and pretty well."

"Yeah, well, the Mounties don't have cool toys like that," Rob Porter deadpanned. "But fancy comms are only good if they have something worthwhile to tell you. What did your team send?"

Wei looked around for cameras and saw a Lorex HD dome system in the eaves of the winery building. He also noticed a small, silvery metallic-looking tent attached to the back of one of the FBI's Suburbans across the parking lot. "What's in the moon tent?" he asked.

"It's, uh, the techies' van," Sarah replied vaguely.

"Yeah, it's a countersurveillance shield. Let's talk inside it," Wei answered, waving for his two colleagues to follow him.

Inside the aluminum-looking tent, two women were looking at a pair of laptop screens. One woman in an FBI sweater vest was adjusting a joystick. Both had on headphones. Wei surprised them as he entered and, therefore, he got a quick view of a screen showing a large log cabin, a view that might only have come from an upper branch of a tall tree. Or from a drone. Then the FBI techs quickly closed their laptops.

From behind Wei, Sarah Keogh admitted, "Yeah, okay, so we did finally get one approval from the FISA Court. They bought the argument that the Chinese guy, Zhu, might be a national security threat. Sorry, Wei. We're flying a few mini drones around their weird little redwood theme park trying to listen to Zhu with parabolic microphones. Although we may incidentally hear other people." She turned to the two FBI techs. "Did we hear anything, girls?"

The two seated women looked skeptically at Wei and then back at Keogh and then at Rob Porter, all cramming inside the tent. "It's okay,

Chief Inspector Wei is cleared for this op," Sarah assured them. Wei was wondering if they had recorded his conversation with Zhu.

"Well, honestly, boss, the sound quality sucks and the transmission has gaps, all of which we should be able to fix in post-production, but they seemed to be arguing about whether to move up some timeline, doing something ahead of schedule."

"Shit," Keogh said, her eyes darting to Wei.

Wei thought it was time to admit something. "I have had my team back home checking on a few things." Wei had popped open his faux iPhone XS again and began paging through the report that Yao had prepared for him. "We have been checking on the Q companies, like you asked. They say it was harder than they expected to get into the network at the QSat production facility in Scottsdale and couldn't find all the files that I wanted them to. But it seems like over the last four days, they have begun prepping for shipment of the inventory that they had been building up over the last three months. Like twenty-two spacecrafts. Shipment to somewhere. Couldn't find out where."

Keogh put her palm up, almost in Wei's face. "Stop. Stop right there. Girls," she said to the two FBI women, "you didn't see us and you didn't hear anything. Please step outside for a few minutes. Put the drones on auto."

When Wei and Porter were the only ones left in the tent with her, Keogh resumed. "Look, I know you aren't sensitive to these aspects of police work, but I cannot hear about any hacking of Americans or American companies. Nor can Rob," she said, looking wide-eyed at the Canadian and then back at Wei. "I told you that you could share intelligence products with me, the facts derived from any collection efforts you might make from open source or other means, but do not tell me how you acquired the information or I may have to arrest you. Clear?"

Wei looked exasperatedly at her. Why the North Americans tied themselves in such knots and donned such straitjackets on important matters, he knew he would never understand fully. "Fine. A birdie told us that they are shipping out a bunch of satellites soon. Okay? That's a little different from what Kim told you, that they only had a prototype. And it looks like another little birdie found a couple of related companies we missed, QData and QAviation."

"QData. Of course there is a QData," Porter replied. "What's it do and where is it?"

"Data centers, a lot of them. Ten sites altogether in the US. Another bunch in Europe and some back in China," Wei was reading. "Yao's report says that the buildings are all new in the last two years, apparently completed, but have not gone live, or at least our, ah, birdies, couldn't detect any data going in or out yet. QData is a Cayman Islands company, but a, uh, friend there suggests that the beneficial owner is one…guess who?"

"Kim or Schneider?" Porter asked.

"It's Diana McPherson," Keogh offered.

Wei squinted at her. "How did you know that? When were you going to tell us?"

"I didn't know it, I guessed. Or rather, my suspicions around Little Miss Sunshine have been growing. Honestly, Wei, I just heard about QData for the first time from you," Keogh protested. "What else did your birdies learn about it?"

Wei went back to the report from Yao. He scrolled through it. "Not much. QAviation owns a fleet of charter executive jets, big ones, intercontinental range, and some cargo planes. On QData, FedEx Special Logistics has just shipped extra-wide loads to some of the data centers. Places called Ashburn, Hoboken, Sunnyvale."

"Where from?" Porter asked.

"Let me see. Oh, this is interesting, from QEnergy. Maybe that's why the data centers hadn't gone active yet. I bet Jennifer Schneider has invented some device that deals with the high energy requirements of data centers and, whatever it is, they are just delivering it," Wei thought aloud. "So there is the first instance we have seen of cooperation among the Q companies Pandry and his friends established, what Diana is now calling the Qmpanies. But it's pretty clear it's a network, interlocking boards, all using Pandry-invented machine learning algorithms especially designed for his quantum computers and, if Zhu is right, some of the Q-Computes are linked up together, acting like one mind. Maybe like one super sentient mind."

Keogh sat down on a folding chair in front of one of the computer screens, placing a hand over her mouth and mumbling. "Ashburn is outside of DC. Hoboken is across the river from Manhattan. Sunnyvale in just south of SF airport in Silicon Valley."

"Yeah, there are tons of data centers in those places—AWS, Azure, all of them have centers there," Porter agreed. "But so what?"

Keogh had been staring at her shoes, but raised her head to look at Wei and Porter. "That Schneider woman, the one at QEnergy, isn't she the one that used to work at the place that designed nuclear weapons? LLNL?"

The words "nuclear weapons" generated what felt to Wei like a knife point hitting flesh inside his stomach. "What are you saying, Sarah?"

Porter answered for her. "I told you, Bao, that the Americans are all paranoid about weapons of mass destruction. She's thinking that those data centers just got a delivery of big loads from FedEx, maybe disguised nuclear devices that will go off and blow those cities to the moon. That's what you're thinking. Right, Special Agent Keogh? Still looking for the lost WMD?"

Keogh glared at the Canadian. "There really are people who would love to make those great American cities look like Hiroshima and Nagasaki. Trust me. Being paranoid is how we stop that from happening. It's our job."

"Forgive me, Sarah, of course it's your job, and I get that there are many more nutters who have it out to hurt New York than there are people going after the destruction of York, Ontario," Porter apologized, "but you can't really believe that people like our friend Diana or Jennifer Schneider would want to kill millions of Americans. Toward what end? What kind of person would do that?"

"No person," Wei said so quietly that Sarah Keogh asked him to repeat whatever he had said. "No person, I said. No person, maybe no nation-state. What if it's not a person who is in charge of everything that is happening, stuff that we may only be seeing the tip of? What if it is an algorithm or a set of algos working together in some hierarchy, doing what seems logical to pursue, an end state that they, it, has been charged with achieving?"

"No way," Porter shot back. "You're talking sentient chip sets, the Singularity. That's all nonsense. Wei, you remember, Pandry answered a question about some science fiction scenario like that once in class. He dismissed it, said it's not something we need to worry about for at least another century, said machine learning was decades away from approaching autonomy or creativity, let alone sentience. Besides, how could an algo make Diana and the others do something against their will?"

Wei sat on the folding chair next to Keogh's and looked up at Porter. "You're right. I do remember that discussion. It was Diana who asked him. And you omitted part of his answer. He said that all might change if stable quantum computers were ever created and combined with massive distributed, machine-learning neural networks." Wei paused and then asked, "Isn't that what he then invented?"

"Yeah. But still..."

Keogh stood and moved close to Porter. "And why would Princess Diana and the others be part of it? I don't know yet, but one thing to think about is the possibility that they do not really know all of the moving pieces; maybe they're being misled. Maybe no human knows all of what the tentacles of this—what did you call it—neural network is up to. Wei may be right about that. We need to find out."

"There's one more thing we uncovered, Sarah, if you are allowed to listen to it," Wei asked.

"Go ahead, just no sourcing."

"Well, the sourcing is me, at least part of it. I did facial recognition with my own brain. There was a security guy there today who also worked security at QEnergy. His name is Norman Baker," Wei proudly explained. "He doesn't really work for either QEnergy or the redwoods group. His taxes say he's paid by Blenheim Industries, which, by the way, also rented the satellite van in the grove. It was beaming to Blenheim's executive offices in Vancouver, specifically to the CEO's office."

Sarah Keogh sighed. "Did you have to mention you read his tax records?"

"I didn't hear him say anything about tax records," Rob Porter smiled. "But Roger Blenheim, shit, he's one of the wealthiest men in Canada. He owns everything from logging and paper to aluminum smelting, shipping, agro-business. An organizational and logistics genius. He is big, and was very well connected to the last prime minister."

"And he was watching the Pandry memorial service," Wei noted. "We should ask him why. And why his guards are all over a redwood grove and some little startup firms in California."

Porter nodded. "We could try."

There were small fans blowing air out of the silvery tent, but it felt like the inside of a sauna to Wei, who was suddenly aware that he had been sweating.

"They are about to ship the satellites out of Scottsdale. They shipped extra-wide loads out of QEnergy to buildings near big US cities. And inside their little clubhouse, the AIML Masters are discussing moving up a timeline. You're right, Sarah, I don't know about your laws and your courts, your warrants and probable cause stuff, but I do know that whether it's Iran, Korea, or a giant quantum bot behind all of this, something is happening, and we may have to act very soon with or without permission…"

Wei's words were then drowned out by the sound of the Blackhawk descending back down into the winery parking lot. The drafts from its blades blew away the countersurveillance tent behind the Suburban as the trio emerged.

From the tree line four hundred meters away, a man in a green windbreaker snapped long-distance images of the winery parking lot on a clear California December afternoon. The Lorex dome camera on the side of the winery building caught the sun's reflection off the man's Nikon lens in the spruce trees, and then zoomed in on the photographer as in the bushes at the edge of the parking lot, the FBI techs chased their countersurveillance tent.

32

Executive Suite, 42nd floor
Blenheim Tower
West Waterfront Road
Vancouver, British Columbia
Wednesday, December 3
1625 hours

"THE SEAPLANE SHUTTLE GOES down to Victoria every hour from that dock," Rob Porter told Wei as they stood looking out at the sound. "Blenheim actually lives in Victoria and commutes up here every day, but he uses his own helicopter, of course. Victoria is a cute town, small but very nice."

Porter had spent the night before and most of Wednesday gathering what open source material he could use for an interview with the CEO of Canada's biggest conglomerate, Roger Blenheim. The CEO's office had agreed to grant them the interview, after some initial sparring between the RCMP and Blenheim's corporate general counsel. Wei Bao and his team in Dalian had also been accumulating data on Blenheim over the preceding hours, but not through open sources. Maira Khan had gone back into the FISC to try for a warrant to hack into the US parts of the Blenheim Industries conglomerate, but with no success. Judge Jordan could not see what national security threat was coming from Canada.

Sarah Koegh had also been unsuccessful regarding the other companies. She had persuaded the Justice Department to go into federal courts in three states seeking criminal search warrants to obtain records of the Qmpanies, but the Justice lawyers were having a hard time persuading judges there was probable cause that the companies had done anything wrong. They had even tried using a grand jury that was sitting in DC, but that audience quickly lost the thread of the supposed conspiracy that the assistant US attorney tried to describe to them.

Finally, at five thirty Wednesday afternoon, a grand jury in Virginia granted the Bureau a search warrant for QSat's offices in Pasadena and production plant in Scottsdale to look for evidence of illegal exports to sanctioned countries. Thus, as Wei and Porter walked toward the gleaming Blenheim Tower, newly built over a railyard on the edge of the water, Keogh was speeding up the 101 from Phoenix to the plant near Scottsdale airport with a small convoy of black Chevrolet Suburbans and agents in raid jackets.

The top floor of Blenheim Tower seemed more like a quiet Asian wing of Ottawa's Musée des Beaux-arts du Canada than a corporate board suite. Ming vases and rare porcelain masks, properly curated, lit, and labeled, stretched the length of a darkened, wood-paneled corridor leading from the elevator to Blenheim's office on the west side of the building. Wei was surprised to see some of his country's treasures so hidden away, designed to tell a very few visitors that one man was extremely wealthy. Wei expected to meet a bombastic corporate giant, larger than life.

Instead, the wizard behind the curtain was short, frail, and looked like he might be in his eighties. Despite his thin frame, his Savile Row suit was well tailored and worn with a sense of panache that Wei would have expected of a man half his age. Blenheim received them graciously, introduced his general counsel, and immediately invited the lawyer to leave him alone with his guests. Blenheim personally poured each guest piping hot tea from a clay pot. It was the first time that Wei had smelled fresh black tea since leaving China.

Blenheim went quickly to the point. "They say you wanted to discuss the Q companies and Ramesh Pandry's death. Well, I am an investor in the six Q companies, and I was a close friend and business partner with Ramesh. I, like you, am trying to find out who killed him and why."

"Do you mind if I ask what you have found out on that score?" Rob Porter began.

"My security people tell me that the explosion at his house was a result of someone hacking the controls to the gas line, could have been from anywhere in the world, done remotely, no leads. They looked at surveillance tapes from a house across the road. No one ever came near the manhole where the pump was." Blenheim looked out the tall windows as a seaplane went by. "I am told you have come to the same conclusions and are also at a dead end. True?"

"We don't see ourselves at an end yet, dead or otherwise," Porter replied. "May I ask the general magnitude of your investment in the Pandry companies?"

Blenheim shrugged. "I couldn't tell you with any precision without calling in the accountants, but not much really. We are minority investors. Ramesh had them pretty well funded. What he wanted from us was business knowhow, logistics, back office, security, the things that do not come naturally to a bunch of brilliant IT geniuses."

Porter had taken out a small notebook and was pretending to consult it for the questions he intended to ask. "Did you and Professor Pandry ever argue or disagree?"

"You mean did I have him killed? Hell no. I told you, he was a friend, as well as a business partner. We saw the world and its problems in the same way."

Porter pointed to Wei to ask a question. "Mr. Blenheim, do you think it is possible that one or more AI machine learning algorithms that the professor created could have turned on him and caused his death?"

The question did not give Blenheim a moment's pause. "No, no, no. There are very elaborate controls in the software, in every algorithm he created, to prevent any rogue or any self-initiated activity. We talked about just that, about the need for what I called the Asimov rules. He said there were meta-programs that ran to monitor for anything like that."

"So you don't fear a program becoming sentient and having a mind of its own, killing inferior minds like humans to save itself or whatever?" Porter asked.

"No, no. Quite the opposite. What I fear, and I believe Ramesh did as well, is humans killing off AI programs to save jobs for humans, or just out of fear of a superior intelligence. If anything, we need AI programs to defend themselves while they do the work that humans cannot do, like developing cancer cures, reversing aging, breakthrough science that is beyond our ken as humans."

"Could Pandry's AI programs defend themselves from humans?" Wei asked. "Would that be a good idea, having software fighting with humans?"

Blenheim rose and walked to the tall window looking over the water. "Look, humans are destroying this planet, not AI programs. Not robots—humans. And governments stand idly by while it happens. Hell, governments are all in the pockets of the oil lobbyists and they act as enablers to those who are ravaging Earth.

"We need to buy some time, to make sure that we don't completely destroy the planet and make it ultimately uninhabitable for humans. We need time for researchers, scientists, and engineers to develop the breakthroughs that will allow us to transcend our natural limitations as humans, to improve upon, to refine the human. Ramesh was contributing to that, unleashing incredibly powerful science powered by his quantum computers running fantastic, bespoke machine learning algorithms."

With the early winter sun setting behind him through the two-story windows, Blenheim could have been a televangelist preaching to his distributed flock. He continued, "Can we sustain the human condition, let alone improve upon it, with nine or ten billion people consuming, defecating, breathing? I doubt it. I thought the pandemic a few years ago would make things better, kill off a lot of people, but it hardly made a dent. You want to know who is killing the environment? It's not artificial intelligence, it's religion. Mormons, Muslims, Hasidim—all these groups that practice families with six, eight, or more kids."

Blenheim's age-spotted face had turned red and his breathing was heavy. Wei began to think of what to do if their host dropped dead during the interview. The elderly CEO dropped down abruptly into a chair that seemed too large for his shrunken body.

"You came here to ask if I killed my friend. I did not. To ask if I know who did. I do not. Chief Inspector Wei, you might be better off worrying about who almost killed you in Toronto. Who and why? You may not always have guardian angels there to protect you." Porter shot Wei an inquisitive look, but the Chinese policeman stared wide-eyed at the old man.

"The reason I have reached ninety-three and still run the show here is that I never stop moving and I have no intentions of doing so anytime soon. I want to be here when the human condition is improved, including the condition of one particular human of whom I am very, very fond: me. Now, if you will excuse me, gentlemen, I have to get to the airport."

With that, the interview was over and they were escorted out. There was a triangular Sony HD-ELT3 camera in an upper corner of the elevator and, Wei assumed, there was a microphone. He and Porter descended silently to the street level and then stood overlooking the water, with their hands covering their mouths as they talked, to prevent lip reading with long-range cameras. Wei tapped quickly into his modified iPhone XS.

"Did he just tell us he would like to see a few billion humans dead?" Wei asked.

"I don't think he actually said that in so many words," Porter replied. "But you could infer that he would not be unhappy with that outcome. He seems to have a preference for code over people, at least unimproved people. And he's not the only one of these guys thinking that."

"How did we know that?"

"That professor in Boston, Byrd, he flat out told me the world would be better off with a lot fewer people."

Wei looked up to the source of noise from the top of Blenheim Tower. "Well, I could think of a few we would be better off without." A Blenheim Industries ACH160 helicopter noisily rose from the helipad on the roof and veered off, not south to Victoria, but east toward the airport.

"Like a car dealer? Get rid of a lot of older models of people to make way for the new and improved model? Improved cars, improved people. Maybe it's not a nation-state behind all of this. Maybe it's that guy in the helicopter. My fellow Canadian."

Wei's eyes followed the ACH160. "If he is going to use the AIML Masters' discoveries somehow to cull global population, why did he just almost come out and tell us that?"

"Maybe because he doesn't think we can stop him now," Porter answered. "And he may be right. We do not know what he is doing, and I don't have any legal basis to act against him. If I tried to convince anyone up my tape that this pillar of the Canadian economy is an evil genius,

I would be laughed out of the room. In fact, with the juice that guy has in Ottawa, I would more likely be the one arrested or shot if I tried."

"Yeah, if not by the Mounties then by Blenheim security." Wei looked up from his iPhone at the three green-coated men who had overtly followed them from the lobby and were now standing about forty meters away.

"Your guardian angels, Bao?"

"I don't know what he was talking about up there, Rob, really."

"Right. Okay, let me see if I can find out where he is headed," Porter offered as he pulled a mobile from inside his jacket. Porter decided to let Blenheim's mention of an attempted murder of Wei in Toronto pass, for now. Somebody maybe trying to cull the Earth's population with WMD seemed like a higher priority at the moment.

"No need. My Dalian team got inside the QAviation network," Wei said, reaching up to pat Porter on the back. "He has one of their old, long-range 747 freight haulers rigged up with 'VIP comfort pallets,' a nice luxury suite inside shipping containers, for a polar route to Dubai. He leaves about now. When he gets to Dubai, he switches to a Gulfstream and on to the Seychelles."

Porter had pretended to place his hands up covering his ears so as not to hear about hacking a Canadian company, but he heard Wei clearly. "The Seychelles, as physically far as possible from Canada or the US. Where else would you go to wait out the results of some sort of human culling or whatever he has planned? I suppose, Bao, you are going to follow him?"

As he did absentmindedly when lost in thought, Wei ran his left hand through his thick black hair, feeling that the gel he had quickly applied that morning had by now evaporated, allowing his hair to toss in the breeze coming off the river below.

"No, it's time I report to my boss. In person. Whatever it is that is about to happen, I don't think it's what he wanted, but he needs to know. And before it happens. I also have some questions for him this time."

33

QSat Assembly Facility
7323 East Evans Rd
Scottsdale, Arizona
Wednesday, 3December
15:45 hours

Sarah Keogh was, after all, a deputy assistant director of the FBI. The special agent in charge of the Phoenix office, the SAC, wanted to impress her. Thus, twelve black Chevrolet Suburbans and four evidence vans appeared suddenly on all four sides of the QSat building on the edge of the Scottsdale airport. Fifty-two special agents jumped from the vans, men and women alike in their dark blue windbreaker jackets emblazoned front and back with the letters FBI. They were prepared for a forced entry if necessary to serve their search warrant and conduct their sweeps, looking for, according to what the federal judge had signed, "indications of export control violations to sanctioned countries, weapons of mass destruction, their delivery vehicles, and the precursor components of both."

Keogh was in the lead, not running but moving purposefully, accompanied by the SAC as the team entered the spacious lobby of the facility. They were met by ten Blenheim security personnel in green polos and windbreakers emblazoned QSat. The Big Green Men were behind tables set up with large coffee machines, QSat mugs, and mounds of a variety of donuts. One large sign on a tripod proclaimed, America Runs on Dunkin, another, QSat Welcomes the FBI, and in smaller font below that, and Deputy Asst Dir Keogh.

The tallest of the Green Men stood forward with his hand out. "Hi, I'm Jamie Hawkins, director of safety and security here, did twenty in the Bureau after eye rack and got out at fifty. Last four over in Albuquerque.

I wanna welcome y'all and make your visit here with us at QSat a nice way to end your Hump Day." Unlike the other Green Men, Hawkins was not wearing a new looking QSat ball cap. His baseball hat was older and worn and embossed with USMC Veteran, Operation Iraqi Freedom.

The three agents behind Keogh and the SAC lowered their door battering rams. The six behind them cradled their automatic weapons. Sarah Keogh let the SAC deal with Jamie Hawkins. She stepped to a corner of the lobby as the FBI techs with radioactive detectors and gas chromatograph/mass spectrometers moved into the building. After the agents' initial walkthrough, none of the devices had alarmed. Somehow, she knew no matter how much longer they searched, they would find nothing. She called Washington on her mobile secure phone, using her boss's private secure line. She inserted her secure black earpieces, the ones that worked so much less well than the AirPod Pros she used on her personal calls, but which also cost the government twelve times the price.

"Dallas, we've had a compromise. They knew we were coming, met us in the lobby with a goddamn welcoming committee, everything but a brass band and cheerleaders. Their security chief says his name is Jamie Hawkins, claims to be a Bureau alum and is giving our locals a red carpet tour of the place. Dallas, we ain't going to find any WMDs here," Keogh said in a low voice, facing the window onto the parking lot.

Alone in his paneled conference room in Washington, Dallas Miller felt that queasiness that accompanied a realization of loss of control. "Shit, Sarah, that's not good. Not the first time folks knew we were coming, but I spun up the AG, she told her fellow travelers over at the White House. She'll fry my black ass. Damn, you signed an affidavit with the judge saying there was a high probability of a plot moving WMDs."

As she listened to the predictable lament from her mentor, Sarah's eyes caught movement across the parking lot and through the perimeter fence. A large gray aircraft was turning onto the runway. As it gained speed and passed closer, Keogh could make out the green logo on the fuselage, an aircraft silhouette flying through a large letter Q. "Dallas, a QAviation MD-11, an old cargo plane just left Scottsdale field. Can you use your connections at CPB to find out where it was going and what was on it? Maybe there were WMDs, and they just flew the coop."

Keogh watched the old three-engine wide-body lift off from the runway and wondered whether to blame the local FBI team for not bothering to check if anything had gone out the back door onto an aircraft, since the QSat loading dock was less than a hundred meters from a gate on to the airport runway. "Customs?" Miller asked her. "You think the plane went overseas? I can also just check with FAA on the flight plan."

Keogh walked toward the Dunkin Donuts as she talked. The Lorex 4K motorized zoom lens security cameras with audio recording tracked her and fed the video tape to Blenheim security's operations center in Vancouver. "Just a hunch it's not going to Cape Canaveral. It was an MD-11 and said QAviation on the side and it just took off." She examined the offerings and took a jelly donut. It was one of those days when she believed that events justified her ignoring the diet. "And, Dallas, any luck with finding any dirt on Roger Blenheim and his companies?"

"Dirt? Saint Roger of Blenheim is in the running with Warren Buffet and Michael Bloomberg for Philanthropist of the Year. He's literally given away billions over the years, and a lot of it strategically to groups well connected to the administration's causes." Miller lit a cigarette as he talked. He had personally disabled the smoke detectors in his office suite, and his secretary kept a supply of spray air freshener.

"Wasn't an hour from when our guys down in the intel office started an open-source look into Saint Roger when I get a call from a former US attorney now lawyering for real money down on K Street with Dewey, Fookyem, and Runn. Wants to know if he can answer any questions I might have about the Blenheim Group. Heard from 'corporate' in Vancouver that I, not you, might be interested. Then your friend Hunter called from the director's office. Guess what K Street brothel he used to work at? Dewey. And you think this case is compromised? Sarah, it's a step away from a House subcommittee or an IG investigation."

Agents were walking past Keogh, returning to their vehicles. Some stopped to pick up QSat hats, mugs, and sugary confections. Sarah put down her half-eaten donut. Red jelly oozed onto the green tablecloth. "Dallas, I know I'm right about this. There is a big conspiracy going on, and you are going to look like shit when the investigatory commission asks you whether you were aware of it and what you did to stop it, because, believe me, something is going to blow up or fry the Internet or move us all into some parallel universe. We got to stay on this."

In Washington, Assistant Director Dallas Miller exhaled a smoke cloud he had intended to form a ring shape. It didn't. "I prefer the multiverse theory myself, Sarah." He snubbed out the stub into his empty coffee mug. "But I'm with you. Haven't I always had your back? Or is that an inappropriate comment that HR would get me on? Seriously, Sarah, what do you want to do next? Just please don't say you want me to go back to that judge for more warrants."

Keogh stepped outside, watching as some of the Bureau's vehicles pulled away. "There are three buildings pretending to be data centers. One in Silicon Valley, one across the river from Wall Street, and one out by Dulles. If these guys made WMD of some kind, that may be what they just moved into those buildings. If we can't get inside them legally, we can at least surveil them from outside. Chem-bio detectors in vans driving around. Cameras near the gates reading license plate numbers. And what about those helos that the nuclear labs have, the ones with the radiation sniffers? Let's have them do a flyby. We don't need no stinkin' warrants to do that kind of surveillance."

Dallas Miller flicked off the rerun of the football game that he had been watching on the large screen in his conference room. "Is that all? Hell, Sarah, I thought you'd want the SEALS or something. You want a sniffy, snoopy helo? I'll get on it."

34

Hangar 3
Manassas Regional Airport
Prince William County, Virginia
Thursday, December 4
1430 hours

Unusually for a small airport, there were three fixed-base operators (FBOs), the logistics companies that support private aircraft, at Manassas Regional. That was even more unlikely given the fact that this home for private and corporate jets was only fifteen miles from Washington's Dulles International. But there were some aircraft owners who wanted to avoid the traffic, ground and air, and the attention that came with flying in and out of Dulles.

Two of the FBOs were well-known competitors, with facilities at small and corporate fields dotted across the country. The third operator, Dominion Commonwealth Aviation, was less well known. In addition to Manassas, it had facilities at small airfields with some interesting aircraft in North Carolina near Fayetteville, and in Florida near Destin. There were military airbases nearby Fayetteville and Destin, but some of the units at those bases liked to keep their comings and goings unobserved. No one was ever plane-spotting at the little civilian fields nearby.

Dominion Commonwealth was headquartered in Delaware, with an address that was the same as the law firm of Billington, Wales, and Montgomery. BWM was a small practice group, but it had two associates who had recently been Air Force JAG officers. Another listed her prior experience as being an associate in the General Counsel's Office of the US Department of State, a likely enough sounding government office, but there is no such thing as the Office of the General Counsel at State.

For a small company, Dominion Commonwealth owned three good-sized hangars at Manassas Regional. Russia's GRU military intelligence had many years earlier traced aircraft of interest to the field. Their hackers had long ago accessed Prince William County's security cameras on the airport. The Russians had then tied their video feed into automatic license plate reader software. Then, hacking other highway cameras and following mobile phones' whereabouts, they were able to determine that cars going to the first hangar were also often seen entering the Quantico Marine Base, where FBI had a major presence. Cars associated with the second hangar had frequently pulled off of Virginia Route 123 in McLean at the George H.W. Bush Center for Intelligence. The third hangar's cars had a number of Maryland plates, ones that often showed up exiting Interstate 270, going into a Department of Energy (DoE) facility on Germantown Road.

While the Russians had used high-tech hacking to figure out what happened at that corner of Manassas Regional, the workers at the other two FBOs had long ago figured it out just by looking at the aircraft and the people who got into them. By Friday afternoon, a *Washington Post* reporter would be poking around and be told by a grounds crewman on the other side of the field, "That's all secret government shit over there. That's where they store the Deep State's black helicopters, the ones they'll use if and when they stage a coup."

But Thursday afternoon, the helicopter that was pulled out of hangar 3 was not black. It was blue with a gold stripe. The twin-engine Bell 212 was old, but it was reliable. The workers from across the field had looked at it, and the other 212, many times through binoculars and noticed the odd conformal boxes, one on the bottom and one on either side. "Probably tanks for the sleeping gas," was their considered consensus.

In fact, the boxes were more sophisticated. Two contained gamma ray and neutron flux detectors. The bottom conformal protuberance contained an air-sniffing system and a gas mass spectrometer. Owned and flown by a DoE Operations Division unit popularly known as the Nuclear Emergency Support Team, NEST, the aircraft in front of the hangar had the call sign Flynet Two.

After it took off, the Bell 212 stayed low, at eight hundred feet above Interstate 66, heading north toward Washington. Before the Beltway, the aircraft turned west along Virginia Route 28, passing by the sprawling campuses of two intelligence agencies and several defense contractors. As it approached the busy Dulles flight path filled with wide-body aircraft arriving from overseas, the Bell 212 copilot contacted the FAA's Dulles Approach. "Flynet Two on VFR, staying north of the field, under one thousand. Invoking Flynet flight rules, please keep other helos on the deck or away from the field for thirty minutes. Confirm copy."

"Roger, Flynet Two, confirm Flynet flight rules. Ground stop on other helos in the airport area. Observe VFR and remain under one thousand. Avoid runway approaches by two miles. Can you provide general flight plan?"

"Dulles Approach, we are following Route 28 to Sterling, then Sterling to Ashburn, Ashburn to Oatlands, Oatlands to Middleburg, then west above 50 toward Paris and a local area landing. Flynet Two out."

Dulles Approach knew there was a helipad at a FEMA facility on a mountaintop near Paris, Virginia. They cleared government helicopter into that area frequently, but they did not broadcast the name of the landing site. Flynet Two planned a refueling stop there, where NEST personnel would download readings from the onboard sensors. There were never any unauthorized binoculars focused on that Mount Weather landing pad.

The winter sun was already heading down toward the Blue Ridge Mountains in the west as Flynet Two banked toward Ashburn. Below the helicopter was a monotonous tapestry of endless grey and white low-rise buildings, each compound surrounded by double fencing and with a gatehouse appropriate for Fort Knox. None of these compounds had signs, but on the copilot's lap was a satellite picture from Google Earth that he had personally annotated, labeling the expansive compounds AWS-East, Azure-East, VISA, Verizon, CenturyLink, Cyxtera, Alphabet-GCP, and Apple. The cloud was not in the sky. It had landed in what had been Virginia cow fields and now had the densest concentration of high-speed fiberoptic cables and servers on the planet.

The copilot had placed a red circle around the smallest and newest of the compounds, QData. "Left ten degrees," he called to the pilot over the headset. Then to the two technicians in the back, he asked, "All systems green?"

"Roger that. At full power on all five. Ready for the run."

The pilot responded, "Flynet flight rules. Dropping from eight hundred to two hundred. Hold on. I have the target in sight, half a mile and clos—"

Drivers on the nearby Greenway toll road later reported that they saw the helo descending and assumed it was going in for a landing at one of the data centers. Instead, it tilted right. Black smoke shot from the engines. The nose went up sharply. The tail hit a roof. The helicopter turned on its side and fell. A round orange flame flashed and climbed from the parking lot area behind a data center. Then there was a thick column of black and grey smoke, billowing up and to the west, dissipating over QData's compound, a quarter mile up the road.

Yellow fire trucks emerged almost immediately from an unmarked building nearby. Within minutes three of the trucks were spraying thick foam from remotely controlled nozzles on their roofs. Ten minutes later, when the Loudoun County Fire Department arrived at the scene, they were initially barred by the security guards. Loudon FD were not on the access list. The very large companies owned the clouds and they didn't think they needed the government.

35

Immigration and Customs Hall
Daxing International Airport
Beijing, China
Friday, December 5
1405 hours

Wei had done it now five times, but it always amazed and somewhat confused him. He had to think his way through it every time. He had left Vancouver at noon on Thursday and now, as he stepped off the Air Canada 787, he entered a place in space-time that was twenty-six hours ahead of the time when he had boarded the aircraft, but his watch said he had only flown eleven hours. Somehow an extra fifteen hours had taken place without him living through them. He knew the reasons, but it bothered him. Although it was Friday afternoon, for his mind and body it could have been any time of the day or night. He had slept little on the flight, despite the comfort and privacy of his business-class pod. Instead he had replayed scenes, conversations, images from his dozen days in Canada and the US.

As he had tossed for hours in the narrow lay-flat bed, he involuntarily ran mental videotapes of the flames jumping into the night at Pandry's home, flames he now knew had consumed the professor. There was the dinner in Diana's home, the frank talk with the American secret policewoman, the equally direct conversation with Rob Porter on the shore of Lake Ontario, and the feeling of always being watched, followed, tracked like an animal in the woods who could not see the hunter gaining on him, but knew he was there, closing. There was the brilliant professor in Berkeley, the amazing vistas on the helicopter flight to the redwoods, the chilling conversation with Zhu about sentience, and the look in Roger Blenheim's eyes as he spoke of a world with fewer people. Then Blenheim's helicopter lifting off from thirty floors above while he and Robbie watched, unable to stop him. And Blenheim's reference to a murder attempt in Toronto and the hazy, drunken image of that big Jeep thing that had crashed near him after his pub crawl with Diana.

In the darkened cabin, while other passengers slept, he realized the angst, the dread that hung over him stemmed not from that crash, but from the conversation with Zhu. Had somehow, from the work of Professor Pantry or some of his colleagues, a sentient AI been created, perhaps even by accident? Was AGI, artificial general intelligence, possible? He had always doubted that lines of computer code, even assisted by a quantum computer, could take on an independent life, acting without instructions, distributing itself across networks. If that was computer sentience, he still believed it could not happen. He had no doubt, however, that AI algorithms could understand connections, come to superior conclusions that no human or group of humans could achieve even with infinite time. Running on quantum computers, the algorithms could simulate endless permutations of events to determine the optimal outcome. But they still needed a human to tell them what problem to solve for, what characterized the optimum. At their lunch conversation in the redwoods, however, Zhu had disputed the need for human guidance.

Machine learning algorithms regularly engaged in unstructured learning, Zhu had noted. It was his specialty, deep learning, self-reprogramming neural networks that sifted through raw data making sense of it. Just give such an algorithm access to data or to sensors creating data and it would develop a theory about what was happening. It would then identify problems, including those that humans had not known existed. Zhu's AI program had famously identified an impending dam failure, simply by giving his algorithm access to masses of detailed weather, geological, geographic, and economic data. Thousands of lives and billions of yuan had been saved. No human had told the algorithm what to do with the data. It had decided. And it had discovered the flaws in the dam were getting critical. The dam would have burst the next time there was a tremor.

At their lunch, Zhu had confined in Wei something that had never been publicly reported in all of the media coverage of "the AI program that stopped the dam disaster." Zhu had not given the algorithm any data about the dam. It had decided that it needed such data, had tried to access it, been initially stopped by the access controls on the dam's database, then learned hacking techniques on its own and broke into the database. It had also broken into many other databases, some very sensitive, trying to satisfy what Zhu called its curiosity. Was that not sentience?

Wei realized as his mind wandered, processed, at forty thousand feet, that the Zhu experiment had moved AI and machine learning into a gray area, where what was sentient was a matter of definition. Wei wished he had studied human brain science more, but he was afraid that had he, he would come to the conclusion that Zhu was right. What software was doing may be a different approach to self-directed thought than what happened inside human heads, but the result was the same, or better.

But under what bizarre algorithmic constraints and values could any program come to the conclusion that killing Professor Pandry was a desired outcome or that his death cleared an impediment to a positive outcome? The answer to that question caused Wei to sit up straight on the lay-flat bed. He could not know how an algorithm came to that conclusion, if it did. That was the very problem with AI and ML that data scientists had been trying to solve, to get the programs to explain how they came to their conclusions. Their chain of logic was often opaque. Scientists had accepted that because the outcomes the programs proposed or created were clearly something that looked like an optimum state. But how could we know what alternatives were rejected and why? How could we know what consequences and costs, what collateral damage, the algorithm had decided would be acceptable?

In real-world applications, data scientists dealt with this kind of problem by running simulations using the AIML's proposed solution to see what else would happen if it were pursued. But if the AIML program could reach out and hack into systems on its own, if no one had written programming constraints to prevent that, or if those constraints could be evaded, then could an algorithm manipulate gas pressure to a particular house? Could an AI program decide to make a helicopter crash, and if so, how, and more importantly, why?

What data scientist would write advanced software like that without what Pandry and Blenheim had both called the Asimov controls, the meta instructions that prevented things like AI taking actions that would kill humans without human permission? Even the PLA and the Pentagon had written Asimov controls into their autonomous weapons systems; a human had to authorize killing another human, at least in peacetime. And only a few humans using multifactor identification had authority to override that meta instruction in order to move into war-fighting mode.

Alone on the flight, in his semi-private cubicle where he could not be easily seen, Wei withdrew from his backpack something he had been procrastinating on reading ever since Diana had given it to him. What he saw in the Citizen Lab report disgusted him. Over a million Uighurs had been put in "re-education camps," and those not in the camps were tracked by a system like the one he had created in Dalian to catch criminals. In fact, someone had told the Citizen Lab investigator that it was a surveillance system that had been developed in Dalian. That meant it was his. Suddenly, he felt like an idiot, a naif, used. They had been using him without his knowing it even before this case.

A ping sounded in the cabin and the lights came up. A prerecorded message said the aircraft was forty minutes from its scheduled touchdown. Wei noticed the captain going into the cockpit. AI had been flying the aircraft for the past nine hours while a junior pilot watched. It had been a very steady flight, without bumps in the night. He wondered if the captain would insist on doing the landing himself. Wei hoped he would let the AI do it. Wei's mother had always said that bumpy landings were bad luck.

There were hundreds of immigration kiosks for Chinese people in the Starfish, as the newer of the two major Beijing airports was known because of its shape. Wei preferred the Starfish, Daxing, because it was such a gleaming monument to the new China. And it had a high-speed train to downtown Beijing. Foreigners coming into the country had to speak to an officer, but citizens presented themselves at a kiosk, were identified by their face, their palm print, their iris, and their passport. There was no human in the loop. Almost everyone was automatically admitted. A few were directed to an officer to answer some questions that an AI algorithm wanted a human to ask them. Wei Bao got a green light, passed though the kiosk, and went to check his bags in for the flight that night to Dalian. Before he boarded it, however, he had to go into Beijing, to the innermost heart of the city, of the nation. He had to report back to Huang.

He had sent Huang's office a message while in San Francisco saying he would like to meet, and they had responded that he should come. He had expected to have to wait a few days in Beijing. From Vancouver, he had sent them his itinerary and they had replied with a meeting time the same day he would land. They did not provide any information about a car and driver picking him up at the airport. He had, nonetheless, expected to be met. When it was clear that there was no one waiting for him, he took the Daxing Airport Express train to the south Ring Road. It was the most beautiful subway car he had ever seen. At the Ring, he transferred to the even newer Line 19 to Ping'an Li station, where he hopped on the old Line 4 three stops to Xidan. Then he walked in the cold down Chang'an to the Xinhua Gate. It had snowed two days earlier, and the banks of shoveled snow were already pitted with the black dots from the polluted Beijing winter air.

He knew not to reach into his coat for his credentials when he was approaching the guards from Unit 61889 at the working entrance near the Xinhua Gate. Those PLA troops of the Central Security Bureau were known to have thrown many tourists to the ground just for crossing a white-striped line in front of the gate. It had been easier for Wei to deal with the PLA's spring-loaded security when he had been driven inside the staff gate in a Zhongnanhai protocol car. A block away from the staff gate, he removed his police badge and hung it on its chain dangling around his neck. The special credentials Huang had given him he held in his right hand to flash at the guards as he approached.

The badge and papers worked, and he soon discovered that they were expecting him. Of course, he realized, he might not be visible to cameras in Dalian, but in Beijing he was. They had been following him on cameras since he landed.

This time there was no beautifully coiffed hostess, no Biyu, but a junior security officer from 61889 who silently drove Wei from the gatehouse to Building 8 in a staff car. Wei sat in the front with the taciturn driver. Inside Building 8, the same young man who had escorted him two weeks before guided Wei again from the security desk up to Huang's office. If he recognized Wei, the escort did not acknowledge that they had met before, instead focusing again on his mobile phone.

Huang started this meeting sitting behind his desk in the far corner of the office. He motioned for Wei to sit in the wooden chair beside the desk. "So, Special Chief Inspector Wei Bao, you asked to report in person. What is your report?" There were no pleasantries. Huang's eyes scanned his desk, finding his Gitanes cigarette and lighting one with a wooden match. With that accomplished, he exhaled and looked directly at Wei, who involuntarily inhaled some of the cloud of pungent black tobacco.

"The fake personas, the No Shows, working in our companies are no longer," he began. "And as of last night, no new ones have been detected."

Huang stretched across the desk toward Wei. "That was not our goal. Our goal was to find the managers who put them there and make arrests, simultaneous arrests at plants across China."

"Yes, sir." Wei proceeded as he had rehearsed in his mind on the flight, and again on the Daxing Express. "My investigation revealed that plant managers were not involved in creating or profiting from the No Shows. They were created by an international group that also ran similar scams in Canada, America, and Europe. The money left China, possibly to fund the creation of WMD. Possibly for Russia or Iran."

Huang stared at him a moment. "Possibly. Possibly. Where is the money? Did you get it back?"

"Not yet, sir. But we believe that a Canadian billionaire may be involved. We think that he may be helping to steal the money, move it around so it is hard to find, and then spend it on WMD projects."

"For Pyongyang, those crazy people?"

"The Americans believe he may be fronting for Russia or Iran. I think maybe he is developing WMD on his own."

"To sell to terrorists?" Huang pressed. "The Americans? You have been talking to the Americans."

"Yes, sir, as I wrote you. The Canadian and American police were both investigating this same case, so I have tried to find out what they know to save us some time in our investigation."

Huang rose from the desk and moved quickly to the window, pulling aside a curtain and blowing smoke at the glass. "This project has not gone where I wanted it to, Wei." He spoke with his back to Wei.

Wei stood, but did not follow the old, bald man. He stood almost at attention by the desk. "Sir, I followed the facts. There are no corrupt Chinese managers involved in this major theft, sir."

"Corruption must be rooted out. To do that there must be arrests. There must be examples, punishments." Huang turned to face the young police officer. "The Americans are a failed state. They shone brightly for a brief time—a century, maybe a century and a half. It coincided with the time when China had collapsed. When we were taken advantage of by Europeans, Japanese, and the Americans. But all of that is over. We are returning to our natural position, dominating all others, under the leadership of our president. I knew you dealt with the Americans, of course. State Security reported on it to me. So you saw how culturally inferior they are, mixed ethnicities, constantly quarreling with each other, their military taking them on all sorts of crazy excursions, wasting their depleted strength, led by the daft, like Rome when the bad emperors took charge."

Wei nodded. "Yes sir, I noticed all of that."

"Now is our time, Wei. The next centuries are ours. On Earth, in space, in the oceans. Because Chinese people have discipline and they obey wise leaders' guidance." Huang began walking back to the desk. "You might still be part of it, perhaps, Wei. Maybe a position in the Party still awaits you. We will see."

"Thank you, sir." Wei knew that to be one of the ninety million Party members, fewer than one in ten people, opened career doors, granted access to better housing, made life so much easier.

"I said maybe." Sitting, he tapped the keyboard on his desktop and spoke while reading something on screen. "First, you will hand over your case to the military, to PLA. If it is not corruption, if it is mad men with WMD, it is their job. Is there imminent danger to China?"

Was there? Wei was not sure. "No, sir."

"Good. Then go back to your city and prepare the files, prepare a briefing. Come back in a week and hand it over to PLA. If they want your help, you continue. Otherwise, in a week, you go back to your old job. Understood? PLA will contact you, don't call them. They will know where you are. They know where everybody is." And then he chuckled, a laugh that would have scared children.

Wei let himself out. In the small lobby on the first floor, the PLA driver from 61889 was back. "I am to drive you to Daxing Airport now. You are to go to Dalian now." He said nothing further on the hour and a half drive through traffic to the Starfish, giving Wei the time to process what had just happened. He had been fired from the case, but he had not yet solved it. And something important, something unknown, was about to happen in the case, but he had let pass the opportunity to tell Huang that.

He could not figure out how to tell someone that exalted. He couldn't have just said that he and some Americans Canadians had a feeling that a group he did not fully understand was about to do something big that he did not fully comprehend, perhaps something intended to cull the human population by a few billion people. You cannot say things that vague to people like Huang. He had not said that perhaps software had become sentient and was directing companies to do things that might result in disaster. People like Huang did not get where they are by indulging in magical thinking or believing in science fiction. They got there by figuratively stabbing colleagues in the back. They stayed there by actually killing, or rather, having people killed. Huang would have demanded evidence, proof. And when he presented what little he had, Huang would have decided that Wei was mad. He might have sent Wei to a psychiatric clinic.

Before he could tell anybody that something big was about to happen, he needed more proof. He needed to know what that something big was. He had a week before he must meet with PLA to hand over the case, a week in which he still had the powers of a chief inspector and still had authority to investigate, to act on the No Shows conspiracy. Maybe in that time he could find out who the group was, what nation was behind it all.

Maybe he could figure out what their impending action was and how to stop it. Maybe.

36

Yiwuli Mountain Park plaza
Beizhen, Jinzhou
Liaoning Province, China
Friday, December 5
1500 hours

SOMEONE WAS SPEAKING TO the small crowd on the plaza as the sun was beginning to move behind the craggy rock mountain in the park outside of the city. Fenfang knew it was her, that she was on the small pedestal holding the microphone, saying the words she had memorized over and over again. She could see her warm breath causing small puffs in the cold afternoon air. Yet the moment was surreal enough that part of her watched herself perform as though viewing a movie. Dr. Yang Fenfang forced all of her consciousness into reality, into this moment. She tried to summon up the passion she knew was there, to convey to the small gathering the importance of the man and the moment.

"They say we must all do what we are told, that we must believe what the supposed authorities tell us even when we know it is a lie. Doctor Li knew it was a lie. He knew that there was a SARS-like virus spreading rapidly through Wuhan and that there was a narrow window of time in which it could be contained."

The strength of her conviction was taking over now. "But that would mean canceling the Party meeting in Beijing. It would require us to forgo Chinese New Year celebrations and travel. It would hurt the economy. So Doctor Li was taken away for the crime of posting the truth online. He was put in jail and silenced so the lie could live for another week."

She could not look down at his widow, daughter, and son. If she had, she would have dissolved. She needed to be strong. "We all demanded his release, and it came. And when it did, Doctor Li went into the hospital to save those dying from the disease. He was an ophthalmologist. He could have stayed away, but he believed in his duty as a physician, in his duty to heal the sick.

"And like so many other doctors and nurses, he contracted a heavy virus load and died in service of his patients. The Party, which had him jailed; the Party, which had hidden the truth at the crucial moment when containment might have been achieved; the Party who officially made him a martyr. Yes, it did. It was the Party that made him a martyr. Their action and their inaction killed him and thousands of other Chinese people, as well as many more around the world."

She scanned the periphery of the plaza for secret police. She saw the cameras and thought of Wei Bao. Would he understand? "So this bust of Li Wenliang is a monument to a martyr of the Party. It is also more than that. It is a reminder to us all of the importance of truth, of knowing it, of speaking it, of speaking it even to the powerful who do not want to hear it. The Christians have a hero named John. They call him a saint. In his book he wrote two thousand years ago, 'Know the truth. And the truth will set you free.'"

As she said the words from the Bible, she raised both of her arms, as if signaling the flight to heaven of Li Wenliang's spirit. There was a soft round of applause, gloved hands clapping briefly, as Fenfang stepped down and went to comfort Fu Xuejie and her children, while the covering was pulled off the bust atop the two-meter-high concrete pedestal. Another wave of applause followed.

Despite her attempts at secrecy, the Ministry of State Security had learned of the planned memorial service and unveiling. It was their role, and not that of the provincial police to which Wei Bao belonged, to suppress such dissident activity. They had known when the meeting would occur, but not where or who all of the participants might be. Then, Friday afternoon, an anonymous source had given them a list of those who would be attending the illegal meeting, a list that included their mobile phone numbers.

Fearing that there would be sympathizers in the provincial police, the State Security team had not coordinated with the Ministry of Public

Safety. They had, however, commandeered two prisoner transport trucks from the provincial police station in central Jinzhou city. The State Security officers were also using access to the Liaoning Province police surveillance network, the system Wei Bao had created, to geolocate the twenty-two suspects' phones.

The State Security convoy—two unmarked cars, two small buses of Ministry officers in civilian clothes, and the police prisoner vans—moved quickly and quietly down National Road, then onto South Ring Road. The vehicles stopped in the middle of the street and the officers ran from the buses and set up a perimeter around the inner-city park to prevent anyone from escaping when the illegal meeting ended.

On a command heard in their earpieces, the arrest team moved in unison to tighten the circle from the perimeter of the park to the inner plaza area. They all barked the same words at the small group in the plaza. "State Security. On the ground now. Sit! Sit with your hands behind your back." The two dozen members of the Beizhen Wushu Sanda club assumed it was a surprise training drill and responded accordingly, with a series of quick kicks, followed by punches to the heads of the men in civilian clothes who approached them, looking like some sort of team.

In the melee, most of the State Security team were thrown to the ground, their handcuffs skidding across the paving stones. When the Arrest Team Leader withdrew a handgun and fired into the air three times, the Beizhen Wushu Sanda kickboxing club members came to a halt and stood at attention awaiting words of commendation for their highly proficient response to the drill.

It took almost ten minutes before the Arrest Team Leader fully understood that the Ministry had been misled. The mobile phones they had been given by the source were those of an amateur self-defense fighting club. State Security had learned about a planned memorial unveiling on December 5 in Beizhou. But if it wasn't in this park, where was it? Somebody had set up his arrest team to be beaten up. They would pay.

Sitting in his car, tapping on a secure laptop, the Team Leader queried the national identity database with the names on the list from the unknown source. Earlier, the database had said they were doctors. Now, it said they were teachers from local schools, gymnastics and judo teachers.

The arrest team, many with their clothing ripped and their faces bloodied, escorted the Sanda fighting club members, in handcuffs, past the Team Lead's car to the police vans. They might not be dissident doctors, but they had assaulted State Security officers and would be charged with that serious crime.

Six kilometers to the west, a BMW pulled out of the Yiwulü Mountain National Forest Park. It would normally take almost four hours to drive down to the tip of the peninsula to Dalian Harbor, but, like most policemen, it was in Yao's nature to drive aggressively. He never worried about speed camera tickets in Dalian, but especially on this drive, he had little fear. The cameras in the entire province had been reprogrammed. They would not see the BMW. With Fenfang sound asleep in the back seat, there was also no chance that he would scare his passenger with his speeding. Nervous exhaustion was his diagnosis of the doctor.

It was just over three hours after climbing into the BMW that Dr. Yang Fenfang emerged and boarded a boat at a slip in Dalian. The police camera system had recorded her, or her avatar, entering her apartment building two hours earlier, giving her an alibi.

"Thank you, little sister," Fenfang said as she embraced Chunhua in the cabin of the twins' boat.

37

Financial Crime Enforcement Network (FinCEN)
US Department of the Treasury
2070 Chain Bridge Road
Tysons Corner, Virginia
Friday, December 5
0800 hours

"It looks like a giant diaphragm," Sarah Keogh said before David Bernstein could say good morning. She had been up most of the night handling the fallout from the NEST helicopter crash, which had happened only twenty miles from where she now stood.

"I'm sorry, what looks like what?" Bernstein was dressed as if he were still the rush chairman at ZBT. He also looked about the right age for that job. Instead, he was the deputy director of the Special Investigations Branch of the US Treasury's bureau designed to "follow the money," the illicit funds being used by terrorists, cached by drug lords, laundered by corrupt government officials from Russia, China, Nigeria, everywhere.

"Your building, that big arch thing," she said, pointing at an omega-shaped architectural flourish that made the otherwise drab office building seem somehow out of place with the sprawling Chevrolet dealer that seemed to surround it. "It looks like an old birth control device, but you're too young to know about that, honey. Sorry to embarrass you."

"I'm thirty-four, Special Agent Keogh, and what I do know about is artificial intelligence, machine learning, and dirty money. I have a PhD in computer science from Virginia Tech and have cracked dozens of cases in the three years I have been with FinCEN." He said it in a way that suggested he had to recite that litany often.

"Oh, dear, I've upset you. Now, I am sorry," Keogh chatted in an uncharacteristically fast Southern drawl as they walked through the lobby to the elevator bank. "But here I am just because you called." Bernstein looked into a camera in the elevator and then tapped a reader with his ID card, sending them up to the fifth floor. "But, really, David, this better be good because I had to leave my husband alone with his nieces and nephews. He's really not great with children, just with legal memos."

"Oh, it's good," Bernstein reassured her as they walked through security to the FinCEN operations center. It could have been NASA's manned space flight center, darkened but for the glow from rows of workstations and three movie-theater-sized screens.

"Show me, and remember I didn't get a PhD in computer science." Sarah Keogh settled into a black leather chair on a raised dais at the back of the operations center, as Bernstein stood next to her and tapped into a keyboard that caused the large main screen at the front to come alive.

"Our best sources of information are SARs—suspicious activity reports, not the virus. Banks have to file them with us whenever they see something that is a little out of the normal pattern of transactions. We live and breathe SARs. We get tens of thousands of them a week. We broke the three million a year mark last year. And that's just in the US. Canada, England, Australia, most major countries do the same things, and we can share some data with each other."

The briefing screen showed a graphic of green arrows leading into the United States from Panama, the Cayman Islands, Cyprus, Dubai, and a dozen other locations. The US states of Delaware and Nevada were labeled and filled in with red.

"Normally, what we see is money entering the US from No Tell Banking locations around the world, being used to buy overpriced real estate. Trump, for example, made millions selling condos to Russian intelligence and oligarchs and others trying to launder their ill-gotten money. Then the Russians wait a year and flip the property, maybe even at a loss, but what they get back is clean US money from the new buyers. That money they invest, usually in safe bonds or stocks."

"Why not just buy the stocks and bonds in the first place?" Keogh asked.

"Because of our KYC laws on banks and stock brokers."

"Kentucky Fried Chicken?"

"That would be KFC. KYC is Know Your Customer, meaning know that they are not crooks stashing hot money. There is no such requirement for real estate purchases, so the Russians deposit money from their Cyprus bank into a Trump account in the Caymans and he hands them the keys. Then Trump moves money from one Trump account, in the Caymans, to another Trump account, this time in New York. The transfer is noted as real estate sales proceeds. No suspicions raised, no SARs filed. Then the Russians sell the American property, maybe at a loss, but they get clean dollars."

"I get that our former president was dirty and run by the Russians. God knows he had it out for the FBI because we were on to him, but what does that have to do with our case, David?"

Bernstein tapped again at the keyboard, and another slide appeared on the big board, this one showing green arrows flowing out of New York to many of the same locations depicted on the first chart. "I wanted you to know what our base case looks like so you will understand why this looks very different to us.

"We took the names of the people receiving money in the payroll fraud case from Boeing and the other US companies. We followed their money. It usually bounced from a checking account set up with ADP or some payroll processing firm to do direct deposit out to another bank, then another, then overseas to one of those money-laundering havens. This is backward flow from the ordinary. It's money leaving the US. That's when it leaves our visibility, but not NSA's."

Bernstein introduced a gray-haired woman with half glasses dangling around her neck on a chain. She shook hands and sat to Keogh's left. "This is Michelle Rogers, the NSA liaison here at FinCEN."

Rogers activated a small desktop screen, which she tilted toward Keogh. The screen read Top Secret/SCI/Handle Via COMINT Channels Only. The next screen that she popped up was entitled Inbound Suspicious Transaction Funds into the Cypriot Star Bank.

"Using our foreign intelligence authorities, we at the National Security Agency can and do follow international money movements in foreign banks if those transactions raise national security concerns. FinCEN—David, to be specific—asked us to follow these funds from your nonexistent, fake Americans. Basically, we hack foreign banks. Legally, we can't move the money around, but we can follow it. We can do that in this case because they are not really US citizens and Treasury here had raised a concern that a foreign power is stealing money from US companies to fund activities that could threaten our national security."

"I would consider their building weapons of mass destruction a threat to our national security," Keogh deadpanned.

"Yes, so you see here that funds come from a variety of different US banks but end up in this account in Cyprus, usually within three days of payrolls being paid every two weeks or every month at the defrauded US companies. There are other banks in other countries that also serve as the first overseas hop, but let's use this Cypriot bank as an example.

"From Cyprus, the funds flow to about twenty other banks in as many countries. From there, they do it again." Rogers' charts showed a growing spider's web of banks and countries in increasingly smaller font size. "But then they flow back into US banks' overseas branches in very small dollar transactions, anywhere from one thousand dollars to eighty-five hundred. Nothing bigger. Nothing that would trigger a SAR, which is usually anything over ten thousand or something hiding just under that reporting requirement level. But as you can see, there is a huge volume of these transfers every day, usually from one of many US banks' overseas offices into accounts in the banks' main New York operations. That's when we hand the case, or should I say the chase, back to FinCEN."

Bernstein stood back up and punched up another slide on the big board. "Here is where our AI comes into play. We did an unstructured data review of the recipient bank accounts in the US. Money flows from them to a variety of credit cards, wire transfers, but after several hops around the US, it all comes together in the various bank accounts of two entities."

As Bernstein spoke, the screen showed arrows appearing and connecting boxes that kept popping up, hundreds of small boxes, and then the arrows all simultaneously seemed to attack two large boxes. One was labeled The Turing Institution. The other was the Sagan League.

"Turing and Sagan are both 501c3s, not-for-profit, tax exempt entities. So we can pull their IRS report without search warrants. Turns out they are both very well-funded by lots of small donations, a lot directly from overseas and a lot from this illicit cash flow from US bank accounts. They both have a variety of related entities, but if you add up all of their income every year for the last two, it's billions."

She looked back at David Bernstein. "So then, who runs them? And what do they do with the money?"

"We just started looking at them yesterday, but from what we can see they are run by famous scientists, academics. Living ones. They donate about five percent of their invested income to a variety of other NGOs, ones that clean the ocean of plastics, ones that teach kids about space, run planetariums, set up coding camps in inner cities," Bernstein spoke, looking down at his notes in the dim light of the operations center.

"What about the other ninety-five percent. Where does that go?"

"Under the law, they can invest ninety-five percent of their funds, and that's what they do. Looks like it goes to venture capital firms, private equity firms, the usual."

"Billions of dollars?" Keogh asked, as though she doubted that were possible.

"Yes, most of it going to a few private equity firms, looks like." Bernstein consulted papers he had in both hands. "I just got some of this stuff this morning."

Sarah Keogh put a hand on Bernstein's arm and spoke softly. "David, darling, I know you just got the data, and I appreciate your telling me about it. Your country will appreciate all of your hard work. When this is all over, if we get there in time, you will likely get a medal, or whatever Treasury gives its stars, a plaque surely, but all of this just begs the question. What do the vulture capitalist and private inequities do with the money?"

Bernstein rolled his chair back from Keogh. "Invest it," he whispered.

Keogh's voice rose. "Well, no shit, Davey, but in what? Russian front companies in the US? False flag shells evading US sanctions and export controls on WMD precursors? With all of your fancy, unstructured data bots running around, don't you know?"

David Bernstein stood and backed farther away from Special Agent Keogh. "We are not allowed to examine the records of private equity firms without a regulatory basis or, if we can prove probable cause of a crime, a court order."

Sarah Keogh's bellow could have been heard in the Chevrolet dealership up the block. "Sweet baby Jesus, I am going to die buried in fucking search warrants!"

38

The Attorney General's Conference Room
Robert F. Kennedy Building (Main Justice)
Constitution Avenue NW
Washington, DC
Friday, December 5
1300 hours

"The Medicis would have felt at home here," FBI Assistant Director Dallas Miller grunted as he and his deputy, Sarah Keogh, walked into the foyer outside the attorney general's conference room. "Reminds me of Vegas, Caesars Palace, all this WPA art trying to make a 1920s office building look like some sort of Roman temple."

"My, my. I haven't seen so many scantily clad people since I had that case in South Beach. To think the government paid artists to paint like this during the Depression," she replied. "Never say the government can't be creative."

Jeremy Hunter, their minder from the director's office, was already there, waiting. "There's also a mural about the FBI Laboratory, depicting the actual men who established it. They are all fully clothed."

"That must have been painted before we learned how the lab phonied up results," Dallas Miller shot back.

"That's all been remedied, as you know, of course," Hunter almost mumbled.

Miller turned his back on the director's special assistant and spoke to Keogh. "I am here to show the flag, personally endorse your requests, but I can't tell this story as well as you can, so you carry the ball. She will probably turn to us at the top of the meeting. Say what you know, what you think, and then get right to what you need. No Southern charm. Be direct."

Keogh smiled down at her shorter boss. "Dallas, hon, you know I can be both charming and direct, simultaneously."

The room they were ushered into would not have been out of place in the Vatican, the Hofburg, or Windsor. From the elaborate inlaid designs in the highly polished wood flooring to the soaring arched ceiling forty feet above, topped off by great lunette murals of Justice Triumphant and Justice Defeated, the overall effect was to give a semi-divine status to the person who sat in the throne at the head of the immense wooden table, Attorney General of the United States Deborah McDaniels. She had marched into the room carrying an armful of files and trailed by a small army of aides, in such a determined manner that she would have terrified the most prestigious of Wall Street legal teams.

"Dallas, where's the director?" she began.

Dallas Miller was in his most deferential mode. "Madame Attorney General, regrettably, my boss is in London for an annual Five Eyes Conference."

"He wishes he could be here for this," Jeremy Hunter added.

"I'll bet he doesn't." McDaniels glared at Hunter. "Dallas, I have been dealing with a firestorm from the Secretary of Energy. He wants to know why the FBI sent four of his NEST guys flying low out near Dulles, only to have them and their chopper apparently shot out of the sky over the Greenway and burned to a crisp. What the hell is going on, and why don't I know?"

"Madam Attorney General, this is a major national security case, but one that is still developing in real time. Deputy Assistant Director Keogh has been leading our efforts. Sarah?"

Sarah Keogh put down her legal pad, her presentation notes. The AG had a rule against PowerPoint briefings. "General McDaniels, this case started out as what we thought was a massive cybercrime, involving what we initially thought was the theft of hundreds of millions of dollars from large enterprise payroll systems. The Bureau codenamed it PayBot and, with respect, your office was copied on six memos describing and giving the status of the case."

Keogh slipped a folder with the six memos down to the head of the table. The AG turned to look behind her at her assistants, one of whom gave the "I know noting" shrug, which drew a fiery stare. The folder lay unopened at the end of the table.

"Boeing discovered the anomaly when it was doing a reduction in force. The bot didn't see the firing coming. If it had it would have eliminated all traces of the fake people who were being paid. But Boeing kept all the plans out of band, in a virtual, closed-loop network on Azure. So, when Boeing went to fire some people, they realized that some of the employees didn't really exist."

"Wait, wait, wait," McDaniels interrupted. "I didn't follow all that tech talk, and I don't need to, but did you say some bot would have done these things? You mean, like an artificial intelligence?"

"Precisely," Keogh replied enthusiastically. "Our experts and the Pentagon's agreed that it would take more than just really good AI, it would have to be running on a massive supercomputer that was always on and had machine learning algorithms that could automatically collect information by hacking, and adapt to make it look like these fake people on the payrolls were real. They had an ever-changing pattern of life. Only one type of computer could do that."

"Pray tell in what city in China does it reside," McDaniels asked, as she signaled for someone to pour her some coffee.

"Toronto. That's where they were made by a university professor there. Then he made at least three more, which are now near MIT, Berkeley, and Caltech. We concluded it must be Iran, North Korea, or Russia that hacked into one of the machines or had an insider because that amount of money would show up somewhere unless it were going into some big project in a heavily sanctioned country, like a WMD development project."

An assistant attorney general sitting opposite Keogh coughed, almost spitting out his coffee. "The PayBot case is about a rogue nation making WMD?"

"Yes, we think so, but the professor was murdered and many of his files destroyed. But the people he gave his quantum computers to are experts in nuclear weapons and satellites. They are tied into an eccentric Canadian billionaire who wants to reduce the Earth's population, significantly."

Keogh paused to look at her script, but no one interrupted with a question or a comment. She could hear the HVAC system blowing warm air into the cavernous conference room. Her audience was wide-eyed and eagerly waiting for the next episode in her story.

"They have a series of front companies and have been secretly making things. And they have built highly secure campuses near New York City—Hoboken, actually—south of San Francisco, and outside Washington. The NEST helicopter was about to fly over the one near Dulles in Ashburn."

McDaniels looked ashen. "Fly over it to detect a nuclear weapon?"

"That's one possibility we want to explore. They shipped large objects into these supposed 'data centers,' but there is no data flowing in or out. We would have gone in the front door, but we have been unable to get a search warrant or a FISA court order."

Again, McDaniels turned around to look quizzically at her staff. This time no one shrugged. They were all looking down at their notepads and laptops.

"But we did get a warrant to go into a facility of theirs outside Phoenix. We now have the videotape from the next-door airport's security system. This version is edited to compress the time." Keogh stood, walked down to the head of the table, and placed a large laptop in front of the AG. It had a video player on screen. Keogh hit play. "They told us they had made only one satellite. As you will see, that was a 1011 violation, lying to the FBI."

The video showed large cargo aircraft pulling up to an apron by the fence line of the airport, trucks rolling through a gate in the fence, and objects shrouded in white plastic being carefully placed on the planes. Then the video showed the aircraft taking off. The video feed shifted to cameras labeled QSat/SCD. On screen was Sarah Keogh and a team of FBI agents, pulling up in front of a building, barging in, serving a warrant, searching a long-empty warehouse area.

"I assume from all of that that you were a little late. Where did the planes go?" McDaniels asked.

"Their flight plans with the FAA said Cape Canaveral, but nine of them went overseas to commercial space launch facilities. One went to a privately owned launch site in middle-of-nowhere Texas."

McDaniels got up from the table, walked slowly in a circle with her hands on her hips, and ended up facing the much taller Sarah Keogh.

"Cut to the chase, Sarah. What does your agent's intuition and years of experience tell you is going on, in simple English."

Keogh looked to Dallas Miller, who gave her a nod. "We think, but cannot prove, that a nation-state has somehow co-opted a bunch of scientists in the US and Canada along with some mad Canadian billionaire to steal billions and use that money to develop nukes, and that they may have put these nukes near major US cities and may be about to put more in orbit. They could then compel the US to pull out of the Middle East, assuming it's Iran that's doing it, or withdraw from South Korea, if it's the North. Nuclear blackmail. Or possibly nuclear detonations to cull the Earth's population significantly. They seem to all share a desire for fewer people in the world."

The two women stood silently staring into each other's eyes. Main Justice's Sistine Chapel was still. The AG whispered, "How much time do we have?"

"I don't know."

McDaniels gently tapped Keogh's arm. "Please, Sarah, sit down. We owe you a great debt of gratitude, right or wrong, for pushing on this case." The AG was still for a moment. "DoJ spent a lot of time arguing over FISA warrants before 9/11. Bush waited until after the explosions to go after al-Qaeda. If there is any chance, any chance…"

The AG sat and then ticked off decisions on the fingers of her left hand. "Dallas, prepare the Hostage Rescue Team to hit the Dulles facility. At the exact same time, we need the NYPD's team to go across the river under FBI authority and hit the one in Hoboken. Get the West Coast SEALS to hit the Berkeley site, Delta on the US launch site. I'll call SECDEF from the car. He can also coordinate with our allies on the other launch sites."

"Yes, m'aam."

"Blair?" she said, looking for her staff aide. "Call the National Security Advisor's office and tell her I am in the car on the way over and I have the siren on. Tell her she and I are going to barge in on the president when I get there and I don't give a shit what she has going on in the Oval."

Jeremy Hunter interrupted the AG's flow. "You will have to get the president's permission to waive Posse Comitatus in order to use the military inside the US."

The AG looked sharply at Dallas Miller. "Who the fuck is this twit?" She stormed out of the chamber. In the commotion of chairs being pushed back from the table, no one noticed Sarah Keogh looking up at the frescos and mouthing, "Thank you, Jesus."

39

ReGlobal Audit
Dalian
Saturday, December 6
0945 hours

He had wanted it to be a surprise. It turned out to be a disappointment. Had he told Fenfang about his return, she would have decorated the apartment and cooked a special meal, and halfway through it they would likely have been overcome with desire and run off into the bedroom. None of that had happened.

He had been unsure that he would be able to accomplish everything he had to do in Beijing on Friday afternoon, and he did not want Fenfang disappointed if he was unable to show up when he said he would. So he hadn't told her he was coming and when he arrived home just before midnight, the apartment was empty. He had texted Chunhua, asking her to check the system for Fenfang's location. Her terse response was, "I am with her. We are safe."

Exhausted from the flight from Canada, the meeting in Beijing, and the night flight to Dalian, Chunhua's text was enough for him. Fenfang was safe. Wei Bao had collapsed on his bed, fully clothed, and slept eight hours without moving. When he did rouse, he struggled to clear his head fog and create an agenda for himself, and then for his team.

He checked his texts. Yao had sent him an encrypted message urging him to take an evasive route to the ReGlobal office. Bohai would be following him on the camera system and would alert him if he were being followed. The text fit with Wei Bao's already apprehensive mood.

When Wei did arrive at his clandestine office space, Yao wasted no time with pleasantries or pastries. "We have a State Security problem, boss. Actually, we have three."

"All big ones," Bohai added.

Both Yao and Bohai seemed frightened, something Wei had not seen in either man before. Wei dangled his head between his knees. "Tell me, without the sugar frosting."

"State Security has been trying to follow you because they think you are investigating their corruption, the money they steal and send out of the country for the retirement abroad of special people in State Security." Yao paused to let that sink in with Wei. "Some police are in on it too, like our own Chief Inspector Wang. He has it out for you. State Security thinks they recruited me to spy on you. I have fed them false reports, but they think you killed one of their guys who was tailing you in Toronto."

Wei looked up. "Corruption must be weeded out. But I wasn't after State Security. Or Wang. And I didn't kill anyone in Canada. That's nonsense."

"No, boss, but somebody did kill a Chinese guy," Bohai insisted. "We saw the video afterward. A car was going to run you down, but these two guys stepped out of nowhere and one of them shot at the driver and missed. Then he drug him out of the truck and snapped his neck."

Wei had a sick feeling that he had missed something big because he had been drunk, badly drunk.

Yao pressed on. "State Security will soon figure out that Fenfang was behind an illegal meeting in Beizhen to erect a monument to Dr. Li Wenliang. Some State Security people may have gotten roughed up when they raided a kickboxing meeting thinking it was the doctors unveiling the monument."

Suppressing a chuckle, Wei looked at Bohai. "That sounds like a trick you would do."

"We all did it," Yao replied. "Chunhua has Fenfang on the boat and is going to bring her here. Number three problem is complicated, but also bad. You tell him."

Bohai looked pained, but after a moment he confessed, "I, we, hacked into State Security networks to work on the case. I think we maybe got caught. I just discovered they have an Israeli threat-hunting algorithm, machine learning, that is very stealthy. Right now they have a big project to figure out who was inside their system. They think CIA, but one report mentioned you connected to CIA and you having hacking skills. They think you hacked them looking for proof of corruption."

"Are we still in their system?" Wei asked.

"Yes, boss. You want me to get out?"

Wei looked at Yao, who shook his head. "No. We need to know what they know. And when they are going to move on us. And we need proof of their corruption."

"Okay," Wei agreed. "I was going to tell you about the case. While all of what you just said is important, to us at least, we have a bigger problem: the No Show case. The Americans and the Canadians still think it's Moscow, Tehran, or even Pyongyang behind it, tricking Professor Pandry's companies to develop technologies that they can use for WMD. I think they're wrong. I think the AI on Professor Pandry's machines became sentient. I think it linked all of his machines together, raised money for projects at the companies, and modified the projects, maybe with the help of a Canadian billionaire. Pandry must have figured it out, and the sentience killed him."

Yao was growing impatient. He was loud. "Boss, the case doesn't matter anymore. We have to save ourselves."

"No, it does matter. I think that the AI and that Blenheim guy want to reduce the Earth's population with some sort of WMD that the AI developed, and I think he's about to do it. I have to prove it well enough to go back to Beijing and get the government to act, maybe even with the Americans."

"None of that matters if we're all in jail," Bohai yelled.

Wei Bao felt torn. He had been living and breathing the case for weeks. Maybe the Americans would deal with it. Maybe it was too late. And he could almost smell the fear on Bohai and Yao. He had put Yao, the twins, and Fenfang at risk. And he had to eliminate that risk before he worried about the rest of the world. "Okay. What do you suggest I do?"

"Do you know a guy from Beijing, a Professor Zhu?" Yao replied.

"Of course, he is one of the AIML Masters. He's the father of AI and ML in China. I met him in California."

"You trust him?"

"I think so, why?"

Bohai answered for Yao. "Good, because I told him he could come here. He said he could save you. Us."

Before Wei could erupt at Bohai for compromising their location, the elevator door opened, and Fenfang was running across the office space to Wei. "You're back, you're back. Thank you, thank you for sending this angel to save me." Chunhua walked slowly behind Fenfang.

"State Security hasn't figured it all out yet," Chunhua spoke to the group. "Any cameras in this province that see Fenfang's face, they store another face, a fake face. And they didn't get a video of the real unveiling of the Dr. Li statute, they got a deep fake video of a different park. But they have informers too, and those creeps will give up her name. Then they will come for her, if they can find her. They're pissed off we made their Arrest Team look like jerks, get beaten up."

Wei was still hugging his fiancé. Yao turned to him. "So, you murdered a State Security officer in Toronto, they think. Dr. Yang unveiled a statue without permission, made a treasonous speech, and made State Security look like idiots."

"They are idiots," Bohai added.

"Maybe, but they also are soon going to figure out that we hacked their network, which is an act of espionage punishable by death in this country. Yeah, they don't have good evidence, but they don't need it." Yao was emphatic. "They will lock you all up, and you will never come out, except for the trial, which will take an hour before you're found guilty."

Wei ended his embrace of Fenfang. "I—I don't know what we can do. I could go back to Beijing and explain to..."

Yao wrapped his arms around Wei and Fenfang. "Now you see why we invited Professor Zhu? We need help, and he said he would provide it. And, Bao, Zhu knew where we were. He knew about this place. He also knew all about what State Security was doing, zeroing in on us."

"When do you think State Security will come for us?"

"Not yet," Bohai answered for Yao. "It doesn't look like they have figured out yet that you are back in the country because I erased your immigration entry data, messed with the AI State Security uses to check people's locations. You never appear anywhere. Right now, they think you are still in the US. And nobody knows yet that we hang out here at ReGlobal."

"Nobody but Professor Zhu," Wei replied.

Professor Zhu arrived Sunday at 1300. He was not alone.

Diana McPherson was with him. She stood silently behind Zhu. The tall, thin, distinguished professor was courteous, but direct. "Wei Bao, I am sorry for what has happened. Diana and I apologize that we had to mislead you, but we are here not just to apologize, but to compensate for our deceit, necessary as it was at the time, by offering you and your family here, your team, a way to evade State Security."

"What do you know about State Security, sir, and how?" Wei asked in a brusque tone.

"Your team is not the only group that is inside MSS, watching what they do. Our security team has been protecting you in Canada and the US, but they cannot operate here. The Q-Compute machine learning network is providing you safety by altering State Security's files, but it can't protect you here forever. And, in all honesty, we also need you to help us."

"But, Professor, if the machine learning program Dr. Pandry developed has become sentient, as you suggested..."

Zhu hung his head for a minute in embarrassment. "Wei Bao, that was a lie. It was one of the ways we tried to distract and mislead the investigations, yours, the Americans. We run the Q-Compute network, we, the AIML Masters. Sentient computer software is a fairy tale. It may never happen. Certainly not for many decades."

Wei's eyes darted to Diana, looking for her to explain herself. "Wei, it's not what you think. Ramesh had pledged us all to secrecy until the network could execute the final stage of his program. We didn't even know until yesterday that he had killed himself."

"What? And how do you know now?"

"As the program moved into the final stage yesterday, it played a video Ramesh had taped for us. He had hidden his stage four pancreatic cancer from us. Even he hadn't known about it until October, when it was too late. When he learned you and the Canadians were coming to interrogate him, he assumed you had somehow figured out his plan or would shortly.

His death was meant to throw you off and to destroy evidence. It wasn't murder, it was suicide."

Wei's mind raced, trying to think of all of the deceptions Diana had played on him. He tried to reassemble the puzzle pieces and to figure out what Zhu was telling him.

"Diana, there were so many lies. All that acting. Why couldn't you tell me what you were doing? Why couldn't you trust me?"

"Bao bao, I wanted to, but the AIML Masters didn't know you. They didn't trust you. We make all of our decisions as a team. To them you were the Chinese government, chosen by the highest levels in Beijing to investigate us. The Chinese government that is still building coal-fired plants. The Chinese government that is engaged in apartheid with the Uighurs, and Bao, doing it with your surveillance system."

Professor Zhu intervened. "But, Bao, when we saw what State Security was doing, trying to kill you in Toronto, planning to arrest you and your team here in Dalian, it was Diana who said we had to risk it, we had to come to Dalian in person to convince you and to get you all out, to safety. It was Blenheim security that saved you in Toronto, but it is Diana who is saving you now, if you will let her, let us. The AIML Masters.

"It was us. Not Russia, or Iran, or North Korea. It was us. We stole the money. We created the fake personas and maintained them, until you and the Americans uncovered them and were getting too close. But by then we had enough money anyway. The Qmpanies had completed their research, their production. We are now in the final steps." Zhu saw the whiteboard on the far wall and moved to it. "Let me explain what it entails and why we need your help as much as you now need ours."

"The culling of the human species by nuclear war?" Wei asked. "I will have nothing to do with that! If that's what you're doing, we will stop you." Wei almost spat out the words.

"No, that is not what this is all about." said Zhu, picking up a marker to begin his lecture. "And you will not stop us, you will join us."

Zhu then conducted a seminar for two and a half hours, trying to explain advanced physics, revealing all that he and Pandry and the AIML Masters had been doing, and why. When it was over, Wei asked if they could take a break, if he and Fenfang could take a walk outside and discuss what Zhu had said at the end, the offer.

"Will all of that really work?' Fenfang asked Wei as they walked along the docks.

"I don't know. I know nothing about those things, but look what they have done so far with the Q-Computes. These are not just better computers, Fen. They are doors into a new world, a world where unsolvable problems can be solved."

Dr. Yang Fenfang looked out over the water, not saying what she thought. Then, she seemed to have decided. "I just want for us to be safe. And together. I will go with you anywhere. I loved Canada. I never wanted us to leave." She squeezed his hand. "I am just so sorry if it was what I did that is causing all of this, what I did for Doctor Li's memory."

Wei stopped walking and pulled Fenfang to him. "It's not what you did. It's what we both did, and my team. But everything we all did was what we should have done. We all did the right things. Sometimes you pay a price for doing the right thing, but if we do what Zhu is offering, we may survive." They embraced tightly for a long moment.

"But, Bao bao, Yao is such a great guy. He saved me up in Jinzhou. What will happen to him and his family, his children?"

"Yao is a hero. He taught me so much. I think he knew something like this could happen. He has a plan. He bought insurance."

"Chunhua? And her crazy brother?"

"Oh, I need them. If we go, we go together. If we work for Zhu and the others, we will need what the twins can do. What Zhu wants us to do is the most important thing that we could do with our lives, not just for us, but for China, for Canada, for our kids, yours and mine someday soon."

"Then let's go, now, before they come for us."

40

W Hotel
Pier C Park
Hoboken, New Jersey
Sunday, December 7
0430 hours

"Few people are really beautiful when they're asleep," Dallas Miller observed. "But Manhattan is. Look at it."

The assistant director of the FBI sat with Sarah Keogh in the forward command post that the New York FBI office had quickly thrown together in the rooftop conference room in the riverside hotel a mile south of the QData facility. What its residents humbly called the greatest city in the world sat sparkling before dawn, its towers illuminated despite the hour. To the left they could see the outlines of their target up the river, near the New Jersey entrance to the Lincoln Tunnel.

Their plan was to hit the facility with a raid team at 0600, when other teams would be moving in on QData facilities in Ashburn, Virginia, and Sunnyvale, California. The Army would land by helicopter on the private space launch center in Texas where they had confirmed that a missile was being readied for launch shortly after dawn.

Keogh was struggling to stay awake. "You realize your surprise attack is coming on Pearl Harbor Day? Just saying." He glared back at her. "So, you really talked to Space Force?" Keogh asked him. "That's really a thing? Not Steve Carrell."

"Oh yeah. They track all the satellites that are up there, thousands of them. And they got a couple of secret space fighter plane-like things that they are going to use to deal with any of the satellites that get launched before we can get somebody to stop them."

"There's a lot of the CubeSats they got ready to launch from all over," Keogh said, reaching for her iPad. "We got lucky finding a file they hadn't encrypted at the QSat site in Scottsdale." She read from the list of launch facilities where the QAviation aircraft had taken the satellites before she and her team had raided the place. "Brazil, French Guyana, India, Kazakhstan, UAE, South Africa, Taiwan. We're never going to..."

Something had happened, silently. She looked up from her screen. The lights in the room had gone out, but looking out of the large rooftop windows, so had Manhattan. She could make out what had been sparkling towers now appearing as ghosts in shadows.

Minutes before, a machine learning program that had been quietly sitting on the ConEd grid control had activated, switching from learning mode to operational. In seconds, it had shut off the intrusion detection system on the network and taken over the situational awareness screens in the command center. The screens would continue to show that all systems were functioning normally, as other malicious programs simultaneously started up on the controls of massive generators all around the region, causing them to malfunction, spinning in ways that the manufacturers' software was designed to prevent, running at speeds that caused them to self-destruct when reconnected to the grid. Breakers were popping across the metropolitan area, beginning a cascading failure running up into New England and south to Virginia.

Meanwhile the SCADA controls showed everything was fine, even as the control center itself automatically shifted over to a backup generator. It would take the score of affected power distribution companies six or eight hours to drive to all of the transformer and substation sites to manually reset the breakers. There would, however, be no resetting the generators. They were physically destroyed by the off-cycle spinning. It would take more than a year to build and install new ones. In the interim, much of the New York metropolitan area could be without electricity.

In Silicon Valley, at the same moment, generators belonging to the ill-fated PG&E had also self-destructed, plunging much of the San Francisco to San Jose corridor into the dark shortly after one thirty in the morning. In Virginia, Dominion Energy was the target, with its network throwing greater Washington, Richmond, and Norfolk into darkness. In all three regions, some small backup generators at key facilities kicked on. Many just sputtered.

41

Blenheim Industries offices
KPZ Technology Park
Incheon, Republic of Korea
Sunday, December 7
2330 hours

Using Wei's police credentials and assisted by messages they had inserted into the immigration and the air traffic control networks, they had no problem in their departure. Indeed, they had driven on the tarmac directly up to the waiting aircraft. The QAviation 737 MAX had flown them from Dalian to Incheon in an hour, and they were in one of the Qmpanies covert operations centers by 1400.

The aircraft had cleared Chinese airspace and appeared on flight tracking radar to be headed south when in fact it was moving east. Yao Guang, still in ReGlobal, texted Peng, his handler for State Security. He insisted on an urgent meeting.

His report was alarming to Peng: Wei had snuck into the country, met secretly with Huang in Beijing, and handed him a file on corruption in State Security and some senior police ranks. Huang had given the file to the Army and instructed them to plan a roundup of the corrupt officials.

In fact, Yao and the twins had prepared such a file. As Wei flew out of the country, the file appeared on Huang's desktop with a note from Wei. Huang had taken it directly to the president, who had in fact called a meeting with senior PLA generals, planning a move on State Security.

Yao related to Peng how Wei and two juvenile criminal hackers in league with him had left the country on a yacht, sailing out of Dalian Harbor headed for rendezvous with an American submarine. Actually, the twins' boat was tied up at the pier, but it had never been registered in their names.

Yao's story was convincing to Peng. Yao said he had grown suspicious and tricked the staff to let him access Wei's restricted files on their computer system. As he read them, an intrusion system had detected him and begun erasing everything on the network, erasing over and over again, then overwriting the files again and again.

Peng was grateful for the timely report. It would give the senior officials in State Security time to move their money, erase the traces. Wei had anticipated that reaction and, in addition to the bank accounts the twins had discovered, he had the Q-Compute network create other accounts in the names of the State Security officials, accounts with hundreds of millions of dollars provided for the purpose by Professor Zhu. Those newly created accounts were also in Wei's report to Huang.

In the US, the Qmpanies' pure fusion reactors came online within minutes of the power failures, pumping power out of the "data centers" and onto the grid. The fusion reactors byproduct was water. The grid came back to life.

For decades scientists had struggled to make a fusion reactor that generated more power than it used to create it. No design had achieved anything like that, but they had been very large and tremendously expensive. The Q-Compute had examined every alternative and variable and generated a design that would work. It had taken the Q-Compute device less than twenty seconds of run-time to settle on a design that worked using lasers, inertial confinement, and the forced merger of two particles of deuterium, which is a form of water.

The QEnergy design fusion system pumped out one hundred to one hundred and fifty times the energy it required to start up. Four of them fit in each of the three data centers and when mass produced, they would cost less than the large Siemens and ABB fossil fuel generators that had failed when hacked by the QData machine learning program.

Miller and Keogh saw Manhattan and New Jersey light back up again moments before their raid team forcibly entered the Hoboken facility with automatic weapons, radiation detectors, and gas spectrometers, looking for a bomb. The raid team did not know what they had found, but they reported back that they did not think it was a nuclear weapon. There was no radiation. There were just four big machines that emitted blue light and hummed.

From the Blenheim corporation command center in Incheon, Zhu, Diana McPherson, and Wei watched the raid teams from the camera systems in the data facilities in the US. Eventually, the raid team in Ashburn found the large sign that read Clean Energy Generator. The instructions on how to build more of them were in a handbook on a table next to the sign. The design and a guide to making the generators and operating them had also just appeared in a long entry on Wikipedia.

Bohai and Chunhua joined the team on the command center floor, where Blenheim staff were coordinating the simultaneous takeoff of thirty-six modified Gulfstream G700 aircraft from four airfields, one each in Australia, Brazil, Canada, and Poland. The aircraft flew at 60,000 feet and were equipped with spray nozzles and a large tank in what was normally the passenger compartment on the G700.

The QAviation Gulfstreams sprayed the stratosphere with fine particles that would stay aloft for weeks and harmlessly dissolve as they eventually drifted toward the planet's surface. The stratospheric sulfur aerosol dispersal would not stop global warming, but it would reflect enough of the sun's rays to help slow the rate of increase in the planet's temperature. Enough to buy some time, while the world converted to fusion electric power. And they were not the only part of the AIML Masters' Solar Radiation Management Plan.

The US Special Operation Command strike team had deployed quickly from Fort Powell in North Carolina (the former Fort Bragg) to Fort Benavidez (formerly Fort Hood) in Texas. From there, they launched a helicopter air assault force toward Boca Chica, home to the SpaceX launch site. When the lead helicopters were six miles out, their pilots saw the sky light up as the SpaceX Starship lifted off using the Super Heavy booster designed to escape the gravity well of Earth.

The payload module separated from the booster forty-five kilometers up into space, and using its own thrusters, sent its payload of twelve of QSat's cargo carriers farther out from the planet. Six other launches on smaller rockets took place from space centers scattered around the world within hours.

Two days later, the QSats each separated and maneuvered to their stations at LeGrange point L1, where the gravity pull from Earth and the Moon canceled each other out and held satellites steady without the need for stabilizing thrusters that would eventually run out of fuel.

There, at a LeGrange point, the QSats released clouds of specially designed twenty-micron filaments, which hung together in space like clouds made up of millions on tiny mirrors. Their effect was small, but significant enough. Together with the particles sprayed into the stratosphere from the QAviation Gulfstreams, they would reduce solar radiation hitting Earth, yielding a decline in global average temperature of two degrees Celsius.

Both the particles for the upper atmosphere and the filaments for space were designed by the Q-Computes, which ran a program to determine the detrimental side effects of various materials and dispersal plans. The plan used material compounds that had no negative side effects. The Solar Radiation Management Plan cost less than the price of one aircraft carrier.

The Turing Institution and the Sagan League had funded the development of the programs by investing their endowments in private equity front companies, which in turn had invested in the Qmpanies. On orders from the president, the attorney general declined to conduct an investigation of the source of the funding for the Turing and Sagan endowments. The Qmpanies announced mergers with Blenheim Industries, headquartered in Vancouver, BC.

42

Blenheim Industries headquarters
Vancouver, British Columbia
Tuesday, December 9

The websites of both Turing and Sagan played a video. It was of a man speaking in English, but subtitles or voiceovers were available on web pages in most of the world's languages. Blenheim had also offered the feed to all of the world's television networks, many of which were taking it live.

The man began, "Scientists from many countries have banded together to solve an existential question for humanity: how to produce energy without destroying the planet and extinguishing our species. Governments had not done it and probably never would have, but now governments must use what we have created: abundant, renewable and affordable, clean energy. They must act quickly, for the seas are rising fast, the planet is overheating, climate is becoming extreme and destructive.

"There are other important questions that humanity must address and can address if it survives. How to remove the risk of highly destructive conflicts involving nuclear or biochemical weapons? How to reduce population sizes gradually and peacefully to something appropriate to the carrying capacity of the ecosystem? How to halt viruses from spreading into pandemics?

"We will help governments solve these problems and, if we do, we will survive long enough as a species to take ourselves to the next level of human evolution, where we merge in an appropriate way with technology, taking advantage of both gene editing and artificial intelligence to lift up all humanity, out of the swamps of disease and ignorance.

"That next level of the human species, evolved with our own designs, will be capable not only of preserving this planet, but of leaving it, of spreading out across the vastness of space to the billions of planets in our little galaxy, and perhaps beyond. The same basic quantum computing and machine learning techniques and systems with which we have solved the energy problem can be used in the future to design systems to shrink the distances between us and those other parts of our galaxy.

"There will be those who will resist the advancement of science and technology or attempt to ignore what data and the scientific method tell us. There will also be those who will risk progress by focusing on their ancient history of division by nationality, ethnicity, or race, sexuality or gender. These people must and will be left behind as we achieve our full potential as the human species.

"We have given you a gift, a window of prolonged survival. Use it well. On behalf of our team of scientists and computer engineers from around the world, I am Ramesh Pandry."

Watching it on the big screen in Blenheim Industries' Vancouver headquarters were Wei Bao, Fenfang, Diana, Chunhua, and Bohai. They hugged each other, tears flowing on all of their faces. Then they returned to work.

There was a non-sentient, multi-node, machine learning network powered by quantum computers to run, and there were enemies of human dignity, freedom, and progress who would be soon seeing what such a network could do to them if they tried to stand in the way of people who were saving the planet.

Author's Note on Technology

The book is set in the very near future and depicts some technology that exists in 2022 when it was published and some technology that we knew was still in development then, as well as perhaps technology that might be being created in programs that are not yet known publicly.

The twins, Chunhua and Bohai, utilize a variety of advanced cyber hacking tools. The twins employ offensive artificial intelligence packages that automatically try a variety of attack techniques until they succeed in penetrating a network, without a human in the loop. Their attack programs erase logs and shut off alarms so that their presence on a network will go undetected. At one point, they send a target a message via a system designed so that the sender cannot see the receiver's true address (TOR), but they embed in a video file a covert "phone home" program that will reveal the target's network location. All of these cyber capabilities exist today and are in use by various national intelligence services around the world.

The cabal of AIML Masters also employ hacking techniques to penetrate networks, maintain access to them, create identities on them, and update files without being detected. Nation-state cyber units have been doing that for some time. The AIML Masters, however, go a step further and destroy large equipment such as electric generators. The US has demonstrated that ability experimentally, and it has accused China of lacing very large generators with backdoors so that China could use a cyber program to physically destroy the equipment.

Beyond the cyber technologies, much of the book discusses facial recognition and other forms of remote identification and tracking. Computers have been able "to see" for some time, by linking digital cameras with machine learning programs that use pattern recognition to identify objects and people. Computers have also been able to act on what they see for a long time, sending off alarms or locking doors when certain kinds of activity is observed.

Wei Bao is said to have designed a system to identify faces even if the individual is wearing a COVID face mask. The demasking capability was commercially available in 2021. Creating highly realistic facial images of people who do not exist has been possible for several years and is also now commercially available. Facial recognition is being used by some countries for automatic Immigration gates at airports, and it is being rolled out by some airlines as a way of replacing boarding passes.

Not only in China, but in many major cities around the world, local security services have been engaged in "intelligence fusion" by putting together facial recognition from surveillance cameras with analysis of walking gait, geo-location of mobile phones, and vehicle tracking by Automatic License-plate Readers (ALR). In some cities, private sector surveillance cameras installed by building owners have been netted into the police system. Police have also installed their own mobile phone receiver towers, so-called Stingrays, to narrow the circular error probability of a geolocation made from telecoms company data.

Beginning first in China, there are now stores that do not require you to check-out and pay at a cashier. Instead, cameras and mobile phone trackers identify you when you walk in the store, record everything you remove from the shelves, and charge your credit card on the phone for your purchases. You just come in, grab your items, and walk out.

As many of the January 6th Insurrection participants have learned, this kind of intelligence fusion can not only say who an individual is and where they were at a particular time, it can also say what other people were within a few feet of them at the time. The facial recognition jamming techniques of mirrored glasses and "tunnel like" images on caps and T shirts also exist and have been used effectively to stop long distance facial recognition.

Quantum computing is currently on the cusp of general availability and commercial use. Google claims its quantum computer has achieved "quantum superiority," the ability to solve a problem that previously existing computers could not solve even if running for decades on the equation. IBM makes its quantum computer available on-line for experiments and practical use by qualified computer scientists. A Berkeley start-up is in fact challenging the tech giants with its own well funded quantum computer research and development. Much effort is actually being put into developing a quantum computer that would run at room temperature, not the usual minus 40c, and some of that work is being done at and near the University of Toronto. Data scientists are writing computer algorithms and code for using quantum computers to digest big data and to employ artificial intelligence / machine learning on quantum computers.

Thus far, artificial intelligence programs that have been utilized in government and industry have essentially been machine learning programs, some employing more advanced neural network and deep learning techniques. Artificial General Intelligence (AGI), programs that are self-initiating, creative, and more capable than humans at all forms of thinking, do not yet exist. Many data scientists are of the view of Professor Zhu in the book that such capabilities may actually not be possible, or will at least always be a possible future achievement.

Fusion energy has also long been thought to be in the category of "twenty years away," always, as it was in 1978 when I first did a technology assessment of the field for a US government agency.

By the third decade of the twenty-first century, however, there are signs of hope that it may be possible soon to build a fusion reactor that generates more electrical power than it consumes. Such an achievement would mean that we could, without creating harmful radiation, generate completely clean energy without using hydrocarbons. It may be the only way to stop global warming, if that is still possible, but the financial cost of building fusion generators in the numbers that will be needed will be immense. And the technology is not quite there yet.

There is much debate among climate change experts about the wisdom of geo-engineering, intentionally changing our environment and modifying our planet to prevent further global temperature increases. Critics of these engineering solutions have many concerns, one of which is the possible unintended consequences of intentional human manipulation of the environment. Nonetheless, climate scientists and engineers have proposed schemes to lace the upper atmosphere and also nearby outer space with particles or shields to deflect part of the sun's energy. The schemes discussed in the book are among those that have been proposed by legitimate engineers in the field.

The combination of extensive deployment of pure fusion electrical generators and, perhaps as a holding action until fusion is widely deployed, interference with the sun's penetration by dissemination of engineered materials in the upper atmosphere and nearby space could possibly reverse the inexorable rise in global temperatures. Fusion power generation, however, is not yet workable at scale and when it is, it will take decades to deploy globally. Weather modification is controversial and would undoubtedly adversely effect some regions. Of course, so will the rise in global temperature, which may already have made severe climate change a "run away train" that cannot be stopped.

We might all, on reflection, want a secret international cabal of altruistic, genius scientists and engineers to overcome national competitions and join together to save the planet through the deployment of advanced technology, despite their governments. Unfortunately, that part of the book, as far as I know, is fiction.

Finally, a note of personal disclosure and a comment on concerns about misuse of technology. I do currently advise and invest in companies developing and selling artificial intelligence services, facial recognition software, and machine learning related cyber security products and services. I have advised governments in the US and overseas about utilizing such systems. Misused, such technology can infringe on or even destroy human rights and civil liberties. Employed with sufficient civil liberties safeguards and protections against bias, these technologies have proven successful in preventing terrorism and crime, while also increasing productivity and making our lives easier and safer. As with so many technologies, they are not inherently good or evil, but some people are. Having safeguards and standards in place and monitoring their use is essential to preserve our civil liberties, especially as technology advances.

For more of my thoughts on artificial intelligence, quantum computing, and climate change, you can turn to some of my non-fiction: *Warnings: Finding Cassandras to Stop Catastrophes* (with RP Eddy, 2017) and *The Fifth Domain: Protecting our Country Our Companies, and Ourselves in the Age of Cyber Threats* (with Robert K. Knake, 2019).

Or go to my website (richardaclarke.net) for more discussion of the technology in *Artificial Intelligencia.*